# ❧ GRAVE ❧
# UNDERTAKINGS

*Also by Ralph McInerny*
*in Large Print:*


Lying Three
Second Vespers
Getting a Way with Murder
Rest in Pieces
The Basket Case
Abracadaver
Judas Priest
Desert Sinner
A Cardinal Offense
On This Rockne
Irish Tenure
Easeful Death
Leave of Absence
Mom & Dead

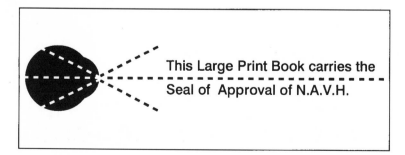

This Large Print Book carries the
Seal of Approval of N.A.V.H.

# ✂ GRAVE ✂ UNDERTAKINGS

*A Father Dowling Mystery*

## Ralph McInerny

Thorndike Press • Thorndike, Maine

Published in 2000 by arrangement with
St. Martin's Press, LLC.

Thorndike Press Large Print Basic Series.

The tree indicium is a trademark of Thorndike Press.

The text of this Large Print edition is unabridged.
Other aspects of the book may vary from the original edition.

Set in 16 pt. Plantin.

Printed in the United States on permanent paper.

**Library of Congress Cataloging-in-Publication Data**

McInerny, Ralph M.
    Grave undertakings : a Father Dowling mystery /
Ralph McInerny.
        p.   cm.
    ISBN 0-7862-2925-X (lg. print : hc : alk. paper)
    1. Dowling, Father (Fictitious character) — Fiction.
    2. Catholic Church — Clergy — Fiction.   3. Illinois
    — Fiction.   4. Large type books.   I. Title.
    PS3563 .A31166 G7 2000b
    813'.54—dc21                                    00-061585

# ❧ GRAVE ❧ UNDERTAKINGS

# ❧ Prologue ❧

When the patient was returned to intensive care from the operating table on which he had lain for eight hours while surgeons removed pieces of metal from his body, stanched the flow of blood, sewed and stitched and taped, it was difficult to tell where he left off and the life-supporting apparatus began.

"Give him absolution, Father," a small woman with intense eyes said to Father Dowling. Her hand gripped the sleeve of his coat.

"Can I be alone with him?" the priest asked a nurse.

"More or less."

"Go downstairs and get a cup of coffee," he suggested to Mrs. O'Toole.

"Coffee! Father, he might die. He hasn't been inside a church for years."

Did she think he could just go in, wave his hand over an unconscious man, and sweep away the sins of a lifetime? A wife can pray for her husband, but he has to feel

7

contrition himself.

The nurse drew a curtain around the bed and Father Dowling pulled a chair up beside it. The murmur and hiss and bubble of medical machinery was background for the rasping breathing of the patient. Vincent O'Toole was unconscious, but Beatrice, the nurse who came and went, assured Father Dowling he should be coming out of it soon.

"If he does, that is."

"What are his chances?"

The corners of her mouth turned down and her rounded eyes rose.

Mrs. O'Toole came back and Beatrice pulled away the curtain. The grieving wife stared at her husband and then looked questioningly at Father Dowling.

"Did you?"

"I'll talk to him when he comes out of it."

"But what if he doesn't!"

She went off again and the curtain was pulled and when Father Dowling turned back to the bed he realized that the patient's eyes were open.

"I'm Father Dowling. Can you hear me?"

The eyes just stared at him.

"Are you sorry for all the sins of your past life?"

The eyes closed. After a moment, tears leaked from their corners. And then he was looking again at the priest. Father Dowling took the tears as sufficient sign of contrition and said the formula of absolution over Vincent O'Toole. The patient followed the movement of his hand as the priest traced the sign of the cross over him.

Mrs. O'Toole flew toward him when he emerged from the room. He grabbed her wrists, as much to defend himself as to arrest her headlong rush.

"He's awake. Go talk to him."

"But did you . . ."

"God is merciful."

She let out a cry of relief and hurried into the room. A moment later the shrieking began. Her husband was dead.

Relief was felt at McDivitt's Funeral Home when it was learned that Father Dowling would lead the prayers at the wake. Floral displays of the gaudiest and most vulgar sort jammed the viewing rooms and McDivitt himself, suffering from an unacknowledged allergy that was triggered by a component of such floral displays, was weeping in his office. It was in this condition that Mrs. O'Toole found him.

McDivitt rose from behind his desk, flustered to be discovered in such discomposure, but the expression on Mimi O'Toole's face told him that his professional mask of grief, perfected over the years, was nowhere near as effective as these quite real tears running down his ruddy cheeks. She actually came into his arms. Behind her, in the open door, stood a large, sullen young man.

"This is Sonny." She stepped back so that McDivitt could get a good look at her child. Sonny was in his early thirties and seemed to be standing at attention, but the effect was spoiled by the pouting expression of his fleshy mouth. A bright-colored skirtlike garment hung below his buttoned topcoat. He shuffled in his sandaled feet.

McDivitt had known Mimi's parents, the Schroeders, who had retired in shame to Tucson when they realized what kind of work their son-in-law Vincent was engaged in. Was Sonny reacting against his father? He had the bland stare of the serial murderer, but he belonged, as Mimi explained while he showed her the casket selections, to a group of monks who begged in airports and lived a communal life in Skokie. He had briefly returned to the Occidental world of getting and spending to support his mother in her hour of grief.

"Where's Dad?" Sonny asked.

The body was still being prepared.

McDivitt deflected the question by displaying a garment.

"This is the suit in which we will bury him."

Mimi threw up her arms. "But I brought clothing."

She sent Sonny out to the car and while the boy was gone, McDivitt urged the use of the suit that O'Toole's associates had brought.

"Who do you mean?"

Even in the privacy of his own office and with no witness but Mimi O'Toole, McDivitt whispered, "The Pianones said they would pay for everything."

For a moment, he thought Mimi meant to refuse that as well. She had taken the suit from him and was examining it in a light that fell from a fixture sunk in the low ceiling of the casket display room. Sonny returned with a complete burial outfit and handed it to McDivitt. Mimi took the Pianone gift suit and gave it to Sonny.

"You could wear that."

"We are buried in our habits."

This reminder of her son's religious enthusiasms caused Mimi to begin weeping again. "Put it in the car," she sobbed, as if anxious to get Sonny out of her sight.

McDivitt sat behind his desk. Miraculously, his eyes had stopped tearing and he fell back on his practiced mask of compassion.

"Father Dowling will lead the rosary at seven-thirty. For the immediate family."

"He was with Vincent when he died."

"God is merciful. The general viewing will begin at eight. Mimi, I have never seen so many flowers."

"Flowers! What good are flowers?"

"You are going to bury that man from St. Hilary's church?" Marie Murkin asked.

Father Dowling thought it best not to respond.

"He never set one foot in that church in all the time I've been here."

"Well, he'll be wheeled in tomorrow."

"He's a gangster. He is tied up with the Pianones." Marie's voice dropped to a whisper, as if she feared being overheard. "It would be a scandal."

Gerry Quinn, one of the small army of auxiliary bishops, called and asked Father Dowling about the newspaper reports that Vincent O'Toole was to be given a Catholic funeral at St. Hilary's.

"A pretty disreputable character, wasn't he, Roger?"

"That's what I'm told."

"Was the chaplain with him when he died?"

"I was there."

"Ah."

Gerry Quinn would not, of course, ask what had gone on between priest and penitent — if that is what O'Toole had been — in that hospital room. But his call prepared Father Dowling for the adverse publicity the funeral would draw.

It began at McDivitt's the evening before. Father Dowling had always thought of the funeral home as having viewing rooms almost too large, making a small turnout seem an adverse judgment on the deceased. But on the occasion of the O'Toole wake, there was far from room enough. As it was, it was mostly women, expensively dressed wives with the look of those who saw no evil, spoke no evil, and certainly did no evil. Those tasks were left to the men of the family.

"What a crowd," he said to McDivitt, who was beaming anxiously in a corner.

"He will be greatly missed." The routine phrase was spoken by the undertaker without thought. Their eyes met.

"If they had missed, Cecil, he would still be with us."

McDivitt's cotton-white brows rose above

13

his gold-rimmed glasses and he pressed fingers to his lips, as if to suppress a giggle.

Driving back to the rectory, Father Dowling wondered why we are inclined to joke in the presence of death, like the grave diggers in *Hamlet*. A kind of psychological protection, of course. But poor Vincent O'Toole apparently was a casualty of a civil war in which there was no good side.

"Look at those cars," Marie cried the following morning, as limousine after limousine pulled into the parking lot behind the church. From them notorious figures with their timid wives emerged. Soon the church, luxuriant with floral offerings, filled with affluent if disreputable mourners. Huge men wept as they carried the casket from the church. Outside, the local media were in full force.

The widow was accompanied by her son, defiantly garbed in the distinctive costume of his sect. Her searching eyes might have been asking sympathy for what she suffered with Sonny as much as for her bereavement. She had adopted the view that God had spared Vincent and he was well out of this world.

"Considering how he went, Father."

She searched Father Dowling's eyes. How

14

she longed for a blow-by-blow description of those minutes he had spent at Vincent's bedside in the hospital. Quite apart from the confidentiality between confessor and penitent, he doubted that she would find her husband's final moments on earth unequivocally reassuring with respect to the state of his soul.

In the following days, newspaper stories continued to appear, suggesting that O'Toole's employers had made a handsome donation to the little parish in Fox River in order that he might receive a fifty-gun Catholic send-off. From being silently disapproving of all this, Phil Keegan began to think of it as an advantage.

"It gave us a chance to take roll call, Roger," he said that night. "We got them on film and they all came."

"They?"

"The underworld."

"I'm surprised Vincent O'Toole had so many friends."

"Friends? Most of them probably wanted to make sure he was dead."

"Who is responsible for killing him?"

Phil shrugged. Clearly this was not a question that weighed heavily on those in law enforcement.

★ ★ ★

" 'Every notable in the local underworld,' " Marie read from the paper she
held. She folded it and slapped her thigh
with it. "Of course they mention St. Hilary's. What are people going to think?"

"Marie, if we had nothing to do with sinners, where would we be?"

"Sinners, yes. Repentant sinners!"

He did not tell her that Vincent O'Toole
had gone into the next world after having
been absolved of his sins. Marie had not entirely accepted the Gospel parable about the
laborers who started late in the day, yet received the same wage as those who began at
dawn. Still, given what Roger Dowling had
learned about Vincent O'Toole, it was odd
to think of him among the saints. Until he
remembered the good thief.

# Heidegger

Heidegger had been sexton at Riverside Cemetery for twenty-three years after serving an apprenticeship of ten years on the grounds crew. He had taken the job because at the time there wasn't anything better. He had never intended to stay, but one day led to another, season blended into season, and he found that he liked outdoor work, even if it was in a cemetery. The fact is, it was hard work only when graves had to be dug or the leaves raked in the fall. Leaves were the bane of cemetery work.

If he could just sit there in his office and watch the trees turn into half a dozen glorious colors it would have been different. In the next office, Annie Ambrose snuffled and hummed, supposedly working on the computer but usually playing solitaire. The sight of leaves drifting down among the markers could stir the soul of any man. But they had to be picked up and carted off to the wilderness area at the west end of the cemetery. Long ago they had burned them and autumnal smoke rose in great sweet-smelling billows toward the sky, making the thin product from the crematorium chimney seem like nothing. At any other season of the year, the smoke from the chimney still got to Heidegger. Burying bodies was best, that was his deep belief. Burning them seemed disdainful, no matter all the good arguments in favor of it. Besides, it stirred up images of hell.

His office, thanks to the addition to the original building, gave him an untrammeled view of his domain. The sexton's office was located a hundred yards beyond the gatehouse. A law student now lived in the gatehouse apartment that was meant for the sexton, but his wife, Dorothy, had refused to move into it. Heidegger was separated from the business office where Annie Ambrose kept the books. Annie talked to herself much of the time, but since she was deaf she might be unaware of it. When people came to ask about plots and burial, he placed their chairs so they could see how serene it was at Riverside. Their beloved would be able to rest in peace under those trees and the gently undulating terrain. Fall was a boom season for burial lots, as if the dying of the year turned people's thoughts to their final resting place. Heidegger used an attractive brochure to supplement the view from the north window.

"They sell themselves," he assured Dorothy.

"I don't want to hear about it."

It was the cross he had to bear. His wife was ashamed of the work he did, put off by it, would never let him talk to her about the satisfactions of being the sexton at Riverside Cemetery. For all that, she was a good woman. He had not told her that two lots awaited them in the area just to the west of the new mausoleum.

Mausoleums were not as bad as cremation, but Heidegger did not in his heart of hearts approve of them either. It was like filing away the remains, as if you might want to come back for them some day. Not that there weren't reburials from time to time. . . .

Outside, the whine of the leaf blowers grew louder and soon the two men operating them came into view. They would not know what an improvement this was over raking. Memories of weeks spent raking between and around the gravestones could call up the constant back pain he had suffered in those days. Heidegger stepped to the window and waved his arms for five minutes before he got the crew's attention. He pointed significantly to his watch. Leaf-blowing was almost addictive. Imagine having to remind men that lunchtime had come.

Lolly and Maxwell, covered with dust from the leaves, ate lunch sitting in the open door of the maintenance shed, looking out at the scene of their labors. Heidegger sat on the tractor to which the suction machine was already attached. That represented phase two. First, blow the leaves into piles close to the roads. Second, suck them up and take them out to the wild area where they would be left to rot. Half would be taken away by truck farmers looking for mulch, bagging it up out there and hauling the leaves away.

"Hallowe'en," Heidegger said.

Lolly nodded and Maxwell said, "Geez."

"Can I count on you both?"

Their shrugs were meant as assent. Hallowe'en called for special precautions, to guard against vandalism.

"Out back is where they're likely to come in."

Out back was the wilderness, but beyond was a housing development filled with teenagers. The cemetery would be irresistible after they had tired of tricks or treats.

He thought of asking Withers, the law student who for the past week had been living in the gatehouse apartment, to keep vigil with them, but decided against it. Withers was preoccupied; he spent all his time studying and never left the apartment.

On Hallowe'en, accordingly, Lolly and Maxwell took up stations out back, where kids were most likely to sneak in. Heidegger took up his vigil in his office. He was dead tired. Dorothy was angry because she was home alone and would have to answer the door all by herself, bribing kids with candy. Throughout the day they had been busy sucking up piles of leaves and trucking them out to the wilderness. Lolly was lying on one of those stacks now, doing sentinel duty.

"Stay awake," Heidegger told him.

But it was Heidegger who fell asleep, tipped back in his chair in his office. He was wakened by the sound of his own snoring and for a wild moment did not know where he was. That was when he looked out and noticed the lights.

He rubbed his eyes to make sure, but there was no doubt of it. Someone was out there doing God knows what. Lolly and Maxwell must have fallen asleep too.

Heidegger slammed the door when he left the office and advanced through the night, shouting toward the lights that flickered through the trees. He knew the cemetery like the back of his hand, but even so he had to be careful not to run into a memorial stone or trip over a marker.

"Hey!" he shouted, waving his flashlight. "Hey, you!"

The lights went out. Heidegger stopped. Had he scared them off? He waited with his flashlight off and had the sense that someone else was waiting a hundred yards away. But the lights did not go on again. Then there was the sound of a motor starting, a powerful motor. To his right came the sound of Lolly and Maxwell approaching, drawn by his shouting. The sound of the motor grew fainter and then, as the vehicle neared the cemetery entrance, headlights went on.

Heidegger moved on then, followed by his men. They came to a halt when they reached the place where the intruders had been. They found a desecrated grave. The large Celtic cross had been tipped over. Signs of digging suggested a macabre purpose.

"Geez."

"Who's buried there?"

Heidegger turned his light on the toppled stone.

"Vincent O'Toole."

# Mimi O'Toole

As the weeks after Vince's death passed, Mimi O'Toole had reached a plateau of resigned loneliness. That last scene in the hospital and the way he handled the funeral drew her to Father Dowling and St. Hilary's. The parish school that had been turned into a haven for senior citizens proved to be just what she needed now and she spent three or four days a week there. There were widows galore but widowers too, and although Mimi never permitted herself to think of it, a world of possibility seemed to shimmer on the horizon of her life.

"One," she would say, when the inevitable question was asked. "A son."

"Is he here in Fox River?"

No need to give details about Sonny. The housekeeper apparently had not noticed Sonny at the funeral, or pretended that she hadn't. She told Marie Murkin that he had a vocation.

"What order?"

"You probably haven't heard of it."

"I know most of them."

23

Marie was nosy but a good woman. She seemed to take special responsibility for Mimi O'Toole, though she became a little starchy and resentful when the subject of Vince's funeral came up. Mimi had finally brought herself to empty out his closets. She took the clothes to Edna Hospers, who seemed surprised when Mimi brought in armfuls of shirts and trousers and suits.

"But why are you bringing those here?" Edna asked.

It had been Mimi's thought that the old people who came to the parish center might want to look over Vince's things and take what they wanted, but it was suddenly clear to her that this was a mistake.

"Where should they go?"

"You might take them to St. Vincent DePaul."

"That's the saint Vince was named after."

"Oh." Edna seemed to think this explained her reluctance to take the clothes to St. Vincent DePaul herself. "I'll take care of it for you, Mimi. They'll get these clothes to people who can use them."

What might have been a bad moment turned into one that began their friendship, though she did not feel as close to Edna as she did to Marie Murkin. All in all, Mimi had convinced herself that she was through the first awful part of being alone. And then out of the blue on Hallowe'en came the desecration of Vince's grave!

Heidegger the sexton was on her doorstep on All Saints' Day when she answered his ring.

"I'm sorry to call so early," he said.

"I am on my way to St. Hilary's."

"There is something I have to tell you."

His manner prepared her for bad news but she listened in disbelief. In a moment, everything she had gained was gone and she began to wail like a banshee. Neighbors appeared, someone called 911, and Heidegger had to explain to the police that he was not molesting her. But it was not until Marie Murkin came that Mimi thought she might just possibly get through this new horror without losing her mind.

"Not even the dead are safe," she said an hour later, sitting at the table in the rectory kitchen, stirring the tea that Marie had put before her.

"Who would do such a thing?"

"As if it isn't bad enough to shoot a man down in broad daylight, they have to —"

She couldn't say it. How could she explain that a body becomes loathsome when there is no longer life in it? She had slept with Vincent O'Toole drunk and sober for thirty-five years, he had tried her patience more than once, but she had never felt disgust or distaste. But when she put her hand on the cool forehead of her dead husband, he had become a thing, a frightening thing. The funeral had seemed an elaborate disguising of that simple fact. The flowers, the music, the ritual, the stately procession across the lawn to the waiting grave. When it was over, when Father Dowling closed his book and she was led back to McDivitt's limousine, Vincent and his casket still sat upon the apparatus whose function she did not want to think of. It would have been too much to wait and see him actually lowered into the ground. Thank God she had been spared that sight.

"Do you know who did it, Mimi?"

"Of course."

Marie leaned toward her and asked in a whisper, "Who?"

"The ones who killed him." Mimi was whispering too.

Father Dowling looked in. "Are you up to talking, Mrs. O'Toole?"

"Mimi."

He smiled. "Captain Keegan would like to have a few words."

Mimi looked pleadingly at Marie. How could they expect her to talk with the police,

26

as if they could possibly care what happened to Vincent O'Toole, alive or dead. Had they even lifted a finger to find the ones who killed him?

"We might stand a better chance of finding out who did that awful thing at the cemetery," Captain Keegan said.

He was a big man, as big as Vince, and had something of the same rough gentleness. Still, he was a policeman, and the natural enemy of her husband.

"What if they try again?"

"Try what?"

"What they tried last night."

"How much have you been told?"

"What do you mean?"

"What exactly do you think went on at your husband's grave last night?"

Mimi looked wildly at Father Dowling and Marie. Heidegger had said that someone had tried to dig up Vince. She said this to Marie, the only way she could answer the policeman.

"Why would they do a thing like that?"

"Let me ask a question," Marie said. "What's to stop them from going back tonight?"

"Police patrols will keep an eye on things out there."

But for how long? Whoever had been

there last night could wait out the short time when the police would patrol the area. Soon they could return and finish what they had started. It was clear that Heidegger and his men had been there that night only because it was Hallowe'en and they had been worried about kids.

"He isn't safe even in his grave."

"Maybe a mausoleum . . ." Marie began, but her voice trailed off. "More tea?"

"Yes!" She pushed her cup toward Marie.

The men left them, as if drinking tea were a peculiarly female ritual. Actually, Mimi did not like tea. But it seemed to be one more of the things she would have to learn to like, now that she was a widow.

# Father Dowling 3

Father Dowling did not find it easy to believe that the Pianones with whom Vincent O'Toole had been connected included Peanuts, the officer on the Fox River police force. But it was almost beyond belief that they were related to Angela, who was a volunteer in the parish senior center once a week.

"This is Peanuts Pianone's family?" he had asked Phil Keegan.

"In several senses of the word."

Marie Murkin contended that St. Hilary's parish had been in steady decline since her first years as housekeeper.

"Are you suggesting a causal connection?"

Marie just looked at him. It was Father Dowling's confessable fault that he could not resist teasing Marie Murkin. She was a valiant woman, a housekeeper *sans pareil,* loyal, efficient, and nosy. Perhaps he should have stopped his inventory with her virtues. But even her nosiness was a virtue. The pastor of St. Hilary felt he had learned at least as much from Marie Murkin about the circumstances of the death of Vincent O'Toole as he had from Phil Keegan. Marie did not befriend Mimi O'Toole in order to pump her, but information came easily over tea. Like most practiced conversationalists, Marie bobbed her head constantly as the other spoke, a metronomic movement that served to keep the story coming. From time to time she breathed a sympathetic sigh or a significant monosyllable.

"She speaks of it as if it were the most ordinary thing in the world," Marie reported, heaving an incredulous sigh.

"What?"

"The way he made a living."

"How was that?"

"He was a gangster."

"Is that what she says?"

"Of course not! I don't think she knows how much she reveals."

From Phil Keegan Father Dowling had learned the nature of the unsavory establishments that had been Vincent O'Toole's responsibility. What a marvel the story of any human life is. To think that a man who had wallowed in such filth ended up the recipient of divine mercy on his deathbed, moments before he passed away. Marie was openly skeptical about those final moments and said so.

"In what way, Marie?"

"I wish the man no harm, Father, and God knows I wouldn't so much as breathe the suggestion to Mimi, but how is it possible for someone who made his living like that to . . ." She waved her hand helplessly as she imagined Vincent O'Toole, white-robed and singing before the altar of the lamb.

He would not berate her about it. Of course he understood her attitude; it was just that he felt no temptation to share it. One who has himself felt the undeserved mercy of God is unlikely to divide mankind into sheep and goats before the final judgment. One does not drink for the sake of drinking, but in quest of some impossible peace or in order to forget an insoluble difficulty. As a member of the archdiocesan tribunal that considered annulment appeals when these were virtually impossible to obtain, Roger Dowling had dealt with couples who had come to the point of repudiating one another, willing to say that no real marriage had ever existed between them, no matter the children, the shared years, the memories good and bad. That whole past was to be treated as if it had never been. It is one thing to want to begin again but something very different to say that one had never begun before. It was the pathetic hope

31

that there was a future waiting that would be wholly different from the past that wrenched the heart. No wonder there were serial divorces, a steady shuffling off of spouses in the mad hope that somewhere a malleable projection of one's desires awaited.

Marie's attitude suggested that there were sinners on the one hand and others on the other and that once upon a time the parish had been made up only of the latter. There was no doubt that the parish area no longer had its former éclat — it lacked the suburban affluence of Buddy Walsh's parish — but Father Dowling hoped to live out his life here. There were tree-lined avenues with fine large family homes set on lots whose lawns had once been the beneficiaries of constant care. Many of these homes had been remodeled and now housed insurance, dental, or legal offices. Some had attracted young families, delighted to find a well-built and affordable dwelling that could accommodate the number of children they hoped to have. But by and large, the average age of parishioners rose, there were few ungray heads when Father Dowling looked out over his congregation, and the parish school, which had been converted into a social center for seniors, attracted more and more people all the time.

"It's a big building," Edna Hospers answered when he asked her if her task was becoming too difficult.

"You should have a staff."

"The volunteers are enough help."

"How do you class Mimi O'Toole, as a volunteer or a client?"

But Edna had been reluctant to talk about Mimi. Did she think that the pastor was likening her own tragic story to Mimi's? Edna's husband was serving a sentence in Joliet. Her children were now in their teens, her own golden years were passing while she supervised the parish center. Edna never alluded to this and certainly never chatted about it. Father Dowling wished that, like a lawyer, he could withdraw the question. Edna's troubles had made her tolerant. She had already welcomed Angela Pianone as a volunteer, so she was unlikely to bridle at Mimi O'Toole.

"Marie's right about one thing," Phil Keegan said, lighting a cigar in the pastor's study.

"What's that?" Phil was referring to his conversation with Mimi O'Toole in the rectory kitchen.

"They'll be back. That wasn't a bunch of kids out there pulling a stupid Hallowe'en stunt. They meant to dig him up."

"Good God."

Phil's eyes narrowed as he drew on his cigar. "I wonder what they're after."

"Maybe the body should be moved," Father Dowling said.

Phil looked at him. "Exhumed?"

"Couldn't he be reburied somewhere that only Mrs. O'Toole would know of?"

"Her and the maharishi." This was Phil's way of referring to Sonny. He would never get over the sight of the corpulent young man sailing down the aisle at his father's funeral with his saffron robe trailing behind. Sonny's head was shaved but Phil discounted that. "His old man was bald as an egg. He probably is too."

Some obscure point lurked in this observation, but it could not compete with Phil's suggestion that the police had an interest in finding out why anyone would want to dig up the body of Vincent O'Toole.

# Monsignor Buddy Walsh

## 4

Monsignor Chester Walsh, Buddy to his family and classmates, had put in a stint as a navy chaplain and returned to face a very receptive appointments board. When they laid out for him the prizes from which he could choose he felt like Christ on the pinnacle of the temple being tempted by Satan. To the surprise of the board he had chosen the semi-rural parish of St. Teresa, west of town, in a place called Barfield that was a town at all only because its grain elevators had once catered to local farmers. But the farms had gradually been taken over by housing developments, giving Barfield a new lease on life and turning St. Teresa's from the sleepy rural parish it had been into one that grew exponentially by the month. Buddy was named a monsignor, put up a huge church and school, postponing the rectory to last. He was obviously pleased when he showed Roger Dowling around.

"When I came here I had visions of spending whole days in my study, reading."

"That's right, you have a degree."

Buddy had earned an M.A. in theology at Notre Dame before joining the navy, but it was fiction, not theology, he had hoped to read. His new rectory had a study of massive proportions, the shelving of white oak, made on the site by craftsmen who obviously took pride in their work. At one end of the large rectangular room was Buddy's desk, at the other easy chairs and bright halogen lamps. There was no television in sight. When Roger Dowling remarked on this, Buddy sheepishly opened a cabinet door to reveal a massive screen.

"I only watch sports." He sounded like an alcoholic who claims to drink only beer.

In any case, the projected reading program was on hold for the foreseeable future. Buddy had two assistants and a theological problem. There was a little cemetery north of the parish plant, an integral part of it because of the way the town had grown around it. In it stood a statue of Our Lady that had spoken to a woman who had knelt before it after visiting a grave.

"She just knelt there, not really thinking about it, and started a Hail Mary when she heard this voice."

Buddy told the story as if he himself did not quite know what to make of it. The woman was no St. Bernadette, nor was she like the children of Fatima. She was in her forties, married to a surgeon, had three kids, and had been runner-up in the state amateur golf championship two years in a row.

"I wouldn't even call her pious, Roger. She's a good woman, don't get me wrong, but there just isn't anything special about her."

"She came to you with this?"

"She said she was ordered to tell me."

Father Dowling waited. He did not want to ask what the message was. Curiosity in such matters could be dangerous. Buddy seemed to be searching for a way to put it.

"Have you been to the cardinal?"

Buddy fell back. "Roger, this can't get out! Can you imagine the effect?"

"I suppose that depends on the message."

Buddy's lips formed a straight line and his cheeks puffed out. There was a little puffing explosion when he spoke. "I can't tell you the message. That's part of the message. Do you think I'm nuts to take it seriously?"

"That's difficult to say."

"It's already begun."

"What?"

"Come here."

Buddy led Roger Dowling to the windows at the far end of the study from which there was a good view of the cemetery. It was a diminutive place, an area perhaps fifty yards square in the middle of which, standing on a high base, was a chalk-white statue of Our Lady. Buddy stepped back so that Roger could have an unobstructed view.

"What am I looking for?"

"Can't you see them?"

Buddy meant the dozen or so people in the cemetery, several on their knees before the statue of Mary.

"Word has gotten out. Don't ask me how. The woman swears she has told no one. She solemnly promised to tell no one but me. But there they are. Every day there are a few more."

"If they're saying their prayers, what's the harm?"

"They want to buy lots, Roger. They want to be buried here."

"Are there still empty lots?"

"It's sold out."

"What's the problem?"

"The parish council had voted to petition for the relocation of the cemetery. It should be out of town, in the open." He looked at Roger. "We need the parking space."

"There's opposition?"

"The Blessed Virgin. At least that's what the opponents say."

"What's the reason?"

"Honor the remains of the faithful departed."

# Cy Horvath

## 5

Cy Horvath's loyalty to Captain Phil Keegan was total. He would not have been on the police force if Phil hadn't remembered his blighted athletic career, rescued him from oblivion, and took him under his wing. In response, Cy became the best detective on the force. Phil had taught him all he knew and made him his right-hand man. If only for these reasons Cy didn't like to hear the snickering about Phil's idea that they exhume the body of Vincent O'Toole. It was received wisdom that a dead mobster was a benefit to the community, no matter how he had managed to get into that condition. O'Toole had been gunned down by people no better than himself. It made no sense to waste scarce resources and overworked personnel trying to figure out who killed O'Toole.

"He wants to find out why they wanted to dig him up," Cy explained.

"Dig him up?" one of the Fox River detectives said. "It was Hallowe'en, a couple of kids fooling around in the cemetery. Come on. You think they buried some treasure with him?"

"Someone wanted to dig him up."

"Have they been back?" another asked.

No need to tell these wiseacres that he and Phil had taken turns since Hallowe'en, volunteering, to keep an eye on Vincent O'Toole's gravesite.

"A patrol car's too conspicuous, Cy. They won't make a move if they see it."

They didn't have a car to spare for such duty anyway. They didn't have the personnel either. If he and Phil hadn't done it on their own, the gravesite would have been easy pickings for the ones who had been there on Hallowe'en. But more than a week had gone by and the cemetery vigil had proved fruitless.

It was eerie, sitting out there in a parked car, surrounded by the dead, the breeze rustling through the fallen leaves. Cars going past on the county road made a mournful sound and there were the far-off whistles of trains. When had he last noticed how many trains blew their whistles as they approached Fox River? As soon as they were on the outskirts, they blew them again, as if in contempt of the statute that banned train whistles in Fox River from dusk to dawn. Cy doubted many people would have noticed if they blasted those whistles all the way through town. What a mournful sound it was, evoking those boyhood dreams of some other place over the horizon, somewhere else.

"That a nightlight in the gatehouse?" he asked Heidegger.

"A caretaker lives there."

"A caretaker?"

"A law student named Withers."

Maybe the fact that someone lived in the gatehouse was meant to provide security. But it hadn't stopped the attempt on Hallowe'en. For that matter, the caretaker showed no curiosity about a car parked in the cemetery for hours each night.

Cy locked the doors of his car while he kept vigil in the cemetery, not really thinking about it, half kidding himself that he didn't realize he was doing it. But it wasn't ghosts he was thinking of. Whether it was Vince O'Toole's friends or enemies who had been here on Hallowe'en, Cy didn't want them creeping up on him unawares. He brought a portable radio, not wanting the car radio lit up. Not much to listen to in the dead hours of night but crazy talk shows, nuts sounding off on everything under the moon, country western, classics. Cy listened to an FM station, classical music, which wasn't bad if you tuned out the wimp who introduced the music. Why did they have to tell you if a piece was in E-sharp or B-flat? One announcer who made little wet sounds between words gave the number of the opus as well, just in case listeners were taking notes. Cy didn't know a sonata from a symphony, but he found the music soothing, particularly piano.

"Any business?" Phil would say when he came at one in the morning.

"I think we're wasting our time."

"Maybe."

"How long do you stay?"

"I'll give it a couple hours."

He found the thought of Phil Keegan sitting alone in his car in the cemetery in the wee hours of the morning sad. His wife was dead, his kids lived in different places around the country, there was nothing to go home to but an empty apartment, but still, it seemed sad that Phil should waste hours out in the cemetery on the remote chance that those ghouls would be back to dig up Vince O'Toole.

After a week of it, Cy decided to have a talk with Mrs. O'Toole.

"You're a cop?"

"A detective."

"On the police force?"

"That's right. I've been assigned to protect your husband's grave."

Her hand went to her mouth and her wide eyes filled with tears. "I can't believe anyone would do such a thing."

"I wonder what they're after?"

"What do you mean?"

"I'm not sure. What if there's something down there, in the casket, something valuable . . ."

She had shut her eyes, put her hands over her ears and was shaking her head hard. Cy waited. When she put her hands on the table, he went on.

"If there is, they are going to get it eventually. We don't have enough people to guard his grave night and day."

"Oh my God."

"There is a way to stop them."

"How?"

He looked her in the eye. He knew his large flat face was reassuring.

"Rebury him."

"What?"

"Change his grave, forget about a marker, they'd never find him."

Even as he said it, he saw the flaw in his suggestion. Anyone really desperate to dig up Vince O'Toole's casket would not rest until he found out where that casket was. Someone would have to rebury Vince. They would find out who and one way or another discover the site. Or they could break into the cemetery office and check the records. Still, if nothing else, reburying the body would make it harder for them.

"Do you think that would work?"

"It's worth a try."

"What do I do?"

"Do you want me to look into it?"

She bit her lips, she made fists of her hands, she looked bleakly out the window. And then nodded, not looking at him.

"But don't do anything without telling me."

He assured her that nothing could be done without her permission. Before telling Phil, he stopped by the cemetery office.

"They haven't been back," Heidegger said, when Cy identified himself.

"We've been keeping an eye on the place."

"Even with the fences, there are lots of ways to get in."

"Only one sure way."

Heidegger thought about it before making a little bark of a laugh.

"How long you been here?"

"All my life."

Would he be buried there as well? Heidegger was like one of those monks with a skull on his desk. Did he ever get a chance to just live?

"I've thought of a way to protect that grave."

"How?"

"Bury him someplace else."

"Another cemetery?"

"Would that be necessary?"

"He could be buried two lots over and who would know?"

"Your crew?"

"Don't worry about them."

Lolly and Maxwell he called them. Cy was going to suggest that he and Heidegger do the job, but why would he think Heidegger was any less vulnerable than Lolly and Maxwell? Heidegger was shaking his head.

"We couldn't do it without permission."

"From whom?"

"The death certificate and an application have to go to Springfield. A funeral director has to be involved."

"That's if we do it legally."

This time Heidegger barked twice. Cy decided that maybe he was kidding.

Phil listened in silence but he began to wrinkle his nose. "We got the widow involved, the sexton, his crew, a funeral director, clerks in state offices . . . We might just as well hire a band and do it at high noon."

"We can't sit out there night after night."

"Yeah."

# Tuttle

6

Tuttle, the Fox River lawyer and sole partner of Tuttle & Tuttle, considered Peanuts Pianone a friend and they were often together, bottom feeders in the tank of life. Peanuts, Tuttle's main source of information about what was going on with the local police force, was not given to displays of feeling. It was sometimes said that Peanuts was taken on as a policeman because he had flunked the exam so resoundingly that his examiners suspected some deep and unusual genius in the candidate. But the fact was that Peanuts would have been accepted on the force, exam or no exam. His hiring was quid pro quo accorded his family, a family in both the Sicilian and ordinary sense. The Pianones had controlled and profited from the misbehavior of their fellow citizens almost from the time of their arrival from Palermo.

By and large, the Pianones were honorable thieves. Extortion, contraband, unsavory bars with questionable entertainment were about the extent of it, and since the will of man is a slender reed, not to be relied upon to do the right thing, evil will exist. No police force can be expected to do what religion, good example, and the fear of being caught have failed to accomplish. Any city, even Fox River, Illinois, must tolerate some evil. The Pianones played an unheralded part in seeing that it did not get out of hand. It did not get out of hand because it did not get out of *their* hands. Violence broke out only when their monopoly on misbehavior was threatened. From time to time some colonizer from Chicago would try to move into Fox River. This became known after the fact when strange bodies showed up in Dumpsters or in the trunks of abandoned cars. A telephone call to the Chicago constabulary sufficed to inform the interested parties to come pick up the departed. Threats from within were seldom even known about because they were handled with dispatch and untraceability.

"I knew you had brothers," Tuttle said to Peanuts. "And you have a sister who is a sister." Sister Maria Madeline neé Laura Pianone was a nun in an enclosed contemplative convent, living a life of penance for sinners, with particular reference to members of her family.

"Better Angela should be a nun too."

"Doesn't she volunteer at St. Hilary's?"

"There aren't any nuns there anymore."

"She looks like an angel."

Peanuts's small eyes peered at Tuttle from under the frown of his single brow. "She is a disgrace."

"That's hard to believe."

Peanuts rolled his eyes and hunched his shoulders. He worked his mouth, seemingly prepared to speak, but remained silent.

"Why?" Tuttle asked.

"She betrayed the family."

Tuttle felt a chill ripple up and down his spinal column. He thought of the recent death of Vince O'Toole. If an enemy is dealt with swiftly, a traitor is dealt with harshly. The Chicago River was said to have a bed of weighted bones, remains of those who had run afoul of the forces of order in the Windy City underworld. The Fox River was a more bucolic waterway, but on several occasions startled fishermen had turned up odd items on their hooks even there. Beyond a certain point, these finds were never investigated. Let deep call to deep, so to say. Some skeletons are best left in Davy Jones's locker.

"Today is her birthday." Peanuts referred to his sister.

"Ah."

"A year older."

"A birthday will do that."

"Than me."

Someone with a vast number of friends might have found Peanuts too demanding a conversationalist and gone on to more congenial companionship. In Tuttle's case, that option was unavailable. If, in the matter of conversation, Peanuts was more a sounding board than an interlocutor, he and Tuttle had enjoyed hours of companionship, over Chinese food, watching the Blackhawks, giving one another professional help. The sister's name was Angela and the normally taciturn Peanuts conveyed quite a bit of information about her over the next hour or two. They were sitting in Tuttle's office, and on the desk were Styrofoam containers of various sizes, testimony to the Chinese meal they had consumed. Peanuts had actually volunteered to pay. That should have alerted Tuttle to the fact that this was no ordinary day. The feast had been in its way a birthday party.

The Pianone women were kept in complete ignorance of the sources of the family's income. Perhaps they actually believed that father and uncle and brothers and cousins were all involved in selling insurance or real estate. There was indeed Pirandello Savings and Loan and Empedocles Investments, both wholly owned and operated by the family. From time to time a policy was sold or a home listed, but that was not what kept these offices humming. Both establishments could have been said to be in the laundry business. It was a fiercely observed part of the family code that the women of the family, innocent and saintly, must not be sullied with the truth about the Pianone affluence.

Peanuts's older sister Laura had heard disturbing things from friends and expected a ringing denial from her father and uncles. Their unwillingness to answer her questions answered her questions. The world suddenly looked completely different than it had before. When she broke her engagement and announced that she had a religious vocation, the men were delighted. Perhaps if the younger sister Angela had been told everything then, she would not later have become involved in a situation all too similar to her sister's. Angela's crime, in Peanuts's eyes, was that she had fallen in love with a man with no connections to the family.

"What's his name?"

Peanuts found it hard to say the name aloud. He hunched his shoulders, squinted his eyes, rolled on his haunches, then barked it out.

"Oscar Hanley!"

Peanuts turned and spat on the floor, then got up and covered it with one of his great flat shoes as if it were a burning cigarette. Tuttle got the point.

Tuttle's friendship with Peanuts Pianone involved a total and willed lack of curiosity about what Peanuts's relatives were up to. The lawyer was in this no different from the local constabulary or judiciary. Even the local newspaper preferred to pontificate on problems pestering far-off peoples rather than comment on the evil beneath its editorial nose. Tuttle had never quizzed his friend about the killing of Vince O'Toole or the attempts to dig him up again once he was buried. Peanuts's unusual confidence about his sister Angela would normally have had no sequel for Tuttle. It was the mention of Oscar Hanley that piqued his curiosity. Surely this was Ray Hanley's son.

"She wants to get married, she marries Giorgio." Giorgio was a cousin of sorts.

"Blood is thicker than water."

"Yeah."

Two days later Oscar Hanley was reported as missing and Tuttle, putting two and two together, wondered if he had a responsibility, as an officer of the court, to

53

relay what Peanuts had said to the authorities. He decided in the negative. The police would not need to be told to suspect the Pianones.

# Mimi O'Toole

## 7

"I never heard of it," Mimi said, taking Marie Murkin's hand.

"Father Dowling has been there. It is taking place in a parish where one of his classmates is pastor."

"The Blessed Mother appears?"

"To a woman." Marie had checked it out with her counterpart, the housekeeper at St. Teresa's, and been told all as if it were a sorority secret.

"Is there a message?"

"It hasn't been revealed yet."

Mimi felt a strange thrill. Ever since Vince had died, she had begun to think that there is only a kind of gauzelike separation between the living and the dead. At first, whenever she had the feeling that Vince was in the room with her, she was a little frightened, but then she found it comforting. Until she began to think he was trying to tell her something. She had asked Father Dowling if Vince had died in the state of grace, forming the question carefully. She had to have a clear answer.

"Mimi, that is something we can't know with certainty even about ourselves. We have that on the authority of St. Paul. *Neque meipsum iudico.*"

It was so nice to hear a priest speak Latin. Her memories of the Mass when it had all been in Latin were dim, but not so dim that they did not tug at her heartstrings. The memories were associated with girlhood and innocence.

"But you gave him absolution?"

Why had he been so reluctant to tell her? Even after he had said he had, and that she shouldn't worry about it, God's mercy is infinite, Mimi was not reassured. She felt that Father Dowling was holding something back. And her sense grew that Vince was trying to contact her, that he was not at peace.

"Marie, let's go to Barfield," Mimi suggested.

"Father Dowling would scalp me if I did."

"Don't tell him."

"How would we get there?"

"I'll drive."

They were like girls sharing a secret, only this was serious. Mimi wanted to visit the place where the Blessed Mother appeared and beg for a sign that Vince was all right, that Father Dowling's absolution had taken effect and her husband was resting in peace.

"I don't know," Marie said, but her tone indicated that she had already made up her mind. "If Father Dowling ever hears . . ."

"He won't hear it from me."

Their grip on one another's hands tightened. After a moment of silence, they made their plans.

It was a sunless windswept day when Marie Murkin slipped into the passenger seat of Mimi's car. Mimi had pulled up on the side street so that the church blocked the view from the rectory, and she kept the motor running. Leaves scudded across the lawn and cartwheeled down the street. Above, bare, brittle branches creaked in the wind. The side door of the church opened and Marie emerged and walked swiftly toward the car, head down, clasping her coat closed with one hand and gripping her purse with the other. Mimi pulled away from the curb as soon as Marie shut the door.

"What did you tell him?"

Marie moaned with a penitent's remorse. "I said we were going shopping."

"I could have picked you up at the front door then."

"He'll think we're taking public transportation."

Mimi did not understand such subterfuge. But then it had always been Vince who deceived her, not the reverse. The memory stirred the ashes of long-forgotten anger, but she did not fan the embers into flame. How much better to have a husband to annoy you than to be a lonely widow. She felt a renewed desire to pray for Vince and ask Our Lady's intercession. She would put in a word for Sonny as well.

For a long time she had difficulty believing that Sonny was the child she had borne in her womb. Even as a little boy he had been strange. Often she would become aware of him, sitting in a corner of the room, staring at her. He stared at Vince too until he got clobbered for it.

"The kid has the eyes of a federal agent."

Neither of them could figure out who Sonny looked like. He was tall like Vince, but soft and shapeless. He had small hands, like Mimi's, and small feet too, which she did not. But it was his behavior, not his looks, that marked him off from every other child. He insisted on clothing two sizes larger than he needed, as if he were wearing a disguise. Real weirdness began when he was a teenager. He let his unwashed hair reach his shoulders and, in response to Vince's threats, he braided it and let it hang down his back.

"I wash my hands of him," Vince said, conceding defeat. Short of disowning him or dropping him out a window, there was nothing to be done. Mimi had been almost relieved when Sonny got religion.

"What kind of religion?" Vince asked.

"Some eastern thing. They meditate."

"He's got a lot to think about."

"He shaved his head."

"Maybe too close."

Before the head shave, Vince had said Sonny's braid was too tight, that was the explanation.

She had expected, half fearing, half hoping, that Sonny would go far away and they would see him seldom if ever again, but the group he joined was located in Skokie. Not that Sonny ever came home. Once Vince thought he recognized him at O'Hare and grabbed the wrist of the man with the bowl and found himself looking into a stranger's eyes.

"He was wearing the same goddamn dress."

"Sonny's like a monk."

"You can say that again."

She didn't press it. Religion was a delicate subject with Vince. Of course there was a fundamental conflict between what he did for a living and basic morality, forget about religion, but he had a residual, almost superstitious faith. Mimi had formed the conviction that, with age and retirement, Vince would withdraw from his old associations and grow closer to God, maybe even become a Knight of Columbus. But Sonny's involvement with the monks in the orange dresses did not help. On that horrible day that she was called to the hospital and told what had happened to Vince, she became hysterical. He must not die until a priest had absolved him of his sins. She was still thanking God for the miracle of Father Dowling's being there.

If only she could be *certain* that the absolution had taken effect. Perhaps today she would get some intimation of that when she prayed before the miraculous statue of Mary in St. Teresa's parish in Barfield.

"Tell me about the apparitions," she urged Marie.

"What apparition? Mary talks to the woman, that's all, confiding a message to her."

"I meant the other ones."

Marie knew about them all, LaSallette, Lourdes, Fatima, others Mimi had never heard of. There were all kinds of apparitions going on all over the world right now, according to Marie, and that made it less surprising that Our Blessed Mother should talk to a lady golfer in Barfield.

They had to park a block away. When they approached, Mimi stopped. "It's a cemetery."

"I told you that."

Had she? If so, it hadn't registered. Mimi looked at the newly painted wrought-iron fence enclosing the cemetery. She saw the neat gravel roads that divided the area into pie slices, the well-tended gravesites. And then, the point toward which the other pilgrims were moving, the statue of Mary in the center where all the gravel roads met. From the outset Mimi knew that something very important was happening.

Many people knelt on the gravel to recite the rosary, but they stood, Marie leaning against a tree to take the pressure off her leg. Sciatica, she said. It made her a restless passenger. All the way to Barfield, the housekeeper had squirmed in her seat, seeking a comfortable position.

There was no contrast between the face of the statue and the garments — all was of uniform white. This gave the statue an ethereal quality, as if it were seen through the gauze that Mimi imagined separated the living from the dead. Mimi had her rosary in her hand but she didn't say it. She just told Mary why she had come. She asked that Vince might rest in peace and she pleaded for some sign that would tell her that all was well with him in the next world. She prayed for Sonny too, the idiot, but he had years in which to correct his mistakes, and her major concern was her departed husband. When consolation came it took an unexpected form.

She found that she intended to have Vince reburied here, in Barfield, in this cemetery, under the protection of the Blessed Virgin. Here he would be safe, from all his enemies in this world and in the next. A great peace came over her with this realization.

"It's just another statue," Marie said on the way back to St. Hilary's.

"I'm glad we came."

"Don't tell anyone. Promise."

Mimi promised, feeling almost selfish as she did because she wanted the cemetery in Barfield to be her secret. Apparently Marie had not felt the power of the place. She thought it was just another statue of Mary! Mimi intended to go back, she intended that both Vince and herself, and Sonny too, if he shaped up, should spend eternity in that blessed place.

"I've been thinking of what you said,"

Mimi said to Cy Horvath the following day. He just waited for her to go on. "About reburying my husband."

He nodded. "It may be the only way to make certain it won't happen again."

"What do I have to do?"

"Who was your funeral director?"

"McDivitt."

"Talk to him. He'll know the procedure."

# Cecil McDivitt

## 8

"It's McDivitt," Marie said, pushing just her head into the study, reminding Father Dowling of St. Denis, who, having been martyred, carried his severed head to the famous church outside of Paris that bears his name. "Why are you grinning?"

"I didn't hear the phone ring."

"He's in the parlor."

Father Dowling rose with mixed emotions. There is a symbiotic — if the word's etymology will permit this use of it — relation between pastor and undertaker. The death and burial of parishioners is a constant factor in the pastor's responsibilities, and this places him perforce into alliance with such professionals as Cecil McDivitt. McDivitt had pretty well commandeered the St. Hilary business, and, given the average age of the parishioners, this was no small coup. In return, he provided elegant calendars for free distribution, bearing, needless to say, a tasteful reminder of the services offered by McDivitt's Funeral Home. The danger in such relations is that they became too cozy. McDivitt sometimes viewed his role in somewhat enlarged terms, and word had come to Father Dowling that the undertaker had invoked his authority on matters that had never been discussed between them. For all that, McDivitt was a good man who knew when to leave off urging the bereaved to spend more than they should on the funeral of the departed beloved.

McDivitt stood by the parlor window, a picture of impeccable elegance, pearl-gray suit, vest, subdued tie, snow-white shirt to complement the cotton-white hair above his ruddy countenance. Despite his lugubrious occupation, McDivitt's smile was prelapsarian in its insouciance. He held out his soft hand and Father Dowling shook it.

"I would ask you into my study but it is foul with the smell of pipe tobacco."

McDivitt, having sat and crossed one creased leg over the other, sighed. *"Ego atque in Arcadia,* Father. It has been a dozen years since I quit."

"Do you miss it?"

"My vice was cigars. Yes, I confess that there are times when the thought of a good cigar can be almost overwhelmingly attractive. But I found that the smell of tobacco can be resented by the bereaved, particularly if their beloved died of —"

"I understand."

"It is hardly the major cause of death, Father Dowling."

"We live in strange times."

"Yes, yes." He uncrossed his legs. "I have come to seek your advice."

"Of course."

"It is about the late Vincent O'Toole."

"Has there been another attempt on his grave?"

McDivitt threw up his hands at the thought of amateurs seeking to undo his handiwork. "Mrs. O'Toole has come to me with the notion of reburying her husband."

"Because of the outrage?"

"Yes."

"That makes sense, doesn't it?"

"There is no need to change cemeteries in order to insure that he will rest in peace."

"Is that what she proposes?"

"Father Dowling, what do you know of the events taking place in Barfield?"

Father Dowling wished he had brought his pipe with him. It was moments like this when the consolations of tobacco were felt most keenly. It would not do to speak skeptically of the alleged appearance of the Blessed Mother to Buddy Walsh's parishioner — after all, it was not his role to pronounce on the authenticity or lack of it in such private revelations — but there was, undeniably, a tendency afoot to put too much emphasis on the extraordinary, as if messages from heaven must compete with news bulletins to guide the faithful through the shoals of contemporary life. The fundamentals of the faith — the sacraments, the Mass — were deemed insufficient and people felt the need for a direct pipeline into the hereafter or, just as frequently, forecasts of what the morrow would bring. Behind it all lay an almost eager curiosity about the end of the world.

"Captain Keegan gave me to understand that it would just be a transfer within Riverview."

"I suppose it's up to the widow."

"Of course. But the police also have an interest."

Father Dowling nodded. Whatever the vandals had been after on Hallowe'en, presuming that a serious attempt to disinter Vincent O'Toole had been interrupted by Heidegger, Phil Keegan would want to know about it. They had spoken of this on several occasions.

Phil felt that the vandals could have been either friends or enemies of O'Toole who thought something had been buried with his body. Did this pique the curiosity of the police sufficiently to exhume the body? Phil just gave him a look, but in this case Phil might not have regretted the indifference of his superiors. In any case, he seemed to think that Mimi O'Toole would seek to have her husband's body exhumed. Cy Horvath had put a bug in her ear. But Cy would not have suggested reburial in Barfield. If Phil had anything to do with it, he would dig up O'Toole and then put him right back where he was. The assumption would be that they had found whatever it was had been buried with the body. But for that a court order was needed, so they were to the intransigent Chief Robertson.

Now, in the rectory parlor, McDivitt was waiting for counsel but Father Dowling could not imagine what the funeral director expected to hear. Mrs. O'Toole had every right to bury her husband's body where she chose. But it was doubtful that it would be in Barfield.

"I think that cemetery is all sold out, Cecil."

"I would have thought so."

"Isn't it?"

"She says she has found two lots."

If true, that would be the end of it. But after McDivitt left, Roger Dowling put in a call to Buddy Walsh. He reached an answering service, but as soon as he began to record a message, Walsh picked up the line.

"I get so many crazy calls, I like to make sure."

"Insurance?"

"Ha! People want the latest bulletin from heaven. What did Our Blessed Mother say today?"

"What do you tell them?"

"Be it done unto me according to thy word."

"Does that satisfy them?"

"Sometimes they ask me to repeat it. I think they write it down."

"It's as good an answer as any. One of my parishioners wants to bury her husband in your cemetery."

"A Mrs. O'Toole?"

"You've talked with her?"

"When she came to me I told her there wasn't a lot left. The following day I got a telephone call from a man who said he was selling Mrs. O'Toole his two plots."

"Hmmm."

"Is there anything wrong, Roger?"

It was a nice moral question. Was he obliged to tell Buddy of the checkered career of the late Vincent O'Toole? Why not let O'Toole's evil be interred with his bones, thus proving the bard wrong for once?

*"De mortuis nil nisi bonum."*

There was a silence. Buddy had been an abominable Latinist. Father Dowling went on. "I was with her husband when he died."

"That's good enough for me."

"Let's hope it was good enough for him."

"She asked me to say some Masses for him."

It was clear that Mimi would not rest in peace until her husband did. Maybe it was just as well that the body should be taken out to Barfield.

"Who was the man who sold her the lots?" Dowling asked.

"Giorgio Pianone? Apparently he had just bought them himself but was willing to let them go."

# Ray Hanley

## 9

Ray Hanley tried with the aid of booze to convince himself that Oscar's disappearance was not sinister. Except for arthritis, sciatica, open heart surgery, and incipient cataracts that made a magnifying glass necessary to read anything but headlines, Ray had been feeling great. It had seemed part of the marriage pact that Eileen would outlive him. She had never known a day of illness, unless having kids could be called an illness, which it never had been until recently, but he didn't want to go into that. Her death was peaceful, he was actually holding her hand at the time and she was as awake as the drugs permitted. One minute she was breathing and then she wasn't. It was like a scene in a movie and it never lost its power to bring tears to his eyes. He was like a kid without her, abandoned, full of a self-pity he did his best to conceal. The kids were wonderful, helping him through it. He told the girls to take what they wanted of their mother's, she would want them to have it. What was he going to do with all the jewelry he had bought her over the years? It had become a habit because he was so lousy at picking gifts. A ring, a bracelet, necklace, simple if expensive, and his shopping was done. Eileen had never really liked jewelry all that much either. Well, the girls loved it. That left him alone in the house with Oscar.

They had named him Oscar because it had taken four daughters before they got him, like a prize.

"You're all Emmies," Eileen had told the girls, not wanting them to take offense.

"Friend and emmies?"

But Eileen took care of them all. She had wanted a son but she loved her daughters. Who ranks kids anyway? They're yours, for better or worse. The girls got married and were living at the four corners of the earth.

"At the round earth's imagined corners," Oscar echoed dramatically, throwing back his head and closing his eyes as he recited the words. Ray would have been worried about the boy but he knew him well enough by then.

"Who said that?"

"John Donne."

"Never heard of him."

Oscar had brains, real brains, everyone noticed. His teachers, his sisters, even his father. The question was, what would he do with his life? He said he wanted to be a poet.

"Sure. Okay. But how you going to make a living?"

Oscar adopted a pained expression, as if the need to earn one's bread was offensive to him. He was at Northwestern then, in a creative writing course, turning out poetry by the yard. Ray had no idea whether it was good or bad. First he would have had to understand it, and Oscar might have been writing in Norwegian. Earl O'Leary, the assistant Ray had hired, said it was good, maybe because it was obvious that the poet would not fill his father's shoes and become Earl's boss. Some of it appeared in a student magazine. Eileen was proud and would have shown it to her friends if it hadn't been for the photographs in the issue. Well, there is an age when the naked human body is of overwhelming interest. Some men never got beyond that age, which was one of the reasons the Pianones were rich.

The thing about writing is that some of it is poetry and some of it is criticism, and a piece appeared on Oscar's poetry in a campus publication suggesting that Keats and Shelley had nothing to fear. The most the critic conceded was that Oscar's poems were technically competent. The critic's name was Angela Pianone. Of course Oscar looked her up.

They became friends.

He brought her home.

Eileen loved her.

Ray faced a dilemma. Angela was a sweet girl, smart, Catholic, serious. But there was her family.

"That what you want to do," Ray asked her. "Criticize poetry?"

"That was for a class assignment. I had no idea it would be published. Actually, I like Oscar's poetry."

"I'm no poet," Oscar said. "You were right. Any idiot can imitate poetry."

"You're too hard on yourself."

She sat closer to him on the couch and put a hand on his arm. Eileen, looking on, smiled beatifically.

"I may go to law school," Oscar announced.

"Just because I'm going?"

"I'm an imitator."

So she was a good influence on him as well. The thought of Oscar taking all his talent into some garret and wasting his life writing sonnets had filled Ray with despondency.

"Either that or go in with Dad."

"Not on your life," Ray said.

"Are you ashamed of being a private investigator?"

"It's better than writing poetry. But not much. You go to law school."

Oscar had shown as little curiosity about what his father did for a living as apparently Angela did about hers. Ray told Eileen the truth about the Pianones and her reaction told him how difficult it would be trying to make Oscar believe it.

Then Eileen died and there was just Oscar and Ray. It was nip and tuck for a while, but Oscar entered law school and Ray began a novena asking that his son stop loving Angela Pianone. He never really believed the prayer would be answered and on the eighth day he called it off, telling St. Anthony he was sorry to have wasted his time. But he was determined to tell his son about Angela's family.

"I've met them," Oscar said.

"You've talked about it with her?"

"Of course. Dad, we're going to get married."

"What's it like when you go home with her?"

"Wonderful. The meals! The wine! The music! Her father is a very cultivated man. Salvatore. That means savior. I'm learning Italian."

"Maybe he'll take you into the business." Ray realized he was jealous. Had a hoodlum replaced him in his son's affections?

"That's a possibility."

"Oscar! What exactly do you know about the Pianones?"

"Dad, they're not mobsters! They sell insurance. They sell real estate. If it was anything else, Angela would know. Of course she has heard those accusations."

"All false?"

"She's got a brother on the police force."

"I forgot that."

That had been as close as he got to spelling it out for Oscar. The engagement of Oscar and Angela was announced, there was an engagement party at the Pianones' and two of Oscar's sisters flew in for the occasion. That made four of them against a small army of Pianones. Talk about an extended family. The women were lovely, the men taciturn, and Sal was the soul of hospitality. He sang along with Vic Damone records and it was hard to say which voice was which. The table groaned under the weight of food. A couple of glasses of the Sicilian red and Ray felt like becoming a wino. It was a great day until Sal made an oblique suggestion that he might throw a little business to Hanley Investigations.

"If I ever expand we can talk about it. I'm a one-man agency." No need to mention Earl O'Leary.

"The best way," Sal said after a moment's pause. "You got a wonderful son."

"Angela is a beautiful girl. My wife loved her."

"My only regret is that we never met her." There were tears in Salvatore Pianone's eyes. How could you hate a guy like that?

Oscar and Angela graduated from college, they entered law school, they were inseparable, they were betrothed. Ray decided that the Pianones had to be schizophrenics to keep such an absolute division between their disreputable businesses and their impeccable family life. In the backyard of Sal's home was a replica of the grotto at Lourdes and there were always candles burning before the statue of Our Lady. Maybe Sal was taking out insurance. It argued for some goodness that the men kept their doings a secret from the women. That suggested both shame for the deeds and respect for women. Ray found himself wobbling, and he didn't like it. In his work he needed a clean, uncomplicated distinction between good and evil. The good guy was his client, the bad guy was the other guy. That's what it usually came down to, a spouse suspicious of a spouse. "Who's he seeing? I've got to know."

Nine times out of ten they would have been better off not knowing, but he should put himself out of business and tell them that?

"They're a lot like you," Oscar said one day. "The Pianones. They make money off the weakness of others."

"How do they do that?" Ray asked carefully. He was rubbing pain killer on his elbows.

"Don't you know?"

"I wonder what you know."

"You tried to tell me once and I didn't believe you. Angela doesn't know, not really."

"So what are you going to do?" He was still feeling the sting of being likened to the Pianones.

"Do? Nothing. What do the police do?"

"That's a long story."

"I'll bet."

"Oscar, don't get involved with them."

"I'm going to marry his daughter."

"Who knows nothing."

"Maybe I'll go in with you."

It was the first time he had hit the kid since he was a teenager. And it wasn't just a pop. He put his arm and shoulder into it, the hell with the pain from his arthritis, and

Oscar careened across the room, hit the wall, and slid into a sitting position, out like a light. Ray poured a pitcher of ice water over his head. He was still mad. When Oscar came to and remembered what had happened he shook him away and went to his room. They never had a real conversation after that. They never had any kind of conversation.

After Oscar disappeared, Ray tried to kid himself that his son had run away because he had hit him.

"I forced his hand," he told Phil Keegan. He had sold the house and moved into an apartment and was surprised to find that Phil Keegan lived two buildings away, his balcony overlooking the same artificial lake. "I hit him and he was going to get even and . . ."

"And what?"

"I don't know. But what could hurt me more than his joining the Pianones?"

"He was going to be a lawyer, Ray. They would have had him doing legit work."

"See, you talk about him as if he were dead. They killed him, you know they did."

"I don't know that, Ray. And you don't either."

After Oscar disappeared, Ray tried to talk to Sal Pianone, but that door was shut and this confirmed his suspicions. He telephoned and asked to speak to Angela but she was never in. She wasn't at school either, she had canceled her courses, her student status no longer active.

"Her love life went sour," the dean's secretary said, whispering. Ray had identified himself as the representative of a relative who wanted to help Angela without the knowledge of her family. A desk plate told him that she was Faye Dupont.

"Financial help?" she asked.

Ray closed his eyes and nodded.

"Apparently her fiancé broke it off and she had a nervous breakdown."

"Of course you wouldn't know his name?" He smiled benevolently at the chubby secretary who had an office of her own and no one to talk to.

"I wouldn't if he hadn't been a student himself."

"Where is he?" He couldn't resist. What if Oscar had left a clue? Faye was grinning as if he had just made the right guess in a quiz. She pulled open a drawer and rummaged around in it. Then she had it.

"This arrived here at this office." The envelope had been opened but still retained its contents. "It is the request for a leave of absence." She looked beyond him. "Why don't you close that door?"

He did and, still whispering, she handed him the envelope. Inside was Oscar's letter requesting a leave of absence and another smaller envelope, still sealed. It was addressed to Angela in Oscar's hand. It was all Ray could do not to tear it open. He put the letter and sealed envelope back into the larger envelope and handed it to Faye.

"She has never returned. I've tried to reach her a million times. It has to be a breakdown. And who could blame her?" Faye's expression hinted at untold depths of emotional response.

Ray thanked her and left. As he passed through the outer office and down the hallway his eyes were photographing everything. He was coming back that night and he was determining the best way to do so unannounced.

What followed later was not a high point in his career. In the dead of night he arrived at the maintenance door of the law school unobserved. The lock gave way easily to the third key he tried. Inside, night-lights enabled him to move swiftly to the dean's office. The outer office was unlocked. He slipped inside and then noticed that the light was on in Faye's office. That was the last thing he noticed before the lights went off in his head. He came to draped over a Dumpster situated just beside the maintenance door. His head had enlarged in a way that made thinking difficult. He had been made a fool of.

The next day when he read the account of the break-in, he thanked God he had given Faye a phony business card. These were tools of his trade, but he might have thought precautions unnecessary when he made inquiries of the law school. Her description of him was flattering. She insisted that he had been a perfect gentleman, implying that he had surmounted all but overwhelming temptation. Maybe she was wrong to single him out. After all, the thief had cleaned out her drawer. She was only now beginning to think of things that were missing.

Earl O'Leary, the assistant who described himself as an apprentice of the master, asked Ray if he had heard of the break-in at the law school.

"Only what I've seen in the papers."

"Any ideas?"

"Not this early in the morning."

He said he wouldn't be taking any calls. There was little danger that anyone would mistake him for the Scarlet Pimpernel who had called on Faye Dupont and stolen her heart away, but you never know.

Obviously the Pianones had a tail on him. Someone had followed him to the law school. The girls in the outer office said that there had been people waiting while the man was in with Faye. She closed the door, they added, but we weren't worried, not about Faye. One of the persons waiting had been listening to a CD player, plugs in his ears, so there was no point asking if he had heard anything, though he had been closest to Faye's door.

That equipment would have picked up Faye's whisper. He had stumbled into their rustling of her office. He was lucky to be alive.

It was not the sort of episode he could talk about, not even to Keegan. But Keegan talked to him about the newspaper reports.

"The guy who spoke to the secretary? That could be you, Ray."

"Ha. That must have been Pianone's guy."

"I wonder what was in the envelope?"

"She says it was from my son."

"You ought to look into it."

"I was hoping you would."

"I'll talk to Cy Horvath about it."

He grabbed Keegan's hand. "God bless you, Phil. I've been praying you'd do something."

"Get off my duff and go to work?"

"You know what I mean."

"You're lucky I do."

# Earl O'Leary

## 10

Earl O'Leary displayed a trustworthy manner and a baby face that either attracted people or put them off. In the case of Ray Hanley it had been a plus all the way; the experienced private investigator had had difficulty keeping condescension out of his manner when Earl walked into his office last winter and applied for the job.

"Job? What job? I haven't advertised a position."

"I know you haven't."

"So what is this?"

There was a smile on Hanley's lips and a guffaw right around the corner as he looked Earl over. Earl was wearing country-bumpkin clothes, a three-piece suit from a discount store that was somewhere between green and beige in color, light brown laced shoes with tan socks, and a shirt whose collar was two sizes too large. The knot of his tie was the size of Sinatra's when he first went on tour. Earl explained that he wanted to be a detective and he had checked out some of the schools and decided that the way to do it would be to apprentice himself to a master.

"The way Abe Lincoln learned law," he added.

Of course Hanley saw himself in the role of Lincoln, which made no sense, but he was clearly flattered by the thought of a young man coming to him as to a master.

"On-the-job training, you mean?"

"The benefit would be mine, so I wouldn't expect much money. I would do it for nothing, the way apprentices used to, only I can't afford that."

Hanley waved away the thought. He was already hooked on the idea. "What did you expect to do?"

"You could call me a secretary. I could be of help to you there." He looked around, as if the idea had just hit him. "And I could help you computerize your operation."

That did it. Like most people who did not understand computers, Hanley was like a member of a cargo cult in the South Seas. He pointed out that he didn't have a computer. Earl told him he could have the office equipped for no more than two thousand dollars.

"And that includes fax."

Hanley found this hard to believe, so Earl got out the cost sheets he had made for various combinations. There were five possibilities running from $1,750 to $2,300, itemized.

"You just carry these around?"

"I came prepared to argue my case."

He won. He got the job. The only thing Hanley said was dress less formally. "You know, jeans, a sweater, a pair of Nikes."

Earl grinned like a kid. "Great. I bought this suit for the occasion."

"See if they'll take it back."

It never seemed to occur to Hanley to check out the man who was volunteering to come into his office, work for a song, and dig around through all his records as he computerized him. A baby face had its rewards.

Giorgio Pianone, on the other hand, had been put off by Earl's cherubic countenance when he walked into Earl's Minneapolis office unannounced last January and said, "I want to see your boss."

"I am the boss."

Giorgio had thought about that. Earl figured they were about the same age. In any movie with a clear story line, Giorgio would be cast with the good guys, not the bad. Maybe it was the red hair. He had said his name was Mosconi.

"Italian?"

"What's O'Leary?"

"Irish. What can I do for you, Mr. Mosconi?"

Earl had assumed the man was using the name for the occasion. Clients in an office like Earl's had problems they did not want to take to the police. Step one was to find out who the prospective client really was. He had found the motel Giorgio had checked into, and the name Pianone didn't ring a bell, but five minutes at the computer turned up the Fox River family. That night, he met Giorgio for dinner, when Giorgio was going to lay out what he would like Earl to do. "Why did you come to me, Mr. Pianone?"

Giorgio's eyes didn't do much blinking and they didn't blink then. "That's the reason. You're smart enough not to trust me."

"Are you dumb enough to trust me?"

"We'll be cute just this one time. I can trust you."

Earl could translate that. As far as Giorgio was concerned, someone working for him was trustworthy or dead. Earl sensed that he had already crossed the line into the danger zone when he told Giorgio that he had found out who he was. He didn't know what this was all about but he already knew too much.

"I don't think I ever met an Italian with red hair."

"It's on my mother's side."

Red hair on your mother's side? I have a mole on my father's side. Things Earl did not say. If he had passed the point of no return with Giorgio, he found it exhilarating. Honesty would have been part of the picture if Earl had become a cop the way his father wanted him to. His father had been crooked in a penny-ante way for most of his time on the Minneapolis force. He cheated, that was it mostly. Earl was shocked. If you can't trust a cop, who can you trust? Just about anyone else, was the cynical answer. His father could have made a pile if he had used the information that came to him in a professional way. But that would have been risky. What if his father had joined the force with the aim of getting rich? Being a private investigator seemed a way in which he could gather all kinds of potentially valuable information, and Earl intended to cash in on it. From the outset, he had the feeling that Giorgio Pianone was offering him the chance of a lifetime.

Not that Giorgio realized it. All he wanted was someone with the smarts to infiltrate

Ray Hanley's operation and tell Giorgio all Hanley knew about things that concerned Giorgio and other Pianones. Particularly everything he could pick up about Hanley's son Oscar. Oscar had just become engaged to Giorgio's second cousin Angela.

"You're asking me to take a job that would take me out of my office for an indefinite period."

"Close your office. You'll work for me."

Earl sat back. He was wearing a black turtleneck sweater, corduroy jacket and jeans. Two-hundred-dollar shoes, pamper your feet. It was the one piece of advice he had taken from his father. "I am very interested to hear how much you are willing to pay to buy my business. That's what you would be doing. Then hiring me to run it."

Giorgio put an envelope on the table, keeping one large hand on it. It looked like a thick envelope. "That's a hundred grand. Tax free, so it is — what's your bracket?"

"That's my retainer?"

Giorgio nodded. "If you're as good as you say you are."

"Did I say I was good?"

"With every breath you take. Get me what I want and you've got another hundred grand."

"Then what?"

"Maybe you will have grown to like us."

Giorgio thought Earl was reaching for the envelope when he put his hand across the table. He had to let go of the envelope to shake. Earl slid the retainer to his side of the table with his free hand.

"What do you want me to do?"

"How would you go about making a guy disappear? Just vanish, no trace of where he had gone."

"But still alive?"

"Still alive."

"Who did you have in mind?"

"You."

So Earl O'Leary died and went to Fox River, invested the one hundred thousand in a stock market that was rising like a rocket, and lived off what Hanley paid him.

"This is no life for you," Oscar said. "You ought to become a lawyer."

"And deal with real crooks?"

It was one of Oscar's gifts that you could not insult him. Negative remarks directed his way were always deflected toward what he took to be their true target. "That isn't where the money is."

"Tell it to the Pianones."

That got home. "I'm not marrying the whole family."

Earl had never got to know the legendary Mrs. Hanley, already raised to sanctity in the memories of those who had known her, but he was assured that she had met and approved of the beautiful Angela.

Law school? Earl dropped by Barnes & Noble and picked up a cram book on the LSAT, took the exam the next opportunity and aced it. He had no intention of going to law school, but it was good to know the choice was his. And he felt it helped understand Oscar.

Earl and Oscar became friends, he met Angela. Hanley neither encouraged nor discouraged this. Later, it gave Earl status in the search for the missing Oscar. And with Giorgio he got credit for looking out for the Pianone interests. Make that Giorgio's interests. It had dawned on Earl that he represented a freelance effort on Giorgio's part and that the rest of the family did not know it. It wounded his vanity to think that this great turn in his luck was due to a rejected suitor's desire to discredit his victorious rival.

"Disappear," Giorgio repeated. "Not snuffed."

This time they were talking about Oscar's fate. Earl assured him that he understood the distinction. At the moment, he had been busy wondering how he could use Giorgio's long-range operation as a means to another and bigger pay off from Salvatore.

"What's he like?" Earl asked Oscar.

"You wouldn't believe me if I told you."

"Crude?"

"No! Earl, he knows more about music than . . . Think of someone who knows a lot about music. Classical music. Opera. And literature?"

"You're making this up."

Incredulity spurs on the effort to prove. Thus, Oscar waxed eloquent about Salvatore's study, the magnificent library, the bindings, the lighting. He made it sound like a shrine.

"So what's he read?"

"The question would be, how many languages does he read."

"English and Italian."

"Those mainly. But he has German and French books as well."

"French?" Earl's eyebrows danced and he dug Oscar in the ribs.

"Listen, that place is like a monastery. Never a word out of line, let alone anything else."

"And it's all financed by Smut City?"

"Paradoxical, isn't it? Maybe none of the great fortunes could stand close scrutiny as to their origins. But Smut City is only part of it, a small part."

"Does he talk business with you?"

Oscar eyed Earl. "I'm going to be his son-in-law."

"You're really going to join the family?"

"It might be tempting. There are slow ways of making money, and there are fast ways."

"Sure. And there are short and long lives."

How much did Oscar know? Earl learned to play his conversations with Oscar against Giorgio's obsession to find grounds to denounce him to Salvatore and discredit him as a suitable suitor for Angela. That way Earl began to get a sense of the operation. Giorgio included him in a few things, no doubt to seal their bargain.

Earl, having given the matter much thought, decided to warn Oscar that he was in danger.

"Get lost. Disappear."

"I don't believe it."

"Believe it."

"But Angela . . ."

"You're no good to her dead."

Oscar's disappearance came as a surprise to Giorgio, but not as much of a surprise as Earl's question.

"Where is he?"

Even the depraved can be surprised by an honest moment. Looking into Giorgio's eyes, Earl knew he had no clue what had happened to Oscar. And Giorgio could read the same message in Earl's eyes and seemed to believe it.

Where the hell was Oscar Hanley?

# Anton Jarry

## 11

As flowers in spring give way to buds and eventually fruit, so construction sites give way in stages to finished buildings. The analogy limps, of course, since flowers are beautiful and construction sites are not. Nor do they suggest the plea, forget me not. Confronted with the building itself — in the case in point, a four-story bank on Dirksen Avenue in downtown Fox River, Illinois — one forgot the ugliness and noise, the dirt, the barriers that prevented proper inspection of the work in progress on the part of citizens whose leisure enabled them to perform this public service. It was not that people stopped and stared in wonder at the building now. We no longer ask so much of our architects in the present age. But it pleased the eye in the sense that it did not arrest it. Once built, it was all but invisible. And it bore the name of a flower, the Crocus Building, whose main tenant was the Pirandello Savings and Loan.

No one looked at that building the way Anton Jarry did. From time to time he came downtown to stare at the site where he had worked as night watchman when the building was under construction.

It was known only to God and Jarry and those involved that one night when the period of construction was just drawing to a close, a van had arrived at the building site and, after a whispered exchange with the watchman, was permitted to drive through the temporary gate onto the building site itself. A small car had followed it in, close as a calf to its mother. What the purpose of the visit was Anton Jarry the watchman neither knew nor dared to ask. This was his last job. His sixty-second birthday had arrived and he intended to retire. Not that he would have indulged his curiosity about this episode earlier in his life. The men who entered the building site that night had expressions one strives to forget as soon as their claim for admission has been acknowledged.

An hour, perhaps two, had passed before the van reappeared at the gate, ready to leave. It was not followed by the little car. The three men in the van had glowered with grim satisfaction. The watchman watched the taillights of the van disappear down Dirksen until it turned off and was gone.

Some time later, making his rounds, Jarry could find no signs of what the men had been here to do. Nor was the little car anywhere to be seen. The area surrounding the building was covered with the usual debris, but it looked as it had looked before. The construction crane was still in place and the basement level, its concrete floor not yet laid, was muddy from the afternoon rain. Jarry was reminded of the springtime fields of his youth. The associations of the men in the van suggested . . . But he shivered and put the thought from his mind. He would leave the workforce with even greater relief because of the night's events.

The construction was completed in due course. He had watched the pilings being sunk and the steel frame raised; now concrete was poured, paint and glass and carpeting installed. Lawn was laid, the sidewalks paved, a ceremony held. The watchman did not attend the ceremony; by then he was retired and had become a frequent presence at the St. Hilary Senior Center. He took comfort from the fact that when Father Dowling said Mass each noon, his commemoration of the dead included all the known and unknown departed, all the poor souls for whom Jesus had given his life in order that they might be saved, no matter where or by whom their bodies might have been consigned to earth.

But Anton Jarry kept his meager savings

in the First Bank, not the Pirandello Savings and Loan.

One afternoon at the senior center a discussion began on the unsolved murders in the area, the theme suggested by the sight of Philip Keegan, captain of detectives, entering the rectory to visit his old friend Roger Dowling.

"There are some they don't care to solve," Hibbs said with a knowing air.

"When the underworld puts one of their own underground," O'Callaghan explained and seemed to have surprised himself by his felicitous turn of phrase.

"Like Vincent O'Toole."

"And the missing people," someone mused.

"Like that law student, Oscar Hanley."

"God rest their souls, I say," said Jarry, and there was the murmur of amen around the table.

"They put some in the river. Some they stash under a highway, before the concrete is poured."

Anton cleared his throat and pulled his chair closer to the table. "Once when I was watchman at the site of the Crocus Building . . . "

But he was ignored. His voice was weak,

and one's tone needed the equivalent of elbows to get into the conversation. Angela, the volunteer, had pushed old Fenster into the room some minutes before and he gaped about, moving his hairless head in a birdlike way. But Angela's sad Italian eyes were fixed on Anton Jarry.

# Marie Murkin

## 12

Marie Murkin answered the door to find Angela Pianone standing on the step. Angela was young and beautiful, yet here she was dressed in black, and not a fashionable black; over her raven hair she wore a babushka that framed the tragic beauty of her face. Angela looked up apologetically.

"Is Father Dowling in?"

"Captain Keegan is with him, but I'm sure he can see you."

"Captain?"

"Of police."

"I'll come back."

Before she could be stopped, she had turned and hurried away. Mrs. Murkin called after her. "In an hour, an hour at most!"

Meanwhile she looked into the study where the pastor, thin, ascetic, wreathed in pipe smoke, was listening to the overweight graying friend of his childhood talk about the Bears draft choices.

"I didn't know there was a war on."

The two men turned to look at her.

"Draft?" She bit her lip, certain she was about to be made an object of fun. "Angela wants to see you."

Father Dowling pushed back his chair. "Is she in the parlor?"

"Oh, she didn't wait. I told her you had company."

"Company?" Phil Keegan was not sure he liked the term applied to so frequent a caller as himself. Marie sometimes wondered why he didn't just move in. They had extra bedrooms because the parish once had prospered and there had been several priests in residence. After his wife died, Phil had sold the house in which they had raised their family and was living in an apartment in a new development that had all the character of an army camp.

"I wish you'd asked her to stay."

"I did. But when I told her Captain Keegan was here she scampered off down the walk."

"Angela Pianone," Father Dowling said to Phil Keegan.

"They're not in this parish!"

"She helps out at the center."

Marie put a hand on one hip and leaned against the door. "She's the one who needs cheering up. She has such a beautiful face, yet she's dressed like a grandmother and looks as if she'll never smile again."

"Oscar Hanley," Phil said.

Marie just looked at him. It could be dangerous to respond to enigmatic remarks made in this room.

"The Pianones chased her lover out of town."

Marie pushed away from the door frame and made an impatient noise. "I knew you'd say something like that. It always has to be a man, doesn't it? Have you ever considered that women might have another thought or two in their minds than some man?"

"No."

"Of all the . . ."

"I mean, I hadn't ever considered it, Marie. Men aren't obsessed with women the way women are with men."

There are moments when anything resembling victory, or at least a draw, depends upon retreat, and this was one of them. Marie turned and stalked regally to her kitchen where she held the swinging door so she could hear if any comments were being made in the study. But the talk had reverted to the Bears' prospects at quarterback.

"If not women, sports," Marie said to herself, and then wished that had been her parting shot when she left them.

With a cup of tea before her, Marie sat at

the table and thought of her own tragic case. Deserted by her husband without fanfare years ago, she had found herself alone and without the least notion of why he had gone. He had been in the navy, proud not to have waited for the draft, and when he disappeared she made inquiries but he had not reenlisted. Her situation had not been enviable. To call attention to it was to invite pity or, worse, the unstated accusation that she had driven her man away. But Marie could with a good conscience hold herself guiltless in the matter. She had two choices. To curse God or to accept this trial and make a life for herself, always hoping and praying that her wayward husband might return. A job in a rectory had seemed to offer the ideal setting for someone like herself. The priests were understanding and unlikely to be surprised by any variation worked on the folly of men. Or of women. She had begun keeping house for priests as a temporary expedient, but when she took the job at St. Hilary's she had accepted it as her destiny. There had been rocky years prior to Father Dowling's appointment, but ever since his arrival, things had been, if not smooth, at least to Marie Murkin's liking.

Feminists who agitated for the ordination of women would receive no aid and comfort from Marie Murkin. She doubted that any of the women who came to Mass at St. Hilary harbored any such ambition.

"Do they want men to become nuns?" she asked Father Dowling.

"Better not pursue it, Marie."

He would know the arguments against it. Marie's knowledge was of another kind. One does not spend as many years in a rectory as she had without learning a thing or two about the human heart. There were occasions, and more than you might think, when a woman's touch was needed, and Marie could supply what a priest could not. Of course she kept her ministry subdued. Father Dowling had an Irish wit, with a keen edge to it, and Marie had learned to avoid being its target.

Suddenly it occurred to her that this was one of those occasions. That poor woman had come to the rectory door with God knows what anguishing problem and had been turned away because the pastor was chatting with his crony about football! Her departure from the study had been an ambiguous move. Had she capitulated or was she declaring victory? Now she had a better response, and one so obvious she scolded herself for not thinking of it sooner.

She let herself out of the kitchen by the

screen door, making certain not to slam it; there was a robin nesting in the dogwood not twenty feet from the porch. Marie moved purposely along the walk toward the school, wondering what might be the best way to elicit from Angela the problem that had brought her to the rectory door.

A throat cleared when Marie hurried past the shrine, so absorbed she had forgotten to stop to murmur an Ave. The cleared throat might have been her conscience. But it was Anton Jarry, smiling at her, eyebrows lifted, his head tipped to one side. He held a bouquet of flowers. Good Lord.

"These are for this Marie," he said, his eyes falling and then lifting suddenly to hers.

Marie did not tell him that the Blessed Mother was more likely to answer his prayers. Anton had come to the kitchen door a week ago and asked if he could take her to a movie.

"I have television."

"For something to eat."

"Mr. Jarry, I spend my day cooking."

"Just a walk then."

"Can you imagine what a pleasure it is just to get off my feet?"

Despite all this, Marie had been tempted. Anton Jarry was a gentleman and he attended the noon Mass each day. He had never married and of course he would assume that she was a widow. She did not care to discuss with him what prevented her from encouraging the interests of gentlemen like himself. Not to lose all benefit from the request, however, she had mentioned it to the pastor. Someone should know that Marie Murkin still stirred the male breast.

"By this time your husband is legally dead, Marie. You could seek a declaration."

She stepped back. "Just assume he is dead?"

"You have to assume that he is alive."

"Are you saying that the Church would consider me a widow rather than a wife if a court declared him dead?" She was shocked.

"The Church does not hold you to omniscience. How long has it been?"

"A long time." She had hesitated, then decided not to be exact. The number of years, when she thought of it, seemed incredible. Who would believe that she had been married all that long ago?

"More than twenty-five years?"

She lifted her chin. "Yes."

"I would say that you can consider yourself a widow, morally. And legally you would have no difficulty having it officially declared. I don't like to see you turning men away from the door."

She had let it go. It was enough that he knew about her caller. Now, seeing Anton for the first time since that conversation with the pastor, she appraised him with a widow's rather than a wife's eye. She gave him a little smile that he might reasonably take for encouragement and went on toward the school. Had she been too abrupt? She turned and to her astonishment saw that Anton had been joined by someone else, a woman in black, Angela Pianone. The woman's beauty had drawn Marie's comment just minutes ago in the rectory. Anton seemed to be speaking to her with great deference. Angela's hand went out and touched Anton's forearm. Marie almost jumped at the contact.

She was tempted to go back. After all, she had come out to talk to Angela. But it seemed that the woman was receiving sufficient consolation at the shrine, and not simply from the Blessed Mother.

# Earl O'Leary

## 13

Earl O'Leary watched Ray Hanley's concern for his son turn into frantic despair. When Earl first met Oscar Hanley last spring, responses to Oscar's applications to law schools were flooding in, but Oscar was less elated by the fact that he had been accepted at the five top law schools than by the return of a sheaf of poems he had sent off to a legendary Chicago literary magazine. His returned poems were accompanied by a printed notice that informed Dear Author that they did not meet the current needs of the editors of *Poetry*. But at the bottom of the printed rejection slip was scrawled in pencil "VG." It was this annotation that brought Oscar rushing to his father's office, the law school acceptance letters in his left hand, the rejection of his poems in his right.

"Good news?"

"Almost," Oscar cried, flourishing what he held in his right hand.

Ray Hanley was dumbfounded. "You weren't accepted!"

Oscar looked at the letters in his left hand.

"To law school? Oh, sure." He dropped the letters on his father's desk, but came around to hold the printed rejection slip under Hanley's nose.

"Look. VG. Handwritten."

But Ray was looking past the slip at the letters of acceptance. He reached for them, ignoring what Oscar held in front of his face. Oscar turned to Earl.

"What do you think of that?"

"Someone's initials?"

"Are you kidding?"

"What does it mean?"

"VG? It means very good! I must have come close."

"From what your father has said, I'm surprised they didn't take them."

This disingenuous remark won a grateful look from Oscar.

"You were accepted by all five!" Ray shouted, leaping to his feet. "Harvard. Yale. Notre Dame, Chicago. Northwestern."

"I'm going to send them something else right away," Oscar said fervently.

It was a revelation of a constant of human nature, Earl decided. The good news received pales beside bad news, but to have the bad news seasoned with the salt of hope completely cancels the taste of the good news. So it was with Oscar and it was left to

Ray Hanley to rejoice in his son's success. Clearly Oscar stood at a crossroads. His youthful, glittering eyes made it clear that he would willingly exchange a brilliant future in the law for a printed page or two of his poems. Earl intervened.

"William Carlos Williams practiced medicine, but who remembers that? Does the name Wallace Stevens suggest insurance to you? Of course not. Oscar will be a brilliant lawyer, but his literary output will assure his immortality."

Oscar responded immediately to the comparisons. In a quince, as at the sound of the depressed key of a clavier, he saw the resemblance. Of course he would go to law school. He would excel at the law, using only a fraction of his talents, and it need not interfere with his true calling, that of a poet. Earl was thus in the position of a bridge player who not only makes his own bid but does so when his opponent has doubled it. Both father and son were grateful to him.

That was the real beginning of his friendship with Oscar and the start of his quiet campaign to enlist Oscar in his project to strip the Pianones of their ill-gotten fortune. He did not of course divulge this to Oscar, who had no idea of Earl's line into the family business via Giorgio. Neither Hanley *père* nor Hanley *fils* would have dreamt that the bright young assistant was a Trojan horse, a representative of the enemy, his mission to discredit Oscar with Angela Pianone, thus restoring Giorgio's chances for her hand. And it never occurred to Giorgio that the man in whom he had invested one hundred thousand dollars would use Oscar as his unwitting accomplice in the impossible dream of stealing the Pianone fortune.

In the event, Oscar went to Loyola law school because that was where Angela was accepted and he could not abide the thought of separation from her.

"You are my inspiration," he told her fervently.

"Oh, no," she moaned. She had no confidence in him as a poet, and doubtless she was right. After all, what was one to make of this one, called *"Parole di Paolo"*?

> *downright*
> *dantelike*
> *to hell and back*
> *I come*
> *bringing*
> *to you*
> *this*
> *kiss*

*of death,*
*Francesca.*

Earl adopted an expression of confused comprehension when Oscar showed him the poem. Oscar was awaiting his reaction. It was difficult to know what to say.

"Why don't you read it to me aloud?"

"Of course."

This did not improve it, but it was clear that Oscar enjoyed reading aloud what he had written. Earl thought for a moment and then said he found the poem amazing, which was true enough.

"I think of it as a variation on Haiku."

"Ah."

Oscar had also written a monosyllabic sonnet, a famous example of which existed in French but which had failed to inspire imitators in any language. Oscar regarded this as a challenge not to be shirked:

> *Hear*
> *my*
> *cry*
> *dear,*
> *dear*
> *dry*
> *my*
> *tear.*

*Cruel*
*rule!*
*One*
*twain*
*one*
*pain.*

"I fear I may be getting too experimental."

"The sonnet is not an experimental form."

"But a monosyllabic sonnet?"

Stroking Oscar's pride of authorship was sinfully easy and effective beyond Earl's wildest expectations. It altered Earl's plan, speeding it up. Much sooner than he would have thought possible, he broached the big topic with Oscar.

"You think that Angela is a prisoner of her family?"

"I suppose I do," Oscar said, after a pause, perhaps wondering when he had actually said the equivalent to Earl's interpretation.

"And you can rescue her from that?"

But Earl had already seen the small spark of avarice in the eye of his new friend. Gallantry and greed could be allied in Oscar's mind. He must be made to imagine that he could whisk away the daughter as well as a good share of the family's ill-gotten gains.

But Earl was not tempted to proceed precipitously. His was the most dangerous of games, and he knew it. Double spies must feel like that, at danger no matter which way they turned. Who knew what Ray Hanley would do to Earl if he learned that his assistant had contracted to deliver Oscar into the hands of his vengeful rival Giorgio Pianone? As for what Giorgio would do if he learned that Earl intended to double-cross him as well as Ray Hanley. . . . Well, the Pianones had a long tradition of sending their enemies cruelly into the next world.

From time to time Earl found himself wondering what, if anything, existed beyond death. He had been brought up a Catholic but during a time when catechetical illiteracy was the rule. Uninstructed savages had a better sense of heaven than did Earl, who was under the impression that religion had something to do with blowing up balloons, acting cheerful in an empty-headed way, and blaming the world's ills on capitalism. His images of the next world came out of a grab bag of odds and ends. He had his doubts about angels, but he firmly believed in ghosts. The air was thick with the spirits of the departed, most of them malevolent. That was part of the attraction of the afterlife: One could go on causing trouble for the living. Meanwhile, he studied his intended victims. Ray and Oscar seemed at best two-dimensional when compared with Salvatore Pianone. The man's cultivated interests seemed genuine, providing him the means of forgetting the sources of his wealth and ease, his music, art, books. Oscar had an advantage on him there: He could talk books with Angela's father and consolidate the position from which he had ousted Giorgio.

# Giorgio Pianone

## 14

Blood is thicker than water but Uncle Salvatore seemed to have ice water in his veins. Sometimes. At others, he would cry unashamedly when he listened to opera; lines from Leopardi had a similar effect. And babies? Put him within sight of a baby and he became an infant himself, down on his knees, cooing, making faces and then holding them so gently in his huge arms, his expression like one of the Madonnas on his wall. Family was the key to everything, blood. That was the theory. Giorgio was not sure that this was an ironclad rule for Salvatore. If it was, Angela would be his and Oscar Hanley would be dead in a ditch for presuming to fall in love with a Pianone. Uncle Salvatore had listened to Giorgio as if he were making a business proposal, wearing his cold fish look.

"Does Angela love you?"

"I love her."

"She's got to love back."

"If she does —"

"Angela will marry the man she loves."

Salvatore didn't mention her, but he had to

be thinking of Laura, the daughter who had gone to the convent when Salvatore would not okay her boyfriend. Religion was all right, but grandchildren were better.

Giorgio accepted the terms. Why wouldn't Angela like him? Women did. He had proof. Not that he could tell Angela that. She was a virgin, you could stake your life on it, and she received Holy Communion every Sunday. She was smart, too, intelligent, and that made Giorgio uncomfortable. She never said that was the reason she couldn't love him, that he wasn't smart enough for her.

"Giorgio, we're cousins."

"Second, third, what's the difference?"

"What do you know about genetics?"

Did she wonder if he knew what to do? "Enough."

"Then I don't have to explain."

"Explain."

He didn't understand the explanation. She seemed to think that if you married your second cousin your kids would be retarded. Where was the proof?

"Uncle Peanuts?"

She might have had an argument there, only Peanuts's parents hadn't been cousins. He saw Angela a lot — at family gatherings, nearly every weekend — but the harder he tried to make her like him, the more distant she became. Not distant. But she kind of kidded with him, as if he wasn't serious. But he was patient. He had time. It was important to his future that he marry Angela, but there was no rush. It wasn't as if he had to live like a monk in the meantime. When men married, they slowed down for a while, but soon they were back at it. Of course they loved their wives and children, but women were something else, a necessity. A commodity too. Sometimes he worried that Angela knew more than she let on and that she had learned that Giorgio now looked after Smut City, Vince O'Toole having been gotten out of the way. But then she ought to despise her father and she adored Salvatore. She obviously had been raised in total ignorance of the operation. In time she would come around.

But what had come around in time was Oscar Hanley. One look at the guy and Giorgio figured, No problem — what woman was going to fall for a guy like that? Half the time you didn't know what the hell he was talking about. But Angela found him interesting, more than interesting, and then she wanted him to meet Salvatore and Giorgio encouraged it, figuring that would be the end of Oscar. Except Salvatore found him almost as interesting as Angela did. On Sundays, Giorgio could hear them in the study, talking low and serious, sharing a laugh, getting thick as blood. Obviously Oscar was a problem he would have to deal with himself. Salvatore put on an iron mask of disapproval now when Giorgio brought up Angela.

"Don't whine."

Whine! Giorgio was enraged, not at his uncle but at Oscar, who had laid him open to such a shaming remark. He needed a careful plan before he could act.

First he tried to handle it without anyone getting hurt. He bought Earl O'Leary and placed him in Ray Hanley's office and counted on Earl to come up with stuff on Oscar that would bring a veto from Salvatore. Earl was good, there was no doubt of that, and he came up with things, but not with anything decisive. There were reasons why Giorgio didn't push him more. For one thing, his own relations with Salvatore improved. Angela still just kidded around with him, but Salvatore seemed settled on what marrying Angela was meant to secure. Salvatore obviously saw Giorgio as the heir apparent.

Salvatore sat him down with Pescatore so that Giorgio would have a sense of the family investments. Angela might talk down to him, but when it came to numbers and money Giorgio could hold his own with anyone. After that first meeting, Pescatore held nothing back. Maybe he thought Giorgio was his replacement.

"What do you think?" Salvatore asked.

"Very impressive."

"If I want to be told how good Pescatore is, I can ask him."

Giorgio got the point, but he did not rush into it. Just a few remarks about mutual funds.

"What's wrong with mutual funds?"

"Nothing. But there are six hundred of them and they almost never repeat a good performance."

Salvatore nodded. Giorgio had the impression he was telling him nothing he did not already know. Tokyo was different.

"Do you know what the Japanese stock market has done during the past couple years?"

"I don't trust it."

"The bankers do."

"They like controlled economies. To invest in. They wouldn't like it here."

"If it's controlled —"

"It can't respond the way the market should."

It was hard to know what Salvatore made of this. Obviously it sounded like heresy at the time. But when the Pacific Rim began to wobble, Giorgio's stock rose as the Oriental markets fell. That was when he learned of the Swiss accounts.

"What percentage of our assets is there?"

Salvatore's eyes looked dead under their purple lids. "Maybe eighty percent."

If what Pescatore handled was only twenty percent . . . It turned out that Pescatore did not know about the Swiss accounts.

"No one does."

Giorgio was reassured that Salvatore took him into his confidence in this way. As long as he kept off the subject of Angela, his relations with his uncle were great. Giorgio was treated as the heir apparent. He wanted that, he wanted it a lot, but he wanted Angela too. Salvatore couldn't or wouldn't help him there. Okay. He would solve the problem himself.

# Dombrowski

## 15

When Dombrowski heard that Oscar Hanley was missing, a chill went through him and for ten minutes he stood immobile at the back of his shop, staring into space. Who would have thought he was in a high-risk business?

Dombrowski had become a book dealer by accident, but then so had everyone else he knew in the business. It wasn't something you majored in at the university or could learn through formal training. He himself had begun scrounging through used bookstores when he was still in high school, at first just looking for raunchy stuff and then becoming interested in the book as a thing. The paper it was printed on, the binding, the date, the author. From used books to rare books, the latter being a subclass of the former. He had first met Oscar Hanley when the young man came into his store on North Michigan looking for a copy of *The Mills of the Cavanaughs.*

"Robert Lowell. That might still be in print."

It wasn't, but it was merely a used book,

not really rare. The kid drooled over the copy and Dombrowski had a sudden memory of himself at that age. He let Oscar have the copy for five dollars. Just giving it to him would have been no way to treat someone who was beginning to have an appreciation for books. And as the interest ripened, he became a frequent visitor to Dombrowski's Rare Books. All the while Oscar was an undergraduate, his interest had been poets. When Oscar entered law school, Dombrowski did not expect to see much more of his young friend. He was wrong.

"What you got in Italian?"

"What are you looking for?"

"Leopardi."

Still poets. Dombrowski dug out an edition that had Italian and English on facing pages. Just what Oscar wanted.

"I'm learning Italian."

"Do you know Eliot's essay on Dante?"

"I'll read it."

"He says he read Italian poetry long before he knew Italian. For the sheer music of the lines."

"Do you read Italian?"

*"Un poco."*

The girl Oscar brought to the store one day was obviously Italian and that seemed to be the explanation for Oscar's sudden interest in the language. When Dombrowski found that she was Angela Pianone, alarms started going off in his head. Salvatore Pianone was one of his best customers. Discretion was always the watchword with clients, but with Salvatore Pianone discretion became a blood oath not to divulge any of their dealings. Early on, Dombrowski had imagined that the notorious hoodlum would be interested in rare pornography. Not at all. His tastes in literature, particularly Italian literature, were astonishing. He seemed half ashamed of his cultivated interests. Perhaps that was why he did not deal with an Italian. All purchases came directly to Dombrowski. Only he knew that they were destined for the magnificent library of Salvatore Pianone. It had been a memorable day when Pianone invited Dombrowski to come see his collection.

The setting, chairs, tables, lamps, the shelving — everything was superb yet subservient to the main purpose of the room: books. Dombrowski's impulse was to ask that he be given the chance to bid first on the collection if Pianone ever . . . But he checked himself before he said it. These were not collectibles for Salvatore Pianone. These were treasures to which he had given a home. They had cost him dear but he no longer regarded his books as commanding a price. They were *hors de commerce,* priceless. It was clear that Dombrowski was now the only bookseller with whom Pianone dealt.

"It was becoming known. That I collect." Pianone shrugged. "Prices started to go up. Supply and demand, I suppose. But I didn't like it."

It seemed a warning. Dombrowski made good money buying for Pianone but he was never tempted to ask for all that he might think the traffic could bear. A reference to Cordelia Fabro, a dealer whose shop in Evanston had simply closed, prompted Dombrowski to ask what Cordelia was doing, now that she was out of the business.

"Don't ask," was the reply from the wily Eddie Abrahms. "She just drove away in her VW."

"Can't they trace the car?"

"They haven't."

On the visit to Pianone's library, he noticed that many of the books had been purchased through Cordelia.

"She closed her store," Dombrowski said.

"I heard," Pianone replied.

The thought had not come in the elegant and refined setting of Pianone's library, but later, putting together what Salvatore had said about soaring prices, his reputation as a mobster, and the remarkable lack of official curiosity about Cordelia's disappearance, Dombrowski wondered if Cordelia had felt the wrath of a Salvatore Pianone who thought that the dealer was overcharging him. He resolved to keep his own transactions with Pianone as straightforward as possible. That seemed somehow threatened when Oscar Hanley brought Angela to Dombrowski's Rare Books. He even became wary of Oscar, particularly when the young man brought up the Pianones.

"He would be a great customer for you."

"I sold him a few things," Dombrowski said carefully, not sure what Oscar was up to.

"You ever see his library?"

"Have you?"

"Every Sunday now. You wouldn't believe it."

The description Oscar gave him matched Dombrowski's memories, but he did not encourage this line of conversation. He was sorry he had mentioned selling anything to Pianone.

As a book dealer he had long since given up trying to form a notion of who might be a collector. There were a few obvious ones — professors, authors — but the majority were surprises. Of course most were just collectors whose books might have been rare coins or old cars, they simply liked the wheeling and dealing. Collectors were young and old, rich and not rich. In that sense Salvatore Pianone was not an absolute surprise.

How long had it been since he had seen Oscar before he heard that the young man was missing?

"He is probably wearing a concrete overcoat at the bottom of the river," Eddie Abrahms said. The fastidious little dealer enjoyed speaking the language of the streets.

"What's he done?"

"He tried to marry into the Pianone family. He got a funeral rather than a wedding."

The next time Salvatore Pianone came into the store, using the alley door as usual, Dombrowski felt an urge to lock himself in his office. But Salvatore had seen him. Besides, Dombrowski wanted to show him the book filched from the Biblioteca Ambrosiana in Milan. He had bought the Manzoni stuff from a man who said he was a professor. So what if the stuff was stolen — half the materials in the Ambrosiana had been stolen from someone else. "Napoleon took his share. You're in good company." While they talked, Dombrowski had thought of Salvatore Pianone, but now that he was in the store he did not want to sell him books and letters that could get him into trouble. That seemed an odd worry about a man like Pianone, but Dombrowski knew what he meant.

"I understand you know Oscar Hanley," Salvatore said, and Dombrowski's knees went weak. He pretended to give the matter thought, then nodded as if the memory were just breaking over the horizon of his mind.

"Sure, sure. A law student."

"He's missing," Salvatore said.

"I read about that."

That seemed to be it. "Dombrowski, I heard about things lifted from the Ambrosiana in Milan. Keep an eye out for them."

It was a triumph of restraint coupled with cold fear that prevented Dombrowski blurting out that he had some of the materials in his safe right now.

"Count on me," Dombrowski managed to say.

Salvatore looked at him for a long time in silence. "The D'Annunzio holograph you found for me? It's gone."

"Gone!" My God. Is this why Oscar Hanley had disappeared?

"Anyone try to sell that, I want to know. I

129

want to know who he is."

Dombrowski nodded. It was only after Salvatore left that it occurred to him that Oscar must be still alive. If Salvatore thought he had the holograph, he would have dealt with the problem decisively. Dombrowski did not often pray, but then and there he said a little prayer for Oscar Hanley.

# Cy Horvath

## 16

"Do you have Vince's death certificate?"

"Death certificate!" Mimi looked at Cy Horvath as if he were mad. "Do you think there's any doubt he's dead?"

"It's just a formality. The doctor signs it after a person dies, stating the cause of death. It's the law."

"I never saw it."

"Maybe you put it away with Vince's papers without realizing it."

"Vince had no papers."

This turned out to be true. Of course in his line of work, keeping records could be dangerous to your freedom. Mimi had grown to trust him now and Cy was not surprised. It was not a knack he had or a skill he had learned. People just trusted him. They told him things they wouldn't tell their best friends. They even got around to talking about how comfortable Vince had left her.

"I live on his pension."

"Social security?"

"That doesn't amount to a hill of beans. I

131

get a monthly check from Pirandello Enterprises. They were his employer."

The Pianone front. How unaware was Mimi of the kind of life her husband had led? Cy tried to imagine a man confiding in his wife that he earned his living on pornography, prostitution, and illegal gambling. Not a plausible sort of pillow talk. Even so, she must have guessed.

"They mail it every month?"

"Oh, they bring it. In cash. They cash the check for me and just bring me the money. It's much easier."

"Not for tax purposes."

"Oh, it isn't taxable."

"Ah."

If the IRS ever got curious about how Mimi O'Toole kept body and soul together she might lose that so-called pension.

"They took care of the funeral, everything. They said it was a fringe. They even wanted to supply the suit Vince was buried in."

"Nice."

"I wouldn't accept it, of course. He was buried in the suit he bought for our thirty-fifth anniversary."

"Thirty-fifth!"

"Whatever people said, he was a good husband." Her lower lip trembled and tears formed in her eyes.

Was it possible that it was the Pianones who wanted Vince dug up? "Did they give you the suit?"

"They brought it to McDivitt's."

"But you didn't accept it."

"I told McDivitt Vince would wear his anniversary suit."

"What happened to the gift suit?"

She had to think. "I'm not sure."

"Did the Pianones take it away?"

"You would have to ask Mr. McDivitt."

"It's not important."

"What about the death certificate?"

In the end he took her down to the county building and up to the sixth floor and records. Birth and death certificates. That about covers it. He held the door for Mimi to go in. There was a counter and behind it, at a distance, two desks at which sat two sullen clerks. One made a face but did not look up from her paper. The other woman, whose hair looked as if it had been shaped by a tornado, sneered at Mimi. But then she saw Cy and scrambled to her feet.

"What can I do for you, Lieutenant?" The other clerk was on her feet too, smiling a toothy smile as she advanced on the counter. Mimi was looking up at him.

"I didn't know you were a lieutenant."

133

"I thought I told you."

"What can we do for you, Lieutenant?"

"A death certificate."

A pad was produced and Mimi printed out the information with a ballpoint that was short of ink. When she was finished the tornado hairdo studied the form.

"That recent? This won't take a sec."

It cost six dollars and Mimi had nothing smaller than a fifty. Her monthly pension was apparently paid in large denominations. Cy put a five and a one on the counter.

"Do you want a receipt?"

"Yes."

Maybe he could get a refund from the department. After all, he had talked Mimi into this. Sort of.

"Do you believe the Blessed Virgin appears to people?" Mimi asked.

"I've never had the experience."

"Oh, neither have I. Have you heard of this woman out in Barfield?"

"What woman?"

"She receives messages from Mary."

"What are they?"

"Oh, they're secret."

"Then what's the point?"

"The priest knows. Her pastor. She was told to tell him."

Mimi was quite excited by all this, and

134

then she told him why.

"I want to bury Vince there. In that cemetery where Mary spoke to that lady."

# Oscar Hanley

Warned by Earl, Oscar Hanley took off and went into hiding and was living in the gatehouse of Riverside Cemetery under the name of Withers. He had ended up there by chance and came to think that the hand of providence was visible in his life.

"Don't go home, just go," Earl had urged him when he caught up with him on campus.

"Why?"

"Giorgio Pianone has decided to remove you as a rival." Earl had spoken in an urgent whisper.

"Remove me?"

Earl drew a finger across his throat, crossed his eyes as he did so, and let his tongue loll out of a corner of his mouth. "So get out of sight, and quick."

"Where should I go?"

"I don't want to know myself!" Earl paused and added in a lower tone, "In case they try to squeeze the information out of me."

Minutes later Oscar saw the notice on a

bulletin board. The deal was that he got the apartment over the gatehouse gratis just for being on the premises when no one else was there. Ideal for student. Oscar tore it from the board and, an hour later, was settled in the gatehouse.

Oscar alternated between thinking his disappearance unforgivable cruelty to Angela and the greatest proof of his love. What had begun as piqued fascination had turned swiftly into the realization that she was the most beautiful girl in the world. It was necessary that his love for her be idealized. Mere selfish possession would not suffice. That might satisfy Giorgio, but Oscar Hanley was made of finer stuff. What Giorgio might be made of had begun to concern him. His easy triumph over his rival created problems of a kind he had little experience with, except from listening to his father talk about his work. To say that Giorgio wished him dead was not simply a figure of speech. That he would like to kill Oscar seemed literal truth. To die for love had its attractions, but Oscar began to think that he had endangered Angela as well. She was frightened of her cousin.

"Hasn't he ever heard of incest?"

"We're second cousins. His parents were second cousins."

"That might explain it."

"Oscar." She gripped his arm. A wave of dizziness passed over him. Dear God how he loved her. Her grip tightened. There was real fear in her eye. "Please don't say anything to anger him."

There was fear in her voice. That she feared for him was a source of joy. Until he realized that she feared for herself as well. What a family. Oscar decided to absent himself from felicity awhile, to create a little breathing space, and to give both Angela and himself time to prepare for exams.

Not communicating with Angela made his exile more real. Besides, it provided food for poetic meditation. From behind the tinted glass of his car he had observed her on her birthday, doing volunteer work at St. Hilary's. It was work that must provide her with a fund of anecdotes that would keep the two of them laughing. But Angela was not laughing now. His heart went out to her through the tinted glass. She was dressed like a widow. Words formed in his mind.

**_unwed widow of my heart_**
**_before our union doomed to part_**

He repeated the lines over and over. He did not want to add to them. If only he had paper with him so he could jot them down. Such on-the-spot inspiration was new to him. His poems had always been retrospective, evoking a lost past.

> *no will-be for you now,*
> *so quickly dead ...*

The tears that formed in his eyes seemed genuine. He was sure they were. The figure in black, bowed under the weight of her sorrow, went out of sight. It had been pure chance that he had had so much of a glimpse. He started the car and resumed his lugubrious anonymity.

When Heidegger the sexton told him his name, Oscar had thought the cemetery must be a place for *noms de plume*. He himself was for the nonce Buz Withers. It was fate that he had acted on the impulse some weeks ago when he sought seclusion to prepare for his law exams. Studying with Angela was a study in distraction. He found himself just gazing at her beauty. Someone in the law school cafeteria began reading help-wanted ads aloud, suggesting possible employment after one flunked the exams. Oscar had been intrigued by the cemetery position. Rimbaud had disappeared — for a time. Robert Graves decamped to Majorca.

Oscar's eyes grew dull with dreams.

"That's all?" he had said to Heidegger when the sexton laid out his task in the office.

"The main thing is, you live here. There is an apartment over the gatehouse."

Oscar asked to see it. One look at it decided him. He took a few things from home, resisted the thought of leaving an enigmatic note for his father, but left a letter for Angela at school and settled into the gatehouse apartment. There wasn't a phone, so he had not called Angela or his father, but then he thought about it and the idea of keeping the whole thing a secret gripped him. Why else had he given Heidegger a phony name?

He had not been prepared for the reaction to his absence. The immediate assumption was that he had been kidnaped by the Pianones and now lay at the bottom of the river. The unease he had felt the first time Angela took him home returned. He knew Giorgio hated him. His exile now took on a different aspect. Maybe his life depended on hiding out in the cemetery. And Angela would love him all the more when he rose from the dead.

When he walked into Dombrowski's he had thought the dealer might not recognize him with a beard, but he took his arm and hurried him into his office.

"Did you tell Salvatore Pianone you were a customer of mine?"

"Sure. Why not?"

"Oscar, he was in the other day. He asked me if I knew you."

"What did you tell him?"

"It's what he said. He said, Oscar is missing, something like that."

"Word is out, Dombrowski."

But Oscar gripped the bookseller's hand. Did he suspect that Oscar was fleeing the Pianones?

"I thought he meant you were dead. When you walked in . . ."

"You want me to leave?"

"By the alley door. But let me check it out first. Salvatore may have this place staked out."

"The papers think I'm dead."

"Don't even say it."

But Dombrowski's shudder seemed prompted by his own danger rather than Oscar's. Of course the papers did not know of the missing holograph, the bookseller said. Salvatore would not consider making it public. He urged Oscar to return it.

"I don't have it."

But Dombrowski closed his eyes and

raised a staying hand. Hear no evil. Oscar did not blame him. That was when his romantic ruse became serious. His life was in danger. If Salvatore thought he had wormed his way into the family in order to rifle his prized collection, death would be too good for him. All he had was a paperback Angela had given him, of little monetary or other value.

He left the bookstore by the back door, stepping into a keen Chicago wind. His car was in a lot near Randolph. He decided to leave it there. He took the train to O'Hare and then jumped a motel shuttle to Fox River and walked to the cemetery. Back in his gateway apartment, he felt safe. He lay on his bed, staring at the ceiling, trying to figure out what was going on.

It had to be Giorgio. And his motive was resentment over Angela. Giorgio could have taken him out, but if he did that without an okay from Salvatore, he would be worse off than before. He had to discredit his rival, stir up Salvatore's anger, so that what then happened to the intruder would have the official seal of the family on it. Giorgio must have removed the holograph and made it look as if Oscar . . . Good God, he might have been falling in with Giorgio's plan, disappearing the way he had. Not that he blamed Earl. If he hadn't gone into hiding, he might very well be dead.

As he lay there, fear gave way to something else. This was a situation worthy of D'Annunzio himself. Safe in his gatehouse apartment, Oscar began to enjoy the danger he now assuredly was in.

# Heidegger

## 18

Heidegger felt he ought to be in charge of the disinterment and he didn't like to be ordered around in front of Lolly and Maxwell but the police had really taken over. They were gathered at the grave of Vincent O'Toole where Lolly used the excavator to get it down to maybe four feet and then he and Maxwell got in there with shovels. Captain Keegan stood at the head of the gravesite and Lieutenant Horvath was supporting Mrs. O'Toole, who looked like she would keel over any minute. This was no sight for a relative, to see the body dug up. Thank God Father Dowling was there. He stood just behind Phil Keegan, keeping a wary eye on Mrs. O'Toole. He had offered to stay with her in Heidegger's office, but she insisted she wanted to be there throughout the whole thing.

Where the men dug now the ground was as soft as if it were midsummer. There had been a frost overnight making the topsoil crisp and brittle, but weather was no longer a factor. The breath of the two men digging was expelled in white puffs and the breathing of everyone standing around was visible too. It was as if they were all proving they were still alive. A car was parked fifty yards away, just visible through the trees, and a man was tending a grave. Up to a point, Heidegger let people decorate their graves, flowers as long as they were in pots — he didn't want planting going on — but from time to time a widow would make a regular little garden around a gravestone before they discovered it.

"Let it be," Heidegger usually advised his crew.

"What if everyone starts doing that?"

"Do you think everyone will?"

Lolly's mouth would open and then form into a smile, revealing an incomplete set of teeth. "You're right."

Lolly was a good worker, better than Maxwell, but every once in a while he went on a toot, usually three or four days, and showed up afterward looking as if he had really been put through the wringer. Lolly knew how they started but often he didn't know where he had been or what he had done. That was how he got married. He woke up in bed with this woman and she said they were married and what could he say? Later he checked it out at the courthouse, just to be sure.

"I signed a false name," he said. "So I couldn't have been too drunk."

"That's a crime," Maxwell said. He was obviously jealous. He was unlikely to get married drunk or sober, he had such a sullen disposition.

"I'd rather serve time for that."

"Than what?"

"Marriage."

He just didn't go back and if the woman looked for him she never found him. Dorothy was disgusted.

"He didn't know what he was doing," Heidegger explained to his wife.

"That's still cruel, just disappearing like that."

"People do."

"Hmph." But she looked at him as if he were threatening something. Heidegger had no desire to disappear. His life wasn't perfect but it was good enough for him. He liked his office and the unexciting but regular rhythm of the cemetery. But he also liked going home at night and listening to Dorothy complain about this and that. It was her recreation, bitching. Well, why not? It was harmless enough and he could just tune her out and let her get it out of her system.

Everyone stepped forward when a shovel

hit something solid, the concrete vault. Lolly and Maxwell proceeded now with exaggerated care, as if you could harm a vault. It was strange to look down at the white concrete top of the vault. When they covered it up less than a month ago it had been meant to be for eternity, and now here they were digging up Vincent O'Toole. Given the anxiety the dead man had caused, Heidegger was glad the widow wanted to have him buried in another cemetery, though he had never heard of the one in Barfield.

"It's very small," Mrs. O'Toole had said. "And full. I was lucky to get two places."

"I'll sell these lots for you."

She seemed unsure she wanted to get rid of them. After all, her husband had lain in one for some weeks at least. Heidegger let it go. She began to sob at the sight of the vault and Horvath turned her away. The people tending the grave across the way were looking at her through the trees, as if they had heard her cry. Father Dowling and Heidegger were the only ones who seemed aware of the observers. Keegan was giving orders now. Maxwell got out of the hole with a boost from Lolly and moved the hoist closer to the hole. Lolly slipped the chains under the vault and Maxwell pushed a lever.

The vault stirred as it freed itself from the clay in which it sat and then began to rise. Lolly rode it up. Mrs. O'Toole's wailing increased. The people at the grave across the way were standing now, looking toward the scene. It would be upsetting, of course, to visit a grave and find another one being opened. Heidegger wished they had put up some screens to block off what they were doing. The thing is, you never knew when there would be people in the cemetery, visiting graves, some walking or jogging. The place was seldom just empty. The vault rose above ground level and Maxwell prepared to swing it slowly over toward the flatbed truck.

"Open it up," Keegan said to Heidegger when the vault, streaked with clay, had been lowered onto the flatbed.

Lolly needed a hand to get out of the hole and Heidegger helped him before acknowledging Keegan's remark.

"That was easy," Lolly said.

"Can you get up there with Maxwell? We're going to open it up."

"Here?"

Again Heidegger was conscious of the curious mourners at the grave across the road.

"We could take it to the maintenance shed," he said to Keegan.

"I want it opened now."

What the hell. Heidegger climbed up on the flatbed too, steadied himself on the vault, and was surprised when it began to move. Maxwell applied a wrench to the bolts. When he turned the first one, the whole vault shifted. Odd. When all the screws were removed, Lolly took one end and Heidegger the other and they lifted the top. Mrs. O'Toole was clinging to Cy Horvath, trying to turn her eyes away from what was going on up there on the flatbed. The mourners were coming across the road, unable to stifle their curiosity. The lid made an odd scraping sound as they lifted it free.

"God in heaven!" Keegan cried.

Below, Mrs. O'Toole let out a wail. One of the kibitzers, a big guy, dashed forward and sprang onto the flatbed. They all looked into the vault.

It was empty.

# Father Dowling

## 19

Father Dowling helped Cy get Mimi O'Toole into a car. They were all going back to the sexton's office to figure out what had happened. Heidegger was almost as disturbed as Mimi. Clearly he thought his own integrity was called into question by the unearthed vault that had proved to contain no casket.

Father Dowling could remember the day of Vincent O'Toole's funeral vividly. How could he have forgotten it, given the turnout? The gravesite had looked different then, of course. A canopy over the rows of chairs, artificial grass covering the mounds of dirt taken from the hole, a gleaming bier spanning it onto whose well-oiled wheels the casket had been slid by the pallbearers. It was a very expensive casket, one for which Mimi herself had not paid, according to McDivitt, the whole funeral being covered by Vince's employers, the Pianones.

Now he closed the car door on Mimi and Cy and turned back toward the gravesite. It was generally understood that no one was better than Cy Horvath with distraught females. Or distraught males, for that matter. His plain Hungarian face had a reassuring receptivity, as if nothing he saw or heard could possibly alter his composure. He got behind the wheel and began to drive slowly off toward the sexton's office near the entrance to the cemetery.

The men Father Dowling had noticed keeping a close eye on Vince O'Toole's grave and who had arrived at the site in time to see that the vault was empty, one of them springing onto the flatbed, turned out to be members of the Pianone family.

"What the hell you doing here, Giorgio?" Phil demanded of one of them.

"Where's the casket?"

"Good question. Maybe somebody dug it up before we did."

But the man called Giorgio shook his head.

"You been watching the grave, Giorgio?"

"Nobody dug up nothing."

"Were you the ones who tried it on Hallowe'en?"

Giorgio did not answer. He was frowning at Keegan.

"What happened to the body?"

The obvious explanation was that the casket had never been put into the vault, that the grave had been filled and the marker raised with no Vince O'Toole six feet under. A remembered image from the day of the burial took vivid shape in Father Dowling's mind. The impressive bronze casket sitting atop the lowering apparatus as the mourners trailed back to the cars that were lined up along the cemetery road. And all withdrew.

Keegan had buttonholed Heidegger and Giorgio and his companion stood by, intent on hearing anything that Keegan did. The workers, Lolly and Maxwell, were sitting on the edge of the flatbed, legs dangling, taking advantage of this lull.

"You suspected when you lifted it out, didn't you?" Heidegger said to Lolly. "It moved too easily."

Maxwell nodded. "There should have been more resistance."

"Leave everything the way it is," Heidegger told his men, and then he led Keegan and Giorgio and his companion on a shortcut toward his office. Lolly and Maxwell looked at one another and shrugged. Father Dowling had put his pipe in his mouth and was searching his pockets. Lolly held out a flaming lighter and the priest dipped forward and lit his pipe from it. Maxwell took out a generic brand of cigarettes and offered one to Lolly. The camaraderie of tobacco soon engulfed the three men.

"I remember the day of his funeral," the priest murmured.

"Me too," Lolly said. "The whole mob was here."

"What do you think happened?"

It was Maxwell who spoke. "The vault was sealed and we filled up the hole."

"You sealed the vault."

They exchanged a look. "Not exactly."

When the mourners of Vince O'Toole had left, Maxwell recalled, the casket stood on the lowering device, ready to be let down into the vault which was already set in the open grave, its lid concealed beneath one of those sheets of artificial grass. The two men had been fascinated by the notorious characters who had gathered around the grave, and they moved off across the cemetery to make an inventory of the luxury cars and stretch limousines, betting one another that those vehicles were armored, all the more so when their occupants thought of how Vince O'Toole had departed this life. When they came back to the grave, the lowering device had been rolled away. Below, the lid of the vault was in place.

"We thought Heidegger had done it. We expected to catch hell for wandering off."

"When he said nothing neither did we."

"Who's that guy that jumped up here?" Lolly asked.

"They call him Giorgio," Dowling said.

Lolly and Maxwell exchanged a look.

Father Dowling said, "You're going to have to tell the police."

As it happened, they were going to have to tell their story again and again. They accompanied Father Dowling to the sexton's office where they told their story, together and separately. Phil Keegan was certain they were lying and right there in Heidegger's office he began to grill them.

"Get out of here," he said to Giorgio.

"You own this place?"

"Tell him to leave," Keegan said to Heidegger, but he had alienated the sexton and was ignored. Giorgio stayed. Phil was more intent on quizzing Lolly and Maxwell than getting rid of Giorgio.

"If what you say is true, someone must have carried off the casket."

"I'm just telling you what I know," Lolly complained.

"Just tell me all you know."

"That's it. You think we stole a body?"

"I think you know who did."

"Who the hell would steal a body?"

Keegan looked at Giorgio. "Why would anyone steal O'Toole's body?"

Giorgio just looked at him, his expression the disappointed one of a taxpayer who felt he was not getting his money's worth. Father Dowling had the impression that Lolly and Maxwell would be dealt with more severely if Giorgio had been able to question them.

Roger Dowling spelled Cy with Mimi, it seemed only fair. She was beyond consolation now, baffled by this incredible turn of events. Anne Ambrose, the cemetery bookkeeper, offered to help but she had such a funereal manner she might precipitate more hysterical weeping.

"To think I've been visiting his grave, bringing flowers, praying, when all the while . . ." A great sob escaped her and she embraced her own frail body. "I'm being punished."

"There, there." He wished Marie Murkin were here. She would be able to soothe Mimi.

"I was sure I was supposed to bury him at Barfield. It wasn't a voice I heard, nothing like that, but I had this feeling when Marie and I were there that Mary wanted me to bring Vince there."

"Marie was there?"

"She told me about it."

Aha. He decided to telephone Marie and ask her to come to the cemetery.

"The cemetery?" Marie asked.

"Mimi will explain it all to you. I mean Riverside, by the way, not the cemetery in Barfield."

When Marie arrived she avoided Father Dowling's eyes, immediately taking charge of Mimi, but Father Dowling could see that she had been pondering his remark ever since he had hung up the phone. The two women left, Giorgio and his companion left, Phil and Heidegger seemed on better terms, allied against the hapless workers. Father Dowling was inclined to believe the grave-diggers' story, but he seemed the only one. Heidegger was particularly offended by their conjecture that he had lowered the casket into the vault and sealed it, leaving the grave for them to fill in.

# Tuttle

## 20

Tuttle got the story from Peanuts whose sources were not confined to the police department, this being an event that involved his family as well. The disappearance of the body of Vincent O'Toole, the Pianone employee who had been cut down by a barrage of bullets as if he had been a duck in a shooting gallery, did not sit well with Salvatore Pianone, the head of the family, nor with Giorgio who had been assigned the task of finding out what had happened. Giorgio had been at the cemetery when the vault was opened and proved to be empty.

It seemed clear that Giorgio had been as surprised as anyone there.

"So who tried to dig him up before?"

Peanuts said nothing. Tuttle did not pursue it. This story was one he could discuss with Peanuts only insofar as it involved the police. When it came to Peanuts's family, Tuttle was a veritable sphinx of ostensible indifference. But in the privacy of his own mind, alone in his office, feet on his desk, tweed hat pulled over his eyes, Tuttle speculated as to what had happened. Weeks had passed since the slaying of Vince O'Toole, and so far as Tuttle knew no retribution had been exacted. The received opinion was that Vince had been killed by rivals, or at least potential rivals, of the Pianones who had decided to make a statement that would catch the attention of the family. If that was what had happened, the Pianones would respond in kind, but at a time and place of their own choosing. Presuming, of course, that they knew who their antagonist was. Like others, Tuttle had pored over the list of mourners who had shown up for the O'Toole funeral, a church full of moral monsters, any one of whom could have cheerfully killed any other. The town of Fox River, the city of Chicago, and most of the suburbs waited for the other shoe to drop. Instead, there was the baffling discovery that the body of Vince O'Toole was missing. If this really came as a surprise to the Pianone family, something very sinister was afoot.

"Giorgio's being there proves it," Falter in the county building press room said, having first coughed to signal that he was about to make a pronouncement.

"Proves what?" demanded Ictus, Falter's natural enemy.

"That the Pianones didn't know."

"Maybe it proves that Giorgio didn't know the vault was empty. He's only one Pianone."

"He was there, representing the family."

"He wasn't alone, either," Suarez said. Suarez was a sickly looking fellow who regularly ran in marathons as an avocation and represented half a dozen county newspapers as a vocation. He was rumored to be writing a novel, which made him an object of envious suspicion. As usual, he was waiting to see which way the conversation went, so that he could join the winning side. His contribution suggested that he had already decided Falter had the better part of this exchange.

"*Was* he surprised?"

There was no firm intelligence on Giorgio's companion at the great discovery. Ictus wanted to know if they really knew someone had been there with Giorgio.

"Maybe it was another cop."

"His name is Healey," Tuttle said.

"Who is Healey?"

"A Pianone driver."

"So he might know something or he might not."

Falter pronounced this indefeasible sentence with a great deal of satisfaction and

Suarez nodded in acquiescence.

"Wasn't he driving the car in which O'Toole got it?"

"I'd have to check," Tuttle said, but he knew that O'Toole had been alone in the car when three gunmen unloaded their weapons on him. Tuttle got up and shuffled out of the newsroom. Clearly there was nothing to be learned there.

He found Cy Horvath in the cafeteria, having a cup of coffee with Dr. Pippen, the assistant coroner. Tuttle joined them, conscious that Horvath resented this. Everybody was half in love with Pippen, who thought it was her medical knowledge that impressed others. Her red hair and green eyes trumped her medical education with everyone but Lubens, her boss, who was jealous of the attention she got, whatever the explanation.

"What would you do with a dead body when you're done with it?" Tuttle asked, adding an ounce of sugar to his coffee.

"Are you referring to Vincent O'Toole?" Pippen asked prettily.

"The same."

"I'd bury him."

"You'd need to dig a hole first."

"Not necessarily."

There was no change in Horvath's expression, but it was clear to Tuttle that Pippen's remark had set his Hungarian mind going. She was saying that getting rid of a body in a cemetery would be easier than elsewhere, but was that true?

"In the newsroom they think only Giorgio was surprised."

Pippen smiled encouragingly at Tuttle, waiting for him to make his remark intelligible. As soon as he began to explain it Horvath pushed away from the table. A lesser man would have whiled away as much time as she would grant him with Dr. Pippen, but Tuttle was intent on seeing where Horvath was going.

"What do they know?" he said, by way of summary, rejecting the boys in the newsroom and getting up.

"Everyone seems to be leaving," Dr. Pippen observed.

It was a novel experience for her to be deserted. Tuttle doubted that she would remain unattended for long in the cafeteria. He doffed his tweed hat and hurried into the hallway. Playing his hunch, he took the stairs and skipped down and outside to his car. He had just driven around in front of the building when he saw the unmarked car emerge from the underground garage. Horvath was at the wheel. Tuttle silently congratulated himself.

He had a pretty good idea where they were headed, but he stayed behind Horvath, following him, not that confident in his hunch. But Horvath's destination was indeed Riverside Cemetery. He slowed as he passed the office but did not stop. Tuttle gave Horvath a little head start and, when he himself drove into the cemetery, took a road that branched off to the left. He could see Horvath's car on the other road. Now that all the leaves were down, it was easy to keep him in sight.

At the far end of the cemetery, beyond the mausoleum and the new section where there were as yet only a few markers, was a wild area, marked off by untrimmed shrubs that had been allowed to grow as they would. One unpaved road ran toward a stand of shrubs and bushes to an opening and seemed almost to tunnel through the bushes. Horvath had driven through and Tuttle followed him. The terrain changed abruptly from level to irregular, the unpaved road dipped and turned, and leaves and cut branches had been piled up out of the way. One depressed area was filled with muddy water on which three Canadian geese floated.

Horvath's car had stopped and Tuttle too

braked and turned off his motor. He watched Horvath wander around. Did he think he would find O'Toole's casket? From the way he suddenly began to act, he seemed to have found something. Tuttle started up his engine and drove on to where Horvath stood. Horvath began to gesture toward Tuttle.

"What's going on?" Tuttle asked, rolling down his window.

"Get out and take a look at this."

Something in Horvath's voice made him hesitate, but he could hardly refuse. Horvath took hold of his arm and led him off the road and pointed.

The bodies lay facedown on weedy ground, the backs of their heads a mess. It looked like an execution.

"Who are they?"

"They worked here. Their names are Lolly and Maxwell."

# Oscar Hanley

## 21

The cemetery had turned out to be as busy as the mall and Oscar decided to get out of there. His car had been left in a lot in the Loop and chances were that it had been impounded. Calling for it would be like making the announcement he was back.

That had its attractions, God knows. He had not believed he would miss Angela so much. He tried to cushion that with the hope that she missed him equally. Telephone her? It would be so simple. But if her family was looking for him they would assume he would get in touch with Angela. The Pianones would know that the newspaper speculation that they had put a hit man on Oscar Hanley was false. At least it wasn't true yet.

Oscar held his hands out in front of him, palms up. Their wrinkled maps led to his wrists and the veins visible there beneath the flesh. How fragile a human being is. Vincent O'Toole had gone down under a barrage of bullets, but any one of them could have been enough. And there are so many simpler ways to make one's quietus short of a bare bodkin. Cut off the air supply, open a vein, introduce some lethal potion into the body, put a little air in the blood supply. Such thoughts of vulnerability did not really affect Oscar's sense that he had a claim on life that could not be broken. Then why was he feeling the beginnings of real fear?

The only solution was to remove the cause of the fear. He felt threatened because Salvatore Pianone thought he had made off with his priceless D'Annunzio holograph. Once he realized that this was false, the danger would be gone.

For all that, he left the gatehouse and the cemetery stealthily, not wanting to bid Heidegger good-bye. A silver car passed through the gate and continued at a fair speed along one of the many roads mourners used to get to their respective loved ones. Oscar waited until it was out of sight, then waited some more. Looking around the apartment he had been occupying, he felt a flood of affection for it. Here he had fantasized about exile, had imagined himself a touchy genius like Gabriele D'Annunzio, needing an appropriate setting if creativity was to put in an appearance. It seemed a shame to study for his law school exams in such a mood.

His books were jammed into a backpack. He got his arms through the straps of the bag. Again he looked around the apartment. He wished Angela could see it. Perhaps sometime he could bring her here and show her where he had hidden from the wrath of her family.

Clouds were very high in the sky and the trail of a jet fattened against the blue. The leafless branches of trees moved in the wind as if they were animate, growths from the Inferno that enclosed the souls of the departed. Oscar headed across the grass, moving among the headstones, reading off the names as if they made a litany. It occurred to him that he was walking on graves. Maybe like O'Toole's they would be found to be empty when the final trumpet sounded.

He realized that it was the ruthlessness revealed by the opening of that grave that had decided him to do what he could to protect himself from the Pianone wrath. As long as Salvatore Pianone thought he had taken that holograph there would be a price on his head. Salvatore would never forget, or forgive. The cultivated exterior had never really negated the corrupt core. To pretend it did was the result of his love for Angela. The best way to convince Salvatore he did not have the holograph was to find out who did have it.

Would Dombrowski know as soon as someone tried to sell it? Probably. But the bookseller had made it clear he did not want Oscar back in his shop, not while Salvatore Pianone was on a rampage.

He had neared the far end of the cemetery that was bounded by trees and shrubs. Beyond was a suburban development and a utility store where he could find a public phone. He hoped he would have decided whom to call before he got to that phone. At the moment, the thick growth in front of him presented a problem. He started into it, shielding his face, parting branches with his arms. Suddenly he became aware of voices, close, and the tone of one of them stopped him. He huddled among the shrubbery and trees.

"Don't," a voice said, strangled with fear.

"Put it away. What can we do to you?"

"Kneel down!"

There was a scuffle, a yelp of pain and then silence. It was broken by an eerie whimpering that sent a chill through Oscar. Grown men were weeping like babies. And then came the shots. Two. The whimpering ceased. Oscar strained forward, trying not to rustle the branches that enclosed him. He moved them in time to see Giorgio staring downward. He looked around, apparently unconcerned, and then walked away. Oscar moved forward and watched Giorgio get into a silver car. He was behind the wheel and had the motor running when the window on the driver's side slid down. He reached out, holding the gun by its barrel, and then heaved it high and far. It crashed into a stand of bushes. The window slid up and Giorgio drove off.

For several minutes Oscar stayed hidden and then he pushed himself free of the bushes. Almost immediately he saw the two bodies. My God. These were human beings who had been alive minutes ago and were now dead. He found that he was moving toward the scene; he had to drink in the horror of it. The thought kept going through his head. That could have been me, that could have been me.

The impulse to run came over him and it was all he could do not to dash back into his hiding place. But his eye lifted to the bushes into which Giorgio had thrown his gun. Oscar ran to it, brought one arm over his face and pressed into the bushes. The gun had not fallen completely to the ground until he moved the bushes. Oscar took out his handkerchief and wrapped the gun in it.

He had to take off his backpack in order to stuff it in there. Then he ran.

Later he would wonder that no suburban housewife, looking out her window to see him dashing past, had not called 911. When he finally got to the convenience store and into the men's room he began to vomit before he could position himself over the toilet. When he looked into the mirror over the washbasin the dreadful thing he had witnessed seemed to have printed itself on his face. His eyes were wild, his hair wild from crawling through bushes, his mouth hung open as if he were about to whimper as those men had before Giorgio shot them.

He took off the backpack but did not open it. He felt through the fabric the shape of the weapon. What impulse had led him to retrieve it? He thought about that after he had cleaned up the washroom and sat at a little plastic table drinking weak coffee out of a large Styrofoam cup. The temperature of the coffee was high enough to disguise its lack of taste. He decided that the gun was insurance. It was proof that the Pianones had assassinated those two men. The silver car was probably untraceable and Giorgio could get rid of the footgear he had worn. Maybe he was right to think that throwing the gun away that close to the scene of the crime was no risk. They would assume he had taken it away.

When he went to the public phone and dialed a number he waited, holding the instrument as if he meant to slam it down at any moment. But the voice that answered reassured him.

"Earl?"

"Who is this?"

"Can't you tell?"

A long silence. "Say something else."

"Where can we meet?"

"Name it."

"Your place."

"Okay. After dark."

# Earl O'Leary

## 22

Earl waited down the street until Oscar showed up. On a bicycle! With his knapsack, he could have been a teenager, except for the beard, but Earl knew immediately that it was Oscar. He watched him go into his building and then he crossed the street and pushed inside.

"You beat me."

Oscar wheeled and, at the sight of the beard, Earl laughed. Oscar's hand went to his facial hair. Stroking it seemed to make his smile emerge.

"I never grew a beard before."

"Now we know why. Want to bring your bike inside?"

"It isn't mine."

"Whose is it?"

"I stole it."

Earl was unlocking his door, trying to stay out of any line of fire that might come from the street. But nothing happened. Apparently Oscar had not been followed. Inside, Oscar headed for the sink where he turned on the water and then dipped into it, letting it run over his face, drinking as if from a pump. When he stood up he looked like a spaniel fresh from a swim.

"I thought you were dead."

"I was in the cemetery."

"You were! Where?"

Oscar's expression changed. "You wouldn't believe what I saw."

"Look. Have you eaten? You look awful. Have a beer."

It seemed best to get busy. Earl put on a kettle of water for spaghetti, put in a loaf of garlic bread, and went to work making a huge bowl of salad.

"There's a jug of red wine in that lower cabinet. Pour us some glasses."

"I'd like to shave off this beard first."

"Don't."

"Do you like it?"

"Hardly. But it does make you harder to recognize."

Preparing their dinner gave Earl time to think and then rethink what he would say to Oscar. Obviously some assumptions of recent days had to be revised. Giorgio had convinced his father that Oscar had made off with the D'Annunzio holograph. Earl saw now that was false, so what was Giorgio's game? The holograph was missing and if Oscar had not taken it, then Giorgio must have, in order to make his uncle believe that Oscar had. All right.

"Where were you hiding out?"

"I had this magnificent apartment over the gatehouse at Riverside Cemetery. Not luxurious, but it had character. You reach it by a stone spiral staircase, you'd think you were in a cathedral bell tower, and it has thick oak doors and a fireplace almost as wide as the room. Beveled glass in the windows . . ."

"How did you find it?"

"There was a note on a campus bulletin board."

"You rented it?"

"No, no. I was a live-in watchman. All I had to do was be there."

"You were hired?"

"There was no salary. The apartment —"

"So someone knows who you are and that you were there . . ."

"No. Heidegger thinks my name is Withers."

"Heidegger?"

"He is the sexton at Riverside."

"Withers" must have been in the apartment when they disinterred Vincent O'Toole and found he wasn't in his grave. Oscar was able to follow it all with his binoculars.

"Giorgio was there, with another man. They waited until the vault was brought up and then they ran over there for the great unveiling. You know what happened."

The whole town knew what had happened then. The vault was empty and the big question was, Who had stolen the casket in which the body of Vincent O'Toole had been during the funeral and the graveside ceremony?

"The Pianones don't know who's doing all that."

"It's Giorgio."

"Giorgio!"

"Earl, I saw him execute two cemetery workers this afternoon. He knelt them down and shot them in the back of the head."

"You saw him?"

"He doesn't know that."

Oh, what a tangled web we weave. Giorgio had told Earl he was getting rid of the workers. "They recognized me when O'Toole's grave was opened," Giorgio had said. "Healy and I showed up just as they were opening the vault, and those two guys knew me."

"I wonder who they told?" Earl had asked.

"I was there when the cops talked to them. They said nothing. But how long will they shut up?"

Giorgio proposed removing the chance that their theft of O'Toole's casket would be revealed. It had been a smooth operation, taking advantage of an unlooked-for opportunity. They had been prepared to dig up the casket in order to retrieve the holograph that had been sewn into the suit McDivitt buried O'Toole in, a suit Giorgio had delivered to the undertaker himself. That is when he recognized Mickey, the chauffeur of the McDivitt hearse, and commandeered her vehicle.

"Was she willing?" Earl had asked.

Giorgio had just looked at him. Obviously Mickey had no choice. Getting rid of those gravediggers had been an emotional release for Giorgio.

Taking the D'Annunzio holograph had been Earl's suggestion, but Giorgio saw immediately that it was the way to turn his uncle against Oscar.

"He's dead meat," he had said with satisfaction.

He was less enthusiastic about sewing it into the suit in which Vincent O'Toole would be buried. Earl told him it was better than a bank. And they could produce it at the appropriate time.

"Dig him up?"

"What are you, superstitious?"

Of course he was. Everyone is when it comes to dead human bodies. Earl had assumed that Oscar was one of those dead human bodies, courtesy of Giorgio. He couldn't wait to get his rival out of the way — that's what Earl had thought. And here was Oscar in the flesh, a witness to Giorgio's killing those two gravediggers. Earl felt that he had been dealt an extra ace. But the best was yet to be.

"I've got the gun he did it with," Oscar said.

"Where?"

He opened his backpack and took out the gun, wrapped in a handkerchief.

"Have you handled it?"

"His prints are on it, they have to be."

Not if he was wearing surgical gloves as per ritual. But even so, this was a sixth ace.

"Let's put it in the freezer, Oscar. And pour some more wine."

# Father Dowling

## 23

Public indifference had permitted, if not justified, the lack of a vigorous investigation of the death of Vincent O'Toole. But now there was a semblance of outrage at the execution of Lolly and Maxwell. Phyllis Lordly launched a week-long series of articles in the *Chicago Tribune* whose upshot was that the cynical acceptance of the death of Vincent O'Toole as a kind of rough justice, an unlooked-for benefit of tolerating the underworld, led directly to the gruesome deaths of two simple workmen in a wooded area of Riverside Cemetery in Fox River. Stung by the implication that the local media had colluded in all this, the *Fox River Tribune* countered with two stories by Cajetan Worth, the venerable editor of its editorial page, that told of the malaise that crept out into the suburbs and surrounding towns and municipalities from corrupt Chicago. The first article, an indictment of the Chicago political establishment and the indigenous crime that had made the city a global symbol of lawless license, was accompanied by a cartoon that depicted an octopus, whose face bore a distinct resemblance to a famous mayoral family, with tentacles slithering to the west and east and south. Two can play at that game. Phyllis Lordly responded with an article asking "Where Is Oscar Hanley?" The disappearance of the brilliant young law student, close friend of Angela Pianone, was one more unsolved mystery in the town of Fox River. But on both sides of this inky battle was a distinct sense of *mauvaise foi* — delinquency enough to encompass both the media and the city along with the surrounding communities.

"You'd think we gunned O'Toole down ourselves," Phil Keegan groused. He had taken the beer brought him by Marie Murkin, but it sat undrunk on the table beside his chair as he glowered at the books on Father Dowling's shelves.

"Who *did* gun him down?" Roger Dowling asked.

"Don't you start."

"Perhaps whoever killed O'Toole killed those two men."

Phil groaned. "What really hurts is that these newspapers sound as if they're published on the moon. Where have they been on all this stuff in the past?"

This was the suggestion of the segment of

a network program that was hastily put together. A correspondent whose face was a mask of wrinkles and whose tone one of unconvincing righteousness portrayed Chicago and environs in such a way that one almost longed for the good old days of Capone and Dutch Schulz. But the coup de grâce was the statement issued by the cardinal. It amounted to a public apology on the part of the Church for its failures in the past to condemn the crimes and mayhem of the city.

All this was bad enough and Father Dowling had little to say that could console his old friend. They had often discussed the moral problem he faced as a member of a police force that operated within a community that, officially at least, had come to terms with the Pianone operations.

"We've talked about it, Roger."

"I know."

"What was that you told me about St. Augustine?"

The tolerance of evil lest a worst evil come about was a principle discussed by Paul and the great Fathers of the Church. Would the elimination of prostitution be for the common good of the community? Augustine had asked. If the hot-blooded young men who availed themselves of the services of fallen ladies became predators of wives and mothers once the opportunities of vice were removed, well, in such circumstances, it could be argued, the common good was better served by turning a blind eye on prostitution.

Whatever the altered shape of society since the fifth century and whatever the facts of the matter at that time, the principle stood out from its application.

"Of course tolerating evil is not the same as doing evil."

"If you don't do something about it, that's doing something, isn't it?"

Father Dowling forbore answering that with "No, it is not doing something." He did draw attention to the difference between those who were directly involved in vice and a government which saw worse consequences from a crackdown.

"That's always been our excuse," Phil said, but he clearly did not savor this doctrine.

"But isn't the accusation that there are officials, politicians and others, who collude with and profit from and don't simply tolerate?"

That accusation was emphatically not applicable to Phil Keegan or to his department in the Fox River police. But the Pianone family allegedly controlled local politics, and their counterparts were not without influence in other communities in the greater Chicago area.

There might have been the lack of an Augustinian nuance in the cardinal's statement, but Roger saw no reason to deflect criticism onto the archdiocese. Tolerance too easily became indifference, an acceptance of crime as part of the natural order of things. And certainly Mimi O'Toole had every right to her suddenly vocal anger.

"I don't know," she wailed to an interviewer who asked if there had been a police investigation of her husband's murder.

"What did he do exactly?"

"He sold insurance." Mimi said this in such a way that she seemed to have no sense at all of the ambiguity of the job description.

"For Pirandello Enterprises."

"Yes."

"Isn't that owned by the Pianone family?"

"What are things coming to if a man can be killed in that way? And then his body stolen!"

"Stolen?"

Thus it was that the missing body of Vincent O'Toole became an item in the news. The discovery of the empty vault had not prompted Heidegger to call a press conference, needless to say, nor had the police made any announcement of it. The news caused a firestorm that made the earlier pious commentary on the execution of the two cemetery workers seem merely a ripple. Camera crews descended on Riverside and Heidegger became a reluctant celebrity. Unfortunately the sexton could not conceal his own sense of responsibility for the missing body and he came through as responsible for the empty vault.

With the help of the *Tribune*, Father Dowling attempted to set down a time line.

*Oct. 2* — *the gangland execution of Vincent O'Toole, member of the notorious Pianone family.*
*Oct. 5* — *a gathering of the clans for the final obsequies of Vincent O'Toole at St. Hilary's parish in Fox River.*
*Oct. 16* — *Oscar Hanley reported missing.*
*Oct. 31* — *desecration of the grave followed by a desultory inquiry by the local police.*
*Nov. 15* — *the widow O'Toole decides to remove her husband's remains from Riverside and rebury them in an undisclosed location since she can get no reassurance that the body would be safe where it lies. The exhumation reveals that the casket of Vincent*

*O'Toole was not sealed in the vault before the grave was closed.*

***Nov. 17*** *— the execution of Lolly and Maxwell, workers at Riverside who took part in the exhumation. They were also at work on the day of the supposed burial of Vincent O'Toole in Riverside.*

The *Tribune*'s map of Riverside Cemetery highlighted the sexton's office, the gravesite, and the wilderness area where the bodies of Lolly and Maxwell had been discovered by Cy Horvath. Mention of the representatives of the Pianones who had been at the cemetery when the body was exhumed was spiked from the story in the *Tribune*, despite the fact that Giorgio Pianone's surprise seemed proof that the mob was not responsible for the empty vault. But there are mobs and mobs and it seemed the part of prudence to leave that detail out of the account.

Mimi enjoyed a brief celebrity at the parish center, though it was one she probably would have been willing to forgo. Other seniors seemed to know more about the associations of her late husband than Mimi did, so hers was an ambiguous popularity.

"She was certain the Blessed Mother wanted her to bury her husband at St.

Teresa's," Marie Murkin said.

"In Barfield?" Dowling asked.

"Monsignor Walsh's parish."

"I am surprised she even heard of it," Father Dowling said.

"Oh, everyone is talking about the appearance of the Blessed Mother there."

"It was nice of you to bring it to Mimi's attention."

Marie made a face. "I was desperate for a way to give her consolation. She prayed before that statue and came away certain she was supposed to have Vincent's body taken from Riverside to St. Teresa's."

"Maybe that's where the body is," Phil Keegan grumped.

"What do you mean?"

"A miracle."

Marie's mouth dropped open and she waited for Father Dowling to chastise Captain Keegan for his remark. Why, it bordered on the sacrilegious. But Phil was not through.

"Maybe someone decided he should be fed to the fish after all."

Marie had had enough. She put her hands to her ears and headed for her kitchen. If Father Dowling had been inattentive during this exchange it was because he was thinking that the body of Vincent O'Toole

184

had been spirited away on the day of the funeral.

"Do you suppose they thought Lolly and Maxwell helped?"

Phil frowned. "Pippen thinks there are signs they were subjected to some persuasion before they were shot. Lubens of course disagrees." There was a long-standing enmity between the medical examiner and his chief assistant.

"What does Cy think?"

"He's still investigating."

# Cy Horvath

## 24

Branches of his family could be traced to both banks of the Danube, to Buda as well as Pest, but doubtless it was even earlier that the elements of the genetic code had been assembled that in unique combination conferred on Cy Horvath a facial expression that seemed designed by a merciful creator to help him withstand the sanctimonious inquiries of the press in an age of moral dissolution.

"You discovered the bodies of the two workmen."

"Yes."

"What were you doing in that part of the cemetery?"

"Investigating the events of November fifteen."

"The exhumation of Vincent O'Toole."

"The exhumation of an empty vault."

"That supposedly contained the casket of Vincent O'Toole."

"That's why it was being exhumed, yes. Mrs. O'Toole wanted to rebury her husband."

"To keep him safe from vandals."

"Is that how she put it?"

"What was your understanding of her motive?"

"We were there because of the vandalism on Hallowe'en."

"Somebody tried to dig up the body."

"It looked like they had that in mind."

"Why would anyone do that?"

"That's what we were trying to find out."

"You think something was buried with the body. . . ."

"The Hallowe'en vandals apparently thought so. Obviously we wanted to know what that might be."

"Obviously?"

Cy's expression did not alter at this expression of incredulity that carried an indictment of himself and his colleagues.

"Lieutenant, if the widow had not insisted on the exhumation of the body, we would never have learned that there was no body buried there."

"Probably not."

"Your assumption is that the workmen were killed because . . . Why do you think they were killed?"

"We are investigating that."

"You must be proceeding on some assumptions."

It went on. Someone had to endure this grilling and Cy was obviously the best man for the task. Phil Keegan would have lost his temper and blown up. Robertson the chief would have tried to ingratiate himself to the press and become a symbol of all that was wrong in the relations between politicians and the underworld. When it was over, Cy went into the cafeteria for a cup of coffee and was half disappointed and half relieved to find that Dr. Pippen was not there. It was a moment when consolation is best received from one's spouse. Or by getting back to work on the investigation he had just been grilled on.

An obvious first step in the investigation of the killing of Lolly and Maxwell was to pay a visit on Giorgio Pianone. The scion of the house of Pianone had been at the cemetery when the discovery had been made and doubtless had gone through the same thought processes as Cy and Phil Keegan. But there were preliminary matters for Cy to look into.

"The casket was there for the taking while we were watching all the hoodlums leave the cemetery."

"We might actually have watched the vehicle that took the casket out."

Phil looked at Cy. "The one that brought it in?"

McDivitt fell back in his chair when Cy asked him if the McDivitt hearse could have left Riverside carrying the same burden that it had brought.

"What in God's name for?"

"Who drives your hearse?"

The driver was a cubelike woman named Mickey, as tall as she was wide as she was deep. She wore a kind of uniform and the look of one whose consciousness had been raised when Cy talked to her.

"How long you been with McDivitt?" he had asked her.

"Does he know you're asking me these questions?"

"I can wait until you get permission to talk."

She had bristled at that, of course. She could talk to anyone she wanted to, or to anyone she didn't want to, for that matter, as in the present case.

"You drove the hearse on October fifth."

"I'd have to check."

"I already have. Who would have driven it if you didn't?"

"Mr. McDivitt drives it himself, for small funerals, where there aren't a lot of people, you know."

Cy had seen his share of Potter's Field burials and he knew that funeral directors cut costs dramatically so as to keep as much as possible of what the state granted.

"He wouldn't have driven the day Vincent O'Toole was buried."

"No."

"So that day, you drove."

"Yes."

"Tell me all about it."

Mickey's face puckered into a frown. Her hair was cut in bangs and when she wore her uniform cap the peak pressed it down and robbed it of any quality of adornment.

"How come you wear a uniform?"

"How come you don't?"

"I'm a detective."

"Well, I'm a chauffeur."

"When did you get your license?"

She rolled to the side and worked a wallet free from her back pocket. She flipped it open and held it toward him.

"That's got two years to go."

She looked at it, then nodded. "That's what it says."

"You going to renew it?"

Her eyes narrowed. "Are you threatening me?"

"With what?"

"A person could get the impression that

you could stop me from renewing my chauffeur license."

"You renewed it when, three years ago?"

"I've had this one three years, that's what it seems to say."

"But you had one before."

She seemed to be reminding herself that he could check her answer. "That's my first." She paused. "Who told you, Heidegger?"

Told him what? Cy let a little silence develop. "I'd rather hear it from you."

She took off her cap and banged it on her knee. With the other hand she fluffed her bangs. That helped a little. Her little mouth turned down and she spoke with a whine. "You never let a person alone. They keep saying, start over, begin a new life, but just try it."

"Your new life began with getting the chauffeur license?"

"I was eligible! And I can vote too. I am not an outcast."

Mickey had spent three years in the Illinois Correctional Institute for Women, which, as prisons go, was almost a country club. Cy could have gone on pretending omniscience and looked up her record later, but he decided against that course.

"Mickey, I had no idea you have a record.

Maybe it's relevant, maybe it isn't. I don't know. You know why I'm here. You drove a hearse to Riverside carrying the casket of Vincent O'Toole. It was taken from your vehicle and carried by the pallbearers across the lawn to the gravesite where it was wheeled onto the apparatus that would lower it into the grave. After the ceremony, the priest, the widow, everyone, went back to their cars. In maybe half an hour everybody was gone. That's when the two workmen found that the vault in the grave had been sealed. The casket was not in sight, they assumed it was in the vault, they filled in the grave. We now know they were burying an empty vault."

"What are you saying?"

"Your hearse was the ideal vehicle to stash the casket in after it had been removed. Where did you drive it?"

"I didn't!"

"The hearse was empty when you drove it out of the cemetery?"

"I would have noticed if there was something in back."

"Did you?"

"And others would have noticed too. Did anyone say they saw a casket in the hearse when it left the cemetery?"

Her answers suggested she was holding

back. Cy took her downtown and called Agnes Lamb into it. Agnes had been brought into the department on an affirmative-action basis but within a month it had become clear that she was one of the best young cops they had. From time to time, she got a little edgy about being black, but since Cy thought that he might have joined up with Farrakhan if he were black, he figured what the heck. By then they knew that Mickey had done time for being a madam in a house where one of the girls had mysteriously died. Arresting the madam for running a disorderly house with a string of other charges was all too typical in such cases. They hadn't nailed the murderer, so they punished the madam in whose domain the crime had been committed. The house in question was part of the Pianone empire. Cy let Agnes lay this out for Mickey.

"Okay. Let's get back to the Vincent O'Toole funeral."

"I didn't drive the hearse back." Mickey spoke as if she had been holding her breath for minutes.

"Who did?"

"I don't know. I was given a ride. The hearse was still there when I left."

"Who took you home?"

"I didn't know him."

"He said, 'Let me give you a ride,' and you said sure?"

"He didn't ask. I know the tone of voice."

"You'd be able to recognize the man?"

Mickey grew terrified. She begged not to be pressed. She had already paid the penalty for someone else's crime and she didn't want to do it again.

"You help us and we'll keep it quiet."

"If I help you, they will know."

Somehow they all seemed to know who "they" were.

"I want you to look at film that was made the day of the funeral and show us the man who took you home."

# Mickey

## 25

When she was a kid the thought of being on her own, away from her mother and the second husband Mickey refused to call Father, seemed the purpose of life.

"Michaeleen!" he had said, the very first time Mickey was introduced to him. His face twisted into what would become a familiar sneer. His main protection against a world he couldn't understand was to convince himself that everyone was nuts but him.

"I call her Mickey."

He called her Minnie, a real wit. His name was Ernie and she thought of him as the Muppet. Mickey was thirteen then and a future outside that house no longer was just a dream. It was a resolve, the point of her life.

She matured early and her breasts seemed never to stop growing. Five-five and overweight, her bosom struck her as grotesque, although girls claimed to be jealous and guys just looked. It was the first thing a guy went for when she was alone with him. Snuggle, squeeze, nuzzle, they acted like babies who had never been properly weaned.

She came to think of men as children and whether she liked it or not she was Mommie. When Ernie came up behind her and put his big hands on her breasts, she raised a foot and brought the heel back into his shin, hard. He yelped in pain and her mother called from the living room. "What's the matter, hon?"

"I got kicked by a filly."

It was the fact that her mother laughed about it rather than got mad that decided Mickey that her time of departure had arrived.

Her travel guide was a recent story in the *Tribune* about late-hour bars on the edge of Old Town. She was fifteen years old, she had thirty-seven dollars in her purse, and she had drunk nothing stronger than beer. The music, the noise, the smoke, the laughter, the lights turned what in daylight would have repelled into a symbol of the good life, meaning an alternative to home. She realized that the dancer on the bar was now totally nude and was writhing and cavorting in a way that brought drunken applause from the glassy-eyed men.

"There's a booth over there." The guy didn't even look at her when he said it, but for Mickey it was a royal welcome.

She sat in the booth and a waitress came

in an outfit that seemed to display her breasts. She was looking back at the dancer. Mickey ordered beer but had to repeat it.

"I'm sorry. I'm on next." For the first time she looked at Mickey. "You alone?"

Mickey nodded.

"I'll see what I can do."

She directed two truckers to the booth, drinks were brought, names exchanged. Mickey realized they assumed she was familiar with the bar whereas this was their first visit. It put her at ease. It was nearly two when she and the truck driver named Leo left. He wanted to show her the cab he drove. It rose above the street, huge, yet odd without the part it pulled. He helped her up. When he drove away he said he would rather go to a motel than one of these city hotels. It all unfolded as if Mickey were fated to spend that night on a queen-size bed with pornography on the television and her companion out like a light after the great secret had been revealed at last. She turned off the television and lay on what he left her of the bed staring at the ceiling. She was a woman now. She began to cry and when she couldn't stop the sobs put a pillow over her face. That made it difficult to breathe. It was the first time oblivion attracted her. All she had to do was hold the pillow more tightly over her face, drift off into nothingness . . .

The man she bummed a ride back to the Loop with rented a motel room and Mickey felt that affording him swift solace was a small price to pay for the room. He couldn't stay so she had it through the night and until noon the following day. That night she went back to the bar. That was the night Vince O'Toole sat across from her and wanted to know all about her.

"You'll never be a dancer," he said, appraisingly.

"Who wants to be a dancer?"

He glanced toward the bar. "It's not bad. They don't last long though."

"Where do they go?"

"Damned if I know."

He paid for a week at the hotel. He was far rougher than the first two men. She felt overpowered, crushed, used. At the end of the week, she was settled in a house run by the outfit. Her size made her a novelty but it turned out that her real future was in management. Where would she be now if she had just gone into the life? If dancers did not last, girls in houses seemed to be used up and discarded by the dozens. Running the place gave Mickey a kind of security. She was twenty-two when she took the fall for whatever monster had strangled one of the girls. Manslaughter.

The years in Illinois Correctional were eradicated like memories of home. When she got out she stayed away from the outfit, got a chauffeur license, rented a little place in Fox River, and landed the job with McDivitt. Cecil McDivitt was such a gentleman. She could not remember ever having been treated with such respect by man or woman. Her feeling went beyond gratitude to something almost like love, which was ridiculous, since McDivitt was in his sixties and only treated her the way he treated every other woman.

She had almost forgotten the outfit when the news of the slaying of Vince O'Toole was everywhere. He was the man who had recruited her for the life, but she didn't resent it anymore. All that was in the past. Until the big guy came up to her when she was sitting behind the wheel of the hearse in Riverside Cemetery on the day Vince O'Toole was buried. Mickey had gotten a look at the body, not during visiting hours, but drifting into the viewing room at an off time and looking at the way McDivitt had restored Vince to some semblance of humanity. Where is he now? she wondered.

It was obvious to her that people didn't just stop when they died. That realization had robbed oblivion of its attractions. If there was nothing awaiting, just a blank, that would be one thing, but if . . . Mickey was as ignorant of religion as it was possible to be. Christian symbols and fragments of the gospels had come into her path but they blended with everything else.

There were beads entwined in Vince O'Toole's hands.

"A rosary," McDivitt answered, really surprised that she had asked.

"I'm not Catholic."

Not Catholic! She could equally as well have said she was not a Moslem or a Buddhist. There was a cross attached to the beads and on it a naked body. Jesus. Jesus Christ. The name had been on her lips many times, part of the slush of communication in a house. The first thing a girl acquired was a dirty mouth. Some men liked to hear a woman swear; it put them at ease. She had a New Testament someone had pressed into her hand at a street corner, bound in green, not much larger than her palm. She read the Gospel of Luke and couldn't put it down. She had been reading the New Testament when the driver door of the hearse opened and the big guy said, "Move over."

"Get out of here."

But she moved the second time he told her. She did not know who he was but she knew what he was. He called her Mickey. She felt that she was under arrest.

"See that car." He pointed. "Get in it and the guy will drive you home."

"I'm responsible for . . ."

"Don't worry, Mickey." He emphasized her name. "I'll get it back to McDivitt's."

Why would he want a hearse? There was no point in asking, she knew that. She got out of the hearse, slammed the door and walked up to the car. The driver nodded at her when she slipped in. The motor was running, he pulled away.

"We never met," he said, being friendly.

"I'm Mickey."

"I know."

All the way back to town she was certain she was being shanghaied, that he would take her to a house and it would all start up again. But he dropped her in downtown Fox River and drove away.

Did they know where she lived? Of course they knew where she lived. Her impulse was to move or to leave town. But she realized she didn't have the energy. She went to her apartment and nothing happened. A day went by and then another and she began to believe that had been it. The exhumation of Vince O'Toole's body was the talk of McDivitt's. And then the vault was brought up and proved to be empty. Mickey was there, in the hearse, waiting to haul the body out to Barfield for reburial. She had an idea why the hearse had been needed the day of the funeral. It was a kind of knowledge she would rather not have, dangerous knowledge. And then the cop Horvath came to see her.

Had she ever really believed that the past could be erased and stop having any effect on her? She had heard the pastor of the church where O'Toole's funeral had been held, Father Dowling, and several times she drove out there, wondering if she could talk to him about things. She wanted someone to give her the ABCs of Christianity. Once she sat in the church, in the back, just staring ahead at the altar. It was not at all like sitting in a viewing room at McDivitt's, even though they were made to look like chapels. She didn't feel alone in the church. If there was a God she had as good a claim on him as anyone else. If he had made her, he was somehow responsible for her. She found herself asking that she would not be bothered anymore about Vince O'Toole. It was her first unanswered prayer.

"I want you to look at some pictures," Horvath had said.

"I don't want any pictures."

"Is he familiar?" He was showing Mickey a photograph of the man who had commandeered the hearse.

"What do you mean?"

"You told me someone took over the hearse on the day of O'Toole's funeral and drove you home."

"That's right."

"Is this guy one of them?"

"Is he in the outfit?"

"He was one of the mourners at Vince O'Toole's funeral."

The other guy was in the same picture, in the background, the one who had taken the wheel of the hearse.

She pointed to the other man. "He is the one who took over the hearse."

"You're sure?"

"No, I'm lying. I'm anxious to stick my neck out."

Horvath just sat there. Was he mad or glad, surprised or what? There was no way of telling.

"Are they all in the outfit?"

He looked at her as if she had touched on his thoughts. "Yeah."

# Salvatore Pianone

## 26

He observed the events as they unfolded, registered them, withheld judgment until a judgment was forced upon him. It was important not to let others know that he was confused by what had happened. He did not understand. One thing alone was clear, the D'Annunzio holograph was missing.

He first became aware of this when a call came to his office. Cornelio wrote down the message and brought it in to him. No indication whether he understood its meaning. Cornelio was a good kid. He let him get out of the room before he turned over the slip. *Gabriele é partito.* Gabriele? Half an hour went by before he thought of the D'Annunzio holograph. Showing no emotion, he had Cornelio drive him home.

The house was full of the smell of candy being made. Christmas preparations. He went into his study and closed the door. He stood for a moment with his hands behind his back, clasping the doorknob. He loved this room. But his eyes had gone immediately to the shelf where the archival box in which he kept the D'Annunzio holograph was still in place. On either side of it, the books that belonged there were still there. Maybe he had guessed wrong.

But as he crossed the room to the shelves he steeled himself. He slid the box from the shelf. When it was in his hands, he could not tell from its weight if its contents were missing. He slid apart the two parts of the box. Empty.

After a moment, he went to this desk and stood the two empty halves of the archival box before him. The precious manuscript was gone, the thick ragged paper on which the great D'Annunzio had written with a pen that traced ink in thick and thin and magnificently formed lines on the page. At its head, *Del libro segreto*. Six and a half pages of the master, verse mixed with the prose. He sat there and remembered how enthralled Oscar had been with it, the poem embedded in the text. Could he make a copy?

> *Tanto sopra me stesso*
> *mi fai, donna, salire*
> *che, non che 'l possa dire,*
> *no 'l so pensar; perch'io*
> *non son più desso.*

"You understand it?"

Oscar made a face. "A little. It's the music . . ."

He recited it then, with a strange schoolish accent, but there was no doubt he really enjoyed what he was saying. There was a music to language independent of the meaning. Salvatore could imagine having a son-in-law like Oscar. He translated the Italian for him and the kid wrote down rapidly what he said.

"That's rough, of course."

Oscar nodded. He had picked up the holograph pages and held them with great care and awe. Then he handed them to Salvatore who put them back in the box.

"It's like being right there at his desk while he wrote."

"Something like that."

Salvatore was not used to talking about his passion for books, but with Oscar it was almost natural. Imagine talking like this with Giorgio.

The next time he came Oscar brought his version of the lines.

> *How far above*
> *myself you lift me, love,*
> *I cannot know or say*
> *since here I do not stay.*

"That's rough, of course."

"Not bad."

It was clear that Angela would go into the convent like her sister Laura before she would marry Giorgio. Salvatore had shown his nephew the study, the books, the paintings, the collection of operas.

"They're worth a lot?"

"They are."

"So what do you do, hold them while the price goes up?"

People did that, he answered Giorgio. There was no point in saying that was not his interest. He would have been willing to pay twice what Dombrowski asked for the D'Annunzio holograph. Maybe the dealer would have asked twice from someone else. Money is money but it didn't matter here except as a means of getting something more valuable than money. Giorgio wouldn't understand that. Which was not a strike on him, so far as the family went, but Angela just didn't like him.

"Not like that. He's always been a cousin, a relative," she said.

"Second cousin," Salvatore reminded her.

"I can't love him."

His heart went out to her. Memories of her sister were too vivid for him to tell her what she was going to do, like it or not. Giorgio looked okay to him but how could a man tell what women saw in any man? She knew Oscar was a poet.

"I thought he was in law school."

"He's got to make a living."

When the holograph was missing, Salvatore knew who had it. Better someone like Giorgio who had looked at the holograph with complete indifference than an Oscar who must have started plotting to steal the thing as soon as he saw it. Then it turned out that the kid was a collector. Dombrowski knew him. Salvatore felt that he had been had. Oscar's interest in Angela, the slow acceptance by her father, finally admission gained to the study and the treasures.

"You tell him what I buy?"

Dombrowski gasped and brought a fat hand to his chest. "Never! Confidential, that's the way I do business."

"What does he buy?"

Dombrowski shook his head. "All dealings are confidential."

But he had been about to speak. If he had asked him before asking if the dealer told Oscar of his purchases, what would the response have been? For a moment, Salvatore imagined a conspiracy that involved dealers as well as predators like Oscar Hanley.

"His father is a private dick," Giorgio had said early on. Another little item that Salvatore wished he had kept in mind.

So who had left the message at his office? Someone who knew Italian. Giorgio?

"How did you know it was missing?"

"I suspected him from the beginning."

"Yeah?"

"I'd rather see Angela in a convent."

Salvatore just looked at Giorgio. Observed. Registered. Withheld judgment. Time passed. Someone fooled around with O'Toole's grave on Hallowe'en, and when the widow decided to have her husband reburied, O'Toole turned up missing. This was a surprise. Who would want a dead body? Who would want Vincent O'Toole, dead or alive? The police? It turned out that the city detective Cy Horvath had guided Mimi O'Toole through the process of getting permission to move the body of her husband. What did the police think was in O'Toole's casket? What did anyone think?

Giorgio reported back.

"I was there when the lid was removed from the concrete vault they took out of the hole. I jumped onto the truck they had hoisted it on. I saw that it was empty."

"So what happened to Vince? We buried him there."

"I know!"

"So who dug him up first?"

It was not a question he expected Giorgio to answer. He sat there, remembering the gathering for the funeral, the large number of cars at the cemetery. Respect. Was stealing the body meant to be an insult?

"Maybe Oscar."

Salvatore looked at Giorgio.

"Maybe he stashed the holograph in with Vince's body," Giorgio said.

"You think that's what happened?"

"Would you look for it there?"

"Someone did."

"Yeah." Giorgio frowned. Then his face cleared. "But then he stashed the coffin too."

That did not make a hell of a lot of sense and it didn't help that Giorgio thought it did. But the central fact was that someone had stolen the D'Annunzio holograph. And whoever the sonofabitch was he was going to suffer for it — after the holograph was back safe and sound.

He could almost feel the sheets of paper in his hands. If you brought them to your nose, they had a distinctive smell, sweet, far back in the ranges of odor. But it was the fragility of the manuscript that brought pain to Salvatore. It could burn, it could be exposed to the elements. He did not like to think of it hidden in a cushioned coffin with the dead body of Vincent O'Toole. But he wanted it back. He would get it back. And he would be avenged for its theft.

His rivals in other parts of Chicago could have learned of his collection, though he had not himself spoken of it. He did not want anyone to think he was soft. And he wasn't. Ask Vince O'Toole about that. But if the others had thought his books and art were a way of getting to him, taking the D'Annunzio holograph would have been a declaration of war.

It was the business with the coffin that he could not understand. Someone had dug up Vince O'Toole, not just to get something out of the coffin, but to take the whole thing. If there was something in there with Vince, you would remove it and put him back where he belonged and nobody need be the wiser. Only you couldn't do something like that without those at the cemetery noticing. Is that why those two grave diggers had got it? Salvatore did not like this sort of thing going on in his domain, when he didn't know what it was that was going on.

As time passed, his repressed fury grew. He had to do something and he didn't know what to do. And then Father Dowling called. Salvatore looked at Cornelio when the kid came in to tell him.

"I put him on hold."

"Did he say what he wanted?"

"No."

Salvatore picked up his phone. "Father Dowling?"

"Mr. Pianone, how are you? I wonder if I could have a meeting with you."

"What about?"

"Many things. But Vincent O'Toole is at the center of it. I want to pose to you a possible explanation of what has been happening."

"Give me your number, Father. I will call you back within the half hour."

"Good."

He looked up the number of St. Hilary's parish. It matched the number he had been given. Now he must exercise caution on this end of the line. He left his office and drove to a mall where on a public phone he called Father Dowling. The same voice answered.

"I thought if you could come here to the rectory . . ."

"When?"

"This evening."

They arranged for a seven-thirty meeting. Salvatore hung up. Cornelio knew that the priest had telephoned and that he wanted to get together. But he would not know when the meeting would take place.

# Father Dowling

## 27

Marie, when he told her of the visit, staggered backward and sat abruptly in a kitchen chair.

"He's coming here?"

Father Dowling pulled back the sleeve of his sweater and looked at the old wind-up watch that had been an ordination gift. "I asked him to come at seven-thirty."

Marie glanced at the window, as if to assure herself that Salvatore Pianone would arrive under cover of darkness. "I can't believe it."

"I would suggest that you go out to a movie, but Amos Cadbury will be here at nine, and I promised that you would make tea for him."

Although seated, Marie staggered again under this second surprise. She admired Amos Cadbury more than any other man, but Salvatore Pianone, whom of course she had never met, was placed firmly at the opposite end of the scale. She stared up at Father Dowling for some explanation of these visits, but in this she was disappointed.

Father Dowling went back to his study

and for ten minutes an almost audible silence occupied the rectory. There was no sound from the kitchen. There was no evidence that Marie had taken the back stairs up to her apartment. No squeak of the door indicated that she had slipped over to the church to pray for the demented pastor of St. Hilary's. Finally, sound resumed and Marie, passing the door of the study, called out, "I hope he comes the back way and parks out there."

Salvatore had been among the mourners at the Vincent O'Toole wake, had attended the funeral Mass and apparently been among those who went on to the cemetery, or so Father Dowling had been assured by Phil Keegan. But which of the stern-faced men in camel-hair topcoats he might have been he did not know, nor, at the time, had he been curious to discover. He regretted not having asked Phil for a photograph of Salvatore as preparation for this visit, but he had not told Phil of it.

During the time before Pianone's arrival, Father Dowling sat in his study, eyes closed, praying that he might say and do the effective thing in his conversation with the mobster.

The doorbell rang at exactly seven-thirty.

Marie, who had put on a lace apron for the occasion, sailed down the hallway to get it. Her voice was high and excited and was answered by a calm baritone: Their exchange had an operatic quality to it, although he could not make out what they were saying. The man who stood in his doorway, announced by a Marie whose voice had regained its normal register, was a surprise. Perhaps Father Dowling had expected someone on the order of Peanuts, the Pianone on the police force. Salvatore Pianone was slightly less than six feet tall, had dramatically silver hair and a broad powerful face. The eyes beneath the generous brows darted to the bookshelves and then he waited to see if the priest would offer his hand. Father Dowling shook his visitor's hand and indicated a chair, but Salvatore was now giving his full attention to the shelves.

"This looks like an interesting collection."

"Well, I've collected them but only at random. Some of them go back to my school days, some I got last week."

Salvatore had stepped closer to one wall of shelves and was scanning the spines of the books. *"Codex iuris canonicae?"* He pronounced it correctly.

"My degree is in canon law."

"Ah. My daughter is studying law at Loyola."

"I know her. She helps out at the senior center one afternoon a week."

The large brown eyes turned to Father Dowling. "Children are full of surprises. My daughter Laura is a nun."

It might have been the beginning of a conversation with any parishioner. Father Dowling had the sense that the suit Salvatore wore would have cost much more than most. He was in fact elegantly dressed, but not ostentatiously. His interest in the books was genuine.

"Do be seated. I understand you are a collector yourself."

"A few things."

He would not mention Dombrowski. Was the man now seated in the leather chair favored by Phil Keegan the king of local vice, responsible for theft and murder and God knows what else?

"And one of them is missing?"

The eyes flickered. This had surprised Pianone. "I wonder how you would have heard that."

"That doesn't matter, does it? I asked you here because I want to say something. You can listen to it as to a fantastic story if you like. But I think it may clear up many things, if true."

The genial book lover gave way to the marmoreal watchfulness of a late Roman emperor. Did he nod? His manner at least suggested that Father Dowling should go on.

He had prayed that the narrative he now began would be effective. Throughout it, Salvatore listened with expressionless attention.

"The story concerns treachery and betrayal," Father Dowling began. "An effort to bring the wrath of a powerful man down on someone who is innocent."

The words and sentences and paragraphs tumbled forth and he had little sense as they did whether they were coherent or effective. He began with the attempted desecration of the grave of Vincent O'Toole on Hallowe'en and then the exhumation ordered by the widow when it was revealed that there was no casket in the vault.

"Giorgio Pianone was there on that second occasion. Was he there at your behest?"

"Yes."

"What if I told you that he could not have been surprised to find that the casket was missing."

"Go on."

The events at the cemetery on the day of the funeral were of course crucial. Father Dowling saw that Salvatore too remembered how they all went away prior to the lowering of the casket into the vault.

"The McDivitt hearse was commandeered, the hearse that had brought the casket to the cemetery. Obviously it was the best way to take it away as well."

"Who?"

"One of them was Giorgio."

He let Salvatore ponder the fact that a man who had apparently been involved in the taking away of the casket could not have been surprised to find that the casket was not in the vault.

"The question is. Was he acting under orders both times, or only on the second."

"You said I could take this as a fantastic story."

"Only you can know if it is anything more."

"Why are you telling me?"

"Because I want to beg something from you."

Salvatore waited as satraps had once waited for the requests of subjects.

"Let Oscar Hanley go. If you think he took the D'Annunzio manuscript, you are wrong."

Silence. Immobility. The eyes alone indicated that Salvatore was sorting out what he had heard. Suddenly he stood.

"Thank you, Father Dowling."

"Don't go yet."

But he was halfway to the door. "I must."

"Will you release young Hanley?"

Salvatore Pianone turned and stepped close to the desk. "Believe this, Father. Oscar Hanley is not in my hands. I do not know where he is. Therefore I cannot do what you ask."

Father Dowling believed him. With his hand on the doorknob, Salvatore again turned toward Father Dowling.

"But what I can do may have the effect of releasing him." His brows lowered slightly. "If he is alive."

# Earl O'Leary

## 28

The gun in the freezer that Oscar had brought from Riverside gave Earl a power over Giorgio he had never hoped for. In a battle of wits, he felt more than a match for Giorgio, who lacked his uncle's sanguine temperament. Giorgio's desire for Angela and his hatred of Oscar clouded his mind. Killing those two laborers had been stupid and maybe even unnecessary. Had Giorgio even bothered to find out if they knew anything? Earl did not fault him for tossing away the gun the way he had. That had not been a bad move. But in the circumstances it had been a fatal one. By doing it he had delivered himself into Giorgio's hands.

"That's your ticket," he said to Oscar.

Oscar was pulled up close to the kitchen table, forking up the spaghetti Earl had prepared, almost gulping his wine.

"Ticket to where?"

"Back into the good graces of the Pianones."

"Listen, all I have to do is talk to Salvatore and explain . . ."

Earl laughed in delighted derision. Oscar looked at him.

"You don't know him, Earl, I do."

"I know what you've told me about him. He isn't going to smile again until he gets back what has been taken."

"Don't worry. He'll get it back."

"But what if you were the one to get it back for him?" Earl said.

Oscar took the toast that popped from the toaster and covered it with butter and strawberry jam. Earl poured the coffee and joined him at the kitchen table.

"You didn't take that manuscript, right?"

"No!" Oscar seemed scandalized by the thought.

"So who did? Giorgio."

"He wouldn't know the value of it."

"He knows the value it has for Salvatore. And by making it look as if you took it, he gets rid of his rival the old-fashioned way, he lets someone else do it."

Oscar chewed while he thought. He shrugged. "Maybe."

"It had to be an inside job. That means either you or one of the Pianones. Who but Giorgio has it in for you?"

Earl's mind was not solely on the argument he was making. The double agent is required to think twice about everything.

Until Oscar called him, Earl had assumed that Giorgio had gotten rid of Oscar. The patience required to discredit Oscar with Salvatore had worn on Giorgio. The way Oscar described him shooting those laborers was Giorgio's style. Fast and brutal and over with. Maybe Giorgio had figured out that turning Salvatore against Oscar would not bring Angela into his arms. He could still make sure that there was no Oscar for her to turn to.

Finished eating, Oscar began to yawn. The sedatives Earl had put in the wine were working.

"I better call my dad."

"Why don't you let me do that?"

Oscar was yawning and his eyes narrowed as he looked up at Earl.

"Oscar, when I heard your voice on the phone I nearly had the big one myself. Let me break it to him gently."

Oscar laughed. "You make it sound like bad news."

Earl picked up the phone and dialed his own number. He held it out so that Oscar could hear the busy signal.

"You want to get some sleep, go ahead. I'll try again in a few minutes."

Oscar looked woozy when he stood up but he made it into the living room where he sprawled on the couch. "I don't know why I'm so tired."

"After what you've been through?"

Within a minute, Oscar was out.

Earl tiptoed into the kitchen and shut the door. He leaned against the sink and looked unseeing out the window. His mind had been going since hearing Oscar's description of Giorgio assassinating those two cemetery laborers. Salvatore would be merciless with anyone who engaged in freelance killing. Only what he authorized could be done with impunity. Of course Giorgio had killed those men to prevent his earlier freelance action from coming to light, the theft of Vince O'Toole's casket. If he does find out, Salvatore will have a big laugh before he takes care of Giorgio. No, Earl amended, Salvatore would not laugh. Not when he found out why Giorgio wanted to open up that coffin.

"You go," Ray Hanley had said to Earl on the day of Vincent O'Toole's funeral. "You won't be recognized."

"So what if they see you?"

Ray managed to say it after a couple tries. Oscar was engaged to Angela, okay, but Ray didn't want people thinking he had somehow become affiliated with the Pianones.

224

"I can't take the chance, Earl. Go."

So Earl went alone, which was better. He was to be waiting in the wild area beyond the cemetery proper where there was a corrugated metal building in which concrete vaults were stacked. Earl had become a student of Catholic funerals, particularly the cemetery finale, during the days after Vince O'Toole died, and had observed that the mourners went off before the coffin was lowered into the grave. Three times he observed this and then he took Giorgio out there to show him. And so the plan was formed.

"How we going to get it into the casket?"

"We will sew it into the lining of Vince's burial suit. You bring that to McDivitt and say bury him in this."

Giorgio shook his head. "That's pretty complicated."

"You want to hold on to that manuscript while Salvatore is looking for it?"

"Geez."

So Giorgio had removed the D'Annunzio manuscript from its box and, still sweating bullets, brought it to Earl. He stood watching as Earl had opened up the back lining of the suit and secured the manuscript pages across the back shoulders, taping them in place. Then he resewed the lining.

"Where'd you learn to sew?"

"The Boy Scouts."

Later Giorgio reported to Earl that the suit had been delivered to McDivitt and that Vince would be buried in it. Removing the casket to one of the vaults in the far shed at the cemetery promised security as well as removing the ghoulish necessity of digging up the buried body.

The snatching of the coffin, getting it back to the McDivitt hearse after Healey drove off with the chauffeur, went off as smoothly as the rest of the funeral ceremony. When Earl saw the hearse coming along the road through the trees he stepped back into the shadow of the shed, but it was Giorgio at the wheel. He drove right into the cool darkness of the shed.

"Where's Healey?"

"Lowering the vault into the grave. He screwed on the top and figured why wait."

"No one saw him?"

"What are they going to see? A worker doing his job."

Earl asked Giorgio if he wanted to check Vince's coffin before they bolted it into one of the vaults in the shed.

"Open it up?"

"You don't want to?"

"I want to get the hell out of here."

Giorgio didn't mind making people dead but he did not want to be around them once they were. At Vince O'Toole's wake he had not gone forward to look at the prettified body of his old associate who had fallen into Salvatore's bad graces and paid the price. Giorgio's edginess had prompted Earl's Hallowe'en excursion. The memory of being out there alone in the dark on the haunted evening, making himself conspicuous so the minor mess he had made around O'Toole's headstone would be discovered, brought a smile to Earl's narrow face.

"What's going on?" Giorgio demanded when he heard about the apparent digging around the grave on Hallowe'en.

"Maybe Vince is trying to get out."

A moment's silence. "But he's not there."

"Kids," Earl explained, and Giorgio accepted it. Earl had hoped to get a bigger rise out of Giorgio.

But Giorgio did show some of the superstitious dread he'd had when in the metal shed they bolted Vince's coffin into a vault, and then stacked several empties on top of it.

"Let's get out of here," Giorgio said.

Which they did. Healey drove the McDivitt vehicle to the point where he had taken the chauffeur. Smooth.

It was some hours later that they telephoned Salvatore Pianone and let him know he was missing something. *Gabriele é partito.* Salvatore liked obliquity, codes, the indirect reference. Earl had no doubt that he would soon discover that his precious D'Annunzio manuscript was missing.

Now, after the execution of those gravediggers, with Oscar in a drugged slumber on his couch, it seemed only right that he should now inform Giorgio where his missing nemesis could be found.

After that, he would let the police know about Giorgio.

# Tuttle

## 29

Ray Hanley was a drinker of the old school. When he opened a bottle and sat down at the table with a fellow drinker, the object of the enterprise was to get drunk. Hanley had been so relieved to learn that his son had been alive and well and living in the gatehouse of Riverside Cemetery that a celebratory drink seemed called for. But when Tuttle led him to believe that Oscar was likely to try to get in touch with him so he should sit tight, Ray agreed.

"So sit and we'll get tight."

Tuttle sat. Alcohol was a luxury, given the parlous state of his finances, so that the opportunity to drink at another's expense was not to be despised. With diminishing coherence, they went through recent events.

"If Salvatore thinks Oscar stole that manuscript, he'll kill him."

"Would Oscar do that?"

"I stopped predicting what people might or might not do a long time ago."

"But Oscar's your son."

The reminder brought moisture to Ray

Hanley's eyes. "I thank God that he's safe."

Affection between father and son touched Tuttle as nothing else could. His own father had retained an unshakable belief in his ultimate success through a seemingly endless series of reversals. Tuttle had gone through law school three times, so to speak, taking classes again and again until eventually he passed them. His father was still alive when he received his law degree and it was as if, his mission on earth completed, he was free to die and he did. His father had been spared the long trek toward admission to the bar, but when Tuttle opened his office he proudly called the firm Tuttle & Tuttle. "Where is your partner?" "In heaven." Tuttle was confident that his departed paternal parent would smile on his effort to reassure Ray Hanley about his son.

"I should let Earl know."

"Earl."

"My assistant. Babyface. You've met him."

Ray went on about how close Earl and Oscar had become. Tuttle dialed the number for him, but Earl's line was busy. Tuttle wrote down the number so he could try again. The address was in the book Ray turned round toward him on the table. Tuttle chuckled.

"What's funny?"

"123 Fourth?"

Ray didn't get it. It was like seeing the test drawing one way rather than another. Tuttle had never been good at such tests so he felt a surge of superiority over Hanley. But then Ray seemed to have started drinking before Tuttle got there.

He finished before Tuttle did too, putting his head on the table, saying he would just shut his eyes for a moment. He left his mouth open and was soon snoring peacefully. Tuttle weighed the wisdom of getting Ray to bed. He decided that the private investigator had probably done his share of falling asleep the way he was and left him as he was.

"I'll stop by Earl's and tell him the good news about Oscar," he said aloud in his car, feeling like a Boy Scout.

"Who's Oscar?"

The voice from the back seat nearly sent Tuttle through the roof. And his heart did not settle down immediately when he realized that it was Peanuts Pianone.

"Good God, you scared me."

"You woke me up when you slammed the door."

"Sorry."

Peanuts's presence posed a problem. This whole business with Vince O'Toole and Oscar involved the Pianones. It was an unstated assumption of their friendship that he never quizzed Peanuts about his family's doings. True, it was Peanuts who had brought up the subject first, complaining about Oscar Hanley and his sister Angela.

"How'd you get here?"

"Agnes Lamb dropped me off."

Tuttle let it go. Agnes Lamb was the cross that Peanuts had to bear as an officer of the law. Agnes was a woman and she was black and she had less seniority than Peanuts but she was a far better cop. Every cop was better than Peanuts, of course, but Agnes was as good as they get. Tuttle had this on the authority of Cy Horvath, who would not be given to affirmative action excess. However Agnes had gotten her job, she deserved it.

"How did you know I was here?"

"Marie Murkin."

"Marie Murkin!"

"She's the housekeeper at St. Hilary's."

"I know who she is!" Tuttle started the car and pulled away from the curb, causing a car approaching from the rear to swerve and blast its horn. Tuttle ignored it. He had a cop in the car if any motorist wanted to make trouble. He must have told Father Dowling he was going to stop at Ray Hanley's. It was odd to think that his whereabouts were being passed from mouth to mouth. It gave him a warm feeling. And he was glad for Peanuts's companionship.

"You smell like booze," Peanuts said. He sat regally in a corner of the back seat, with a good grip on a safety strap.

"I was being a good guest. Ray Hanley just found out his son is still alive."

Silence from the back seat.

"It turns out he has been hiding in an apartment in the gatehouse of Riverside Cemetery."

"Two guys got killed out there."

Tuttle waited. Would Peanuts say more? Did he know more? Peanuts was an enigma when it came to the doings of his family. It was unclear how much they told him or what he picked up without being told. But then it was unclear what information he could give them of the police department that would be helpful. The family need have no fear that Peanuts would betray them. The police gave him little opportunity to undermine their work. In any case, the relationship between the police and the Pianones was largely a stand-off, live and let live.

"Workers," Tuttle said.

The manner of their going pointed to the mob. But then Peanuts surprised him.

"We're clean."

"Yeah?"

"Pass the word. The Pianones had nothing to do with those two guys in the cemetery."

"I'll pass it on."

"Don't quote me."

"I understand."

Peanuts settled back. "Where we going?"

"1234."

Peanuts accepted this mystery as he accepted a hundred others in the course of an ordinary day.

When Tuttle got on to Fourth Street he turned west and as he passed 123 a car backed out of the driveway and went in reverse several doors and stopped. The headlights had not been turned on. When Tuttle passed the stopped car, on his left, he glanced at the man behind the wheel. Earl O'Leary. Even as he recognized him, the young man slid lower in the seat, resting his head against its back.

Two intersections further on, Tuttle made a U-turn and came slowly back on Fourth. Before crossing the intersection he pulled over and turned off his lights.

"This the place?"

"Let's keep an eye on the car parked in the next block."

Peanuts thought about it. "I wish we had something to eat."

Tuttle handed him a bag of M&M's. "To tide you over. This shouldn't take long. Then we'll hit a Chinese restaurant."

Do we ever really see the street on which we live? Most of the time Earl just pulled into or out of the driveway and once inside the house the street was only what he happened to notice from the windows. Sitting slouched down behind the wheel of his parked car, Earl had the opportunity to contemplate the stretch of Fourth Street he had come to think of as home. It was in what is now called the Inner City, meaning the decaying center that has been abandoned for the suburbs that encircle it. There were pockets and islands that resisted the descent into shambles, but Fourth Street was not one of them. His house, 123, had an impressive history, if one believed the plat book. Earl had examined it one day when he had been on an errand in the courthouse for Ray Hanley. The house had been built by an alderman whose family had occupied it continuously from 1903 until the Depression. It had then passed through half a dozen owners until the Second World War when it was sold for four thousand dollars, just before its value rose suddenly like a

rocket in the wartime economy. Since 1950, it had passed from hand to hand, and the fact that it was now in his seemed a seal on its decadence.

From this vantage point his house seemed narrow and high. He had never thought of it that way. He stared at the darkened window of the room in which Oscar lay in drugged sleep. The gun with which Giorgio had killed two men was in the freezer still, but Giorgio would not search the place. By delivering the witness of the killing up to Giorgio, Earl caused the value of the gun as leverage to decrease, but his perfidy had much to commend it.

First, the only serious rival for Angela Pianone's hand would be removed. He had stopped resisting the thought that Angela was too beautiful for either Giorgio or Oscar and had himself become an unannounced claimant for her hand.

Second, Giorgio would thereby come doubly into his power — the gun would enable him to make the case against Giorgio with Salvatore.

Third, this should ingratiate him with the man whose son-in-law he intended to become, with an eye ultimately to inheriting the Pianone operation. If a Pole could become pope, surely an Irishman could rise to the top of the mafia.

Fourth, while Giorgio was busy taking care of Oscar, Earl would retrieve the holograph from the O'Toole casket. This was not a task he looked forward to with anticipation. He would wear the nose plugs he wore while swimming. He would wear dark glasses to blur the images. What does a body look like weeks after death? But Vincent had been embalmed, so corruption should not be too far advanced. In any case, all he had to do was remove the suit jacket and shut the casket. He must seal it up again in a vault in case Giorgio decided to check the site to see that all was well.

He had persuaded Giorgio that by returning the D'Annunzio holograph, presumably stolen by Oscar, he would discredit Oscar and have a powerful advocate in Salvatore, who would force Angela's consent. Giorgio wanted to possess Angela more than he wanted to win her heart. Earl's altered plan was a variation on the one he had sketched for Giorgio. Giorgio would be revealed as the unauthorized executioner of the two workmen and of Oscar. Retribution would be swift and final. Subsequently, Earl could present the holograph to Salvatore, covering it with a plausible story. He was developing such a story when the Lincoln

Town Car came slowly down the street and then swung abruptly into the drive of 123.

The Lincoln was out of his line of vision when Earl heard the slam of its doors. Giorgio was certainly not arriving unannounced. Two minutes passed, what might have been the sound of the door, and then window after window of 123 lit up. Earl straightened in his seat, imagining the drama within. Giorgio coming upon his drugged and defenseless rival. Images of the scene at the cemetery as Oscar had described it sent a tremor through Earl's tensed body. For a moment the depth of his treachery was starkly outlined against a vestigial memory of honor, but then he embraced the image of his supposed friend being brutally executed by his supposed ally.

Earl had never read Machiavelli, but he thought he understood the gist of *The Prince*. His own handbook was a much-thumbed paperback edition of *Thus Spake Zarathustra*. The nihilist assumption was that moral rules were simply devices to keep the peasants down, that the informed realized that rules were simply arbitrary and to be used to one's advantage. Aphorisms soothed what might have been called his conscience. He had risen to the heights, a moral superman. To betray others was highest virtue, whether to advance self-interest or merely as a whim. But of course he had in mind a very distinct prize as a consequence of Giorgio and Oscar canceling one another: Angela. But then he smiled. No, Angela too was merely a means, the path to the usurpation of Pianone power.

No very cosmic point of view is needed to appraise the scale on which Earl O'Leary's deeds must be placed. A western suburb of Chicago, a community all but anonymous in the state in which it is found, unknown beyond and virtually nonexistent as the horizon expands. *What does it profit a man if he gain the whole world and suffer the loss of his own soul?* This verse was painted on the back wall of Our Lady of Hungary, the church Earl attended with the Hanleys, keeping up his persona, and he had often read it on his way down the aisle after Mass. Now he thought of Richard Rich and Wales, but what was the Pianone underworld outfit compared to Wales? Each Alexander must conquer the world at his disposal. Napoleon could only be present in one subjugated country at a time. It might have been Fox River. In any case, Earl had made his choice and he felt no urge to rescind it.

He had rolled down the window on the

passenger side and now he picked up the sounds of the door opening, movement toward the driveway, heavy breathing under the burden being carried. A sound that he retrospectively identified as the trunk door opening when he heard the unequivocal sound of its closing. There was the unmistakable sound of two car doors closing almost simultaneously, an engine started, and then the Lincoln Town Car slid unlighted into the street. Earl had just ducked out of sight when the headlights came on and lit up the inside of his car as if it were a store window. His heart was in his throat while he wondered if Giorgio would recognize the car, check it out, look in and find him hiding here. . . .

But the engine raised its voice slightly and the car and lights went by, leaving Earl in darkness. Five minutes later, he drove again into his driveway and on into his garage. The raising and lowering of the garage door violated the relative silence of the night, though he was aware again now as he had not been in his car of the incessant hum of traffic on the interstates that formed a concrete triangle around Fox River.

His front door was ajar. He pulled it shut behind him. The lights had been left on as well.

The couch was empty.

In the freezer, still wrapped in Oscar's handkerchief, was the gun Giorgio had used to execute the two cemetery laborers.

# Cy Horvath

## 31

The lab had made casts of tire prints at the scene of the execution of Lolly and Maxwell, the fatal bullets had been found, footprints examined, the usual routine gone through conscientiously but without the remotest hope that it would produce evidence that would be crucial in the conviction of the killer. Killers. Hit men. This was a professional job and it pointed in one direction without the aid of any other data. The mob.

"But which one?" Phil Keegan grumbled. "Not ours."

Phil brushed aside the confusing conduct of Giorgio and stuck with the notion that the Pianones had nothing to do with the theft of Vince O'Toole's casket.

"The ones that got Vince O'Toole."

Some gang other than the Pianones must have gunned down Vince O'Toole and then stolen his coffin before it got buried. Why?

"Check it out?"

Cy had just waited, and then Phil said, "The casket. There's something about the casket."

So Cy went back to McDivitt and checked the records of purchase of the casket he had sold to Mimi O'Toole, he examined what McDivitt assured him was the exact duplicate of it. With the help of the undertaker, he established a schedule of the days from the time the body had arrived until the first viewing and wake, the sealing of the casket before the trip to St. Hilary's the day of the funeral. Cecil McDivitt, aware of the special character of the deceased and moved as well by his affection for Mimi and her family, had supervised the process from one end to another.

"Why would anyone steal a body?"

Cecil McDivitt found the topic painful. "God only knows."

"It sounds as if it would have been hard for someone to slip something in with the body."

"Absolutely impossible!"

Nothing helpful emerged from that visit. But that still left a stolen body and two grave diggers dead in a way that seemed clearly connected to the missing casket. Cy was about to inquire into the manufacture of the casket, to see if some explanation could be found there, when yet another call came from Riverside Cemetery. It was Mrs. Heidegger and she was hysterical.

"My husband has been attacked, the body has been desecrated, you have to do something."

"Are you at the cemetery?"

She was furious with him because he did not know where she was. When it became clear she was in the sexton's office, Cy assured her he would be there immediately. On the way he spoke with the officers who had arrived on the scene. That is why, at Riverside, he drove past the sexton's office and continued through the cemetery to the far end and the corrugated shed where there were now three patrol cars and a van from the lab. Cy found Heidegger sitting with a haunted look in his eye, staring into space. Cy sat down beside him and put a hand on his shoulder. The sexton flinched, ducking away, and then, recognizing Horvath, said, "What in the name of God is going on? Is nothing sacred anymore?"

"Tell me about it."

"Where is Dorothy?"

"Mrs. Heidegger is in your office."

"I don't want her back here."

Cy spotted Agnes Lamb and called her over. He wanted Heidegger to hear him ask the young officer to go to the sexton's office and reassure Mrs. Heidegger that her husband was fine and that everything

245

was under control.

"Under control," Heidegger repeated.

"We don't want her worried."

"No," the sexton agreed. "No, we don't."

Heidegger was much calmer now and Cy let him gather himself more before asking what had happened to him. Meanwhile, Cy went to the shed. Inside, those who weren't wearing medicinal masks were holding handkerchiefs to their faces. It looked as if a stack of concrete vaults had toppled. One had its top removed and a casket had been pulled from it, its lid raised. The shirted body of the late Vince O'Toole hung over the side of the casket, facedown. The scene came and went with the photographers' flash bulbs. Cy was a stolid man whose emotions were ever under control, but this was a scene out of a bad movie, ghoulish.

"Nothing been moved?" he asked Lubens.

"Nothing."

Cy then went out to Heidegger, helped him to his feet, and took him to his car. It was then that he heard the sexton's tale.

Still bearing the burden of the loss of Lolly and Maxwell, Heidegger had driven out to the far shed for the excavator, intending to dig a grave for a burial scheduled for the following day. When he approached

246

the shed, he heard noises from within. He broke into a run and began to call out.

"I didn't feel any fear. I was angry. I was reminded of Hallowe'en."

If he thought at all he thought it was kids fooling around in there. He ran into the shed whose door was open and the passage from light to darkness blinded him. But not so much that he did not see the activity going on by the light of a flashlight.

"The coffin was open and he was doing something with the body."

"Removing its coat?"

Heidegger looked at him. "Yes! That's what he was doing."

He'd had only a glimpse until the flashlight went out. The man moved in the dark. Heidegger had thought he would be trying to flee, but then the lights really went out. The lump on his head, the bruised and scraped side of his face, suggested being hit and then falling on the rough concrete floor of the shed. He was lucky to be alive.

"Can you describe him?"

"He was just a figure."

"But a man?"

"Yes, of course."

"Large, small?"

"I don't know. What in the name of God is going on?"

Cy did not say so but for the first time he felt that events were less mysterious than they had seemed. Apparently it was the clothes in which Vince O'Toole had been buried that had been the object of all these strange happenings. The Hallowe'en night, the curiosity when the vault was brought up and shown to be empty. Someone had taken the casket because they wanted Vince's burial clothes. Lolly and Maxwell had been killed because they were suspected of what? Maybe simply of having seen too much.

Heidegger was able to drive himself back to his office. Cy followed him and went in and watched the reunion of the Heideggers. Mrs. Heidegger's relief soon gave way to re-crimination and she began threatening to leave him if he did not get a decent job at last. Phil Keegan arrived and Cy told him what he knew.

"His clothes?"

"His coat. He could have taken more once Heidegger was subdued, but he settled for the suit jacket."

"Something in its pockets?"

"I'm going back to talk to Cecil McDivitt."

"I'll come along. Agnes can handle this."

# Giorgio Pianone

## 32

Giorgio was in Racine with Healey when Salvatore got him on the phone and told him, *parlando Italiano,* that O'Toole's casket had been found in a shed at the far end of Riverside Cemetery. The sexton had surprised a man who had pulled the body out of the casket.

"Who was it?"

"I want you to find out."

"The police don't know?"

"They say they don't. I don't care what they know. I want that guy."

"Just one."

"If there's more than one, I want them all."

After he hung up, Giorgio sat looking out at the roiled winter surface of Lake Michigan. Earl. It had to be Earl O'Leary. Why? He forced himself to sit still, to sip his mineral water, to look out at the water rising high as it hit the pier, adding to the icy stalagmites that formed in the freezing cold. It was possible that Earl had just activated their plan, but Salvatore had made no mention of Oscar Hanley. The plan was to use the stolen manuscript to discredit Oscar and get him erased so that Giorgio had a free track with Angela. Earl had the coat, so he had the manuscript. He hadn't acted yet. But why had he gone to that shed without telling Giorgio?

Earl O'Leary represented an important basis for Giorgio's belief that he was capable of taking over from Salvatore, eventually, as designated successor. Going to Minneapolis and enlisting the baby-faced private investigator as permanent ally had been accomplished without anyone else being involved. Only he and Earl knew what Earl had been hired to do. When Earl got a job with Ray Hanley, Giorgio was sure that he had made a good pick. But he remembered now that he had wondered if maybe Earl wasn't too good. He had gotten the job with Hanley first and then told Giorgio. The guy was a self-starter. Until now, Giorgio had quieted any incipient doubts with the assurance that he owned Earl, the guy was entirely in his power. He could destroy him anytime he wanted. Sitting in Racine, looking out at the lake, it dawned on Giorgio that he had given Earl equal power over the man who had hired him.

For a moment, apprehension rose in him,

real fear, not of Earl, but of his uncle Salvatore, if Earl should . . .

He shrugged the thought away. He wouldn't dare. You didn't betray a Pianone and live.

That went for Pianones too, however. His apprehension did not go away.

Maybe Earl was looking for him, wondering where he was. He would want to talk to him before he talked with Salvatore. Giorgio heaved himself from his chair and called to Healey.

"Let's get on the road."

"You figured it out?"

Giorgio made an enigmatic movement with his head. It was important that Healey not suspect he didn't know what the hell was going on. Earl better have a very good reason for taking that coat off Vince's body when he did. It couldn't have been planned. Acting alone, no wonder he had been surprised by the sexton. Heidegger. The cemetery guy was becoming a real celebrity. Giorgio thought of him coming into the shed and finding Earl stripping a corpse.

"What's funny?" Healey asked.

"Everything."

After a moment, Healey grinned confusedly at the road that was taking them back to Fox River.

Giorgio said, "Did you check the trunk?"

"He's okay."

"We gotta feed him."

"We gotta change him too." When Giorgio did not respond, Healey added, "Like a baby."

"In my car!"

"He's still wrapped up."

Giorgio's nose wrinkled as he cautiously inhaled. He detected no evidence of what Healey was saying.

"What we gonna do with him?"

Driving around with Oscar in the trunk was not smart. When Earl called to tell him that he could pick up Oscar at Earl's apartment if he wanted him, Giorgio had been delighted.

"Where's he been?"

"Ask him."

"He's there?"

"Of course you can't talk to him right away. He won't come out of it for hours."

"Where is he?"

"I'll leave him on the couch."

"Leave him?"

"I have something to do." Riding back from Racine, Giorgio remembered that remark. Something to do must have meant get the coat off Vince. Meanwhile Giorgio would be occupied taking care of Oscar. His idea had been to do the job in Wisconsin and get rid of the body there. The call from Salvatore had saved Oscar, or at least postponed his fate.

Salvatore had not mentioned Oscar.

"What are we going to do with him?" Healey asked.

"Him in the trunk?"

"Yeah."

Ideas are marvelous things. This one just lit up Giorgio's mind without preamble. He laughed again.

"We're going to take him back where we got him."

# Cecil McDivitt

## 33

No one even asked him anymore why he had adopted his profession, doubtless because no one could imagine him doing anything else. Those who could remember Cecil McDivitt before he became an undertaker were a dwindling band, many former members of which had been the beneficiaries of his skills, but Cecil himself could remember those earlier days. There was a part of his soul that was able to see the decades in which he had escorted body after body to the grave as insignificant, not the true story of his life. But even when he traveled, he found himself eventually wandering the path of some cemetery, marveling at the cultural differences his trade exhibited as the result of being practiced in this country or that. He had spent hours in Montmartre, he had lingered in the cemetery in Florence with its rows of miniature basilicas and cathedrals, its life-size *cararra* marble likenesses of the departed. He had developed a sense of the dignity and importance of the work he did. But the events surrounding the death of Vincent O'Toole threatened the whole edifice of his self-esteem.

Dealing with Mimi had brought back memories of early days, memories of her parents. That had made it possible for him to treat the preparation of the slain mobster who was Mimi's husband not as simply another job but as a favor for old friends. He had had to relive those days again and again, most recently when Lieutenant Horvath had led him painstakingly from moment to moment, in search of some explanation of the incredible happenings at Riverside. Could anyone blame Cecil if he now steered clients away from Riverside? It was the claim that his hearse had played a role in criminal doings that particularly wounded Cecil. Mickey the chauffeur stood before his desk with her uniform cap in her hand and cried without facial expression.

"You should have told me, Mickey."

"Told you what? They drove me away a couple blocks and fifteen minutes later turned the hearse back to me."

It seemed to Cecil that such information would have told him something was wrong. But would it?

"That's all there was to it," Mickey wept. "The vehicle was in perfect condition. If they had done any damage . . ."

"I don't blame you for what happened, Mickey."

Her tears stopped flowing. She put on her hat, then took it off again. McDivitt realized she was still standing. Her stature was such that she might have been sitting. He asked her to be seated. She shook her head.

"Did they force you out of the hearse?"

"They didn't have to."

"Did you know them?"

"Him."

"You have to tell the police."

"I already have."

"You have! How long have they known this?"

McDivitt's confusion and anger were transferred to Cy Horvath. If he had known all along about the hearse, why . . .

The phone rang and he picked it up in midring. "McDivitt's Funeral Home," he said unctuously.

"Lieutenant Horvath. O'Toole's casket has been found."

"My God! Where?"

"I'm on my way there now."

The line went dead. Mickey still stood before his desk.

"They found the casket. He's coming here. Lieutenant Horvath."

Did Mickey salute before she left his office? Perhaps it was just the way she put on her cap before turning on one heel and marching to the door. McDivitt sat in wordless perplexity, dreading the arrival of Cy Horvath.

His mood was not brightened by what Horvath told him when he arrived. McDivitt closed the door carefully. Whatever horrors were to come, he did not want them bruited about the funeral parlor. Horvath sat without being asked.

"The casket was stashed in a shed at the back of the cemetery. Apparently since the day of the funeral. O'Toole was pulled halfway out of the casket. It was the coat they were after. The coat had been stripped from the body."

McDivitt put his face in his hands. "Poor Mimi O'Toole. This will kill her."

"Did you dress the corpse?"

"I supervised it, yes."

"Did you notice anything peculiar about the jacket you put on him?"

"Absolutely not!"

McDivitt stopped and for a moment it wasn't Horvath he saw, but Mimi and her boy. Sonny.

"What is it?" Horvath said.

"Let me think, let me remember."

He should have remembered to mention

that the Pianones had paid for Vincent O'Toole's funeral.

"They brought a suit for him to wear."

"Who brought it?"

"The Pianones. Giorgio. That's it, isn't it? There was something in that suit."

Horvath was on his feet. "We'll find out."

After the door closed, McDivitt felt as he often did after sustaining a client through the ordeal of a funeral: depleted, collapsed, without strength. Listlessly he turned the pages of his appointment calendar, looking for clear days during which he might flee Fox River and sit like a vegetable in the southern sun, his mind blessedly free of grief and death and floral arrangements that made him sneeze.

But the call of duty was relentless. He picked up the phone, dialed St. Hilary's, and asked to speak to Father Dowling. He must be forewarned that Mimi would soon be confronted with another test of her resilience. As for himself, he must face the unsavory task of preparing Vince O'Toole one more time for consignment to the earth. This time he would not leave the grave site until he had personally supervised the filling in of the hole with the dirt that had been dug from it.

That done, out of relief, as a reward, he

258

slid open a drawer of his desk and took from it a bottle of scotch. He had just put it on the desk when the door pushed open and a young man with a baby face stepped in. He closed the door behind him.

"Could I have a few minutes of your time?"

The politeness of his tone seemed to cancel out the rudeness of just walking in as he had. "I am about to have a drink."

"By all means."

The young man acted as if he were giving Cecil permission. He sat, unbuttoned his coat, crossed his legs. "Can I record our conversation?"

"Who are you?"

A merry laugh. "Don't be alarmed. I am a detective. A private investigator. I work with Ray Hanley."

"I don't care who you work for. I have already talked with the police."

"Good. Let's go over what you told them."

Cecil rose to his feet. "Please leave. I have no intention whatsoever of discussing such matters with you."

He seemed to have done something to a small recorder he had taken from his pocket. "Why?"

"I will not talk about it."

"Is it true that the mob provided burial clothes for Vincent O'Toole?"

"My God." Cecil sat. "Who told you that?"

"Then it's true?"

Cecil sipped his scotch, watching the young man over the rim of his glass. He put the glass down. The police had asked him about this and he had told them that Giorgio had brought a suit for the burial. But now he remembered the sequel of that, when Mimi and Sonny O'Toole had come to him.

"No, it is not true."

"It's not?"

"The widow brought a suit for the funeral."

The young man frowned. "That isn't what my other sources tell me. I was told that clothing was delivered here by the Pianones."

"But it was not used. Mrs. O'Toole wanted her husband buried in a suit he had worn for their thirty-fifth anniversary."

Why was he telling this annoying young man these things? Perhaps because they seemed to upset him so.

"What happened to the clothes the Pianones brought here?"

He had to think. He closed his eyes and

suddenly felt the effect of the scotch on his frazzled nervous system.

"She took them."

"Mrs. O'Toole?"

He nodded. "Please leave me alone."

The young man surprisingly sprang to his feet. "You're absolutely sure?"

"Absolutely."

And he was gone. Several drinks later Cecil was not sure whether or not he had dreamt the visit.

# Earl O'Leary

## 34

Earl hurried through McDivitt's parking lot
to the side street where he had left his car.
Unpleasant thoughts, maddening thoughts,
pursued him. He had been double-crossed
by Giorgio. Worse, he had been outsmarted.
His hubris had brought him to this. Giorgio,
the whole Pianone family, had seemed ci-
phers he could manipulate to his own advantage. His own treachery would be so total as
to be indiscernible. He would betray Giorgio,
he would betray Ray Hanley, he would betray
Oscar, and he had, all these things had been
done, but to no purpose! When he went to
claim the prize it was not there.

He sat at the wheel of his car, letting the
thoughts torment him. But it was what
McDivitt had just said that oddly provided
relief. When the undertaker denied burying
O'Toole in the clothing provided by the
Pianones, Earl had not believed him. Why
would the man lie? Why not? Had he
made the same denial to the police? A small
question formed in his mind. What if
McDivitt was telling the truth? His hand

reached out to the ignition key.

Mimi was not at the O'Toole residence so Earl settled down to wait. It was a mark of his profession, waiting. Stakeouts might try the patience of a saint, but they were the daily bread of investigators. He would not want to add up the hours he had sat in a car, waiting for someone to appear, waiting for something to happen, waiting. One learned to think of such time as unlike ordinary time. It came in such big chunks that a needle moving over a gauge, a hand across the face of a clock, did not suffice. It was all already there.

Can one who doubts the existence of God be a determinist? If there is no God, and all is random, nothing is determined. Events occurred and what we call causes are merely elements of the events. So much for logic. Earl was a determinist, a fatalist, he believed that he was acting in a drama that was fore-ordained, every jot and tittle of it predestined to unfold necessarily from their antecedents. Of course, this left room for wondering what would happen next. Or, under these circumstances, wondering when Mrs. O'Toole would come home.

The answer was seven fifty-one. Unless Earl was mistaken, the driver of the car that brought her was a city detective, Keegan. He had his arm under Mimi's elbow as he took her to the door, he stood there until she had closed it on him, then went stolidly back to his car. Doubtless out of habit, his eyes went up and down the street before he got into his car once more. He drove away immediately.

Earl waited until a minute after the hour before knocking on the O'Toole door. He stepped back when the light over the door came on so she could get a reassuring look at him. He wore a serious expression.

"What do you want?"

The door had not opened. She must have a system for communicating without opening the door.

"That's very wise of you, Mrs. O'Toole. You can't be too careful." He smiled at the door. "Ray Hanley sent me."

This was met with silence. Then he said what he wished he had said at first.

"I have just come from Mr. McDivitt."

Open sesame. He heard the chain removed and the dead bolt slid away and the knob turned. He waited. The storm door too was locked. He waited until she pushed it open.

"This will only take a minute. I can imagine how distraught you must be."

The coat she had worn was thrown over a chair and there was a glass on the table. She had had time to make herself a drink.

"I am nearly out of my mind."

"Go ahead and have that. I don't want anything."

She actually thanked him and picked up the glass. She sipped and then kept on sipping. Why didn't she just take a healthy swallow?

"They have been pestering McDivitt about everything preceding your husband's funeral." He made a disgusted sound. They had moved into the living room. Mrs. O'Toole sat in the middle of the sofa, holding her drink with both hands. Earl took an upright chair with padded arms. "Of course they are concentrating on the clothes."

"He was buried in the suit he bought for our thirty-fifth anniversary."

Earl nodded. His mind was reeling. McDivitt had been telling the truth. But if the suit was his . . .

"It's a matter of interest because of the claim that the Pianones provided clothes for your husband's burial."

"I refused to accept them."

She would not have noticed how his hands gripped the padded arms of the chair in which he sat. What had McDivitt done with that suit? Earl wished he had stayed with the undertaker, pursued the implications of his denial. Where was the suit Giorgio had brought him, the one with the precious manuscript sewn into the jacket?

Earl felt badly dealt with by fate. He might have been spared the horrible experience of getting that vault out from under the others, unbolting its top and dragging the casket free, opening . . .

"What's wrong?" Mrs. O'Toole was looking at him strangely.

"I was thinking of all you've been through."

He thought she was going to hug him. "Let me get you something."

"Do you have a soft drink?"

"Are you sure?"

"Well, maybe a beer."

She brought him a beer. His impulse was to fly back to McDivitt and choke out of him what he had done with that suit.

She said, "I suppose that suit they brought went to St. Vincent DePaul with everything else."

"You gave away his clothes?"

She looked guilty. "I don't need those to remind me of Vince."

"Of course not. You donated them to

St. Vincent DePaul?"

She smiled. "Actually, I brought them to St. Hilary's center. I don't know what I was thinking of. Those people don't need secondhand clothes. They offered to take them to St. Vincent DePaul's for me. Of course I agreed."

"Of course."

"Vincent. St. Vincent. It seemed right."

"How long ago was this?"

"The week after the funeral."

Earl's heart sunk. How long did clothes stay on the racks at St. Vincent DePaul? It was not easy to tell himself that all this had been predestined. Fate had made a fool of both Giorgio and himself.

It was an hour later that he let himself into St. Vincent DePaul's through a door next to the loading dock in back. He found himself in a large room filled with pasteboard boxes. Contributions received but not yet put on the shelves of the store in front? He searched among the boxes and came upon a pyramid of them wedged into a corner. Each box was labeled ST. HILARY.

He heard the sound of someone approaching and saw the beam of a flashlight moving erratically through the store. Earl slipped back to the door he had left ajar and was soon outside. As he drove away he sang aloud. He would go back in the morning. No need to run any risks. Once more he had moved into an advantage over Giorgio.

# Father Dowling

## 35

Phil Keegan came into the rectory with an ebullience that had been missing from his manner in recent weeks. He went to the dining room door and called hello to Marie in the kitchen, then came and stood in the doorway of the study, arms akimbo, smiling benevolently at Father Dowling.

"There you sit," he said with a smile. "Pipe going, book in hand, at peace with the world."

"While you wear the smile of satisfaction."

Phil swung out of his coat and took it down the hallway to the rack inside the front door. Returned, he plunked into his favorite leather chair and beamed at the pastor. Under the circumstances, it would have been unfriendly to deprive Phil of his moment of triumph and tell him that Cecil McDivitt had telephoned to tell Father Dowling to ready himself for a relapse on Mimi O'Toole's part.

"We found Vince O'Toole."

"In heaven, I hope."

"In a corrugated shed. At Riverside. Someone must have removed the body to the shed the day of the funeral and been waiting for things to cool down. Today they opened it — and guess what?"

"Don't tell me the body was missing."

"Oh, no. They pulled poor Vince half out of his casket and stripped him of his coat."

"What in the world for?" In the long history of the popes there was one who, allegedly, dug up his predecessor and propped the corpse up so that the departed could be accused of his many crimes and turpitude. Macabre cashiering. Vince O'Toole had been guilty of much in his life, but surely not anything that required posthumous punishment.

"That's what it's all been about, obviously. The coat."

"And now they have it."

"Giorgio brought a suit to McDivitt and asked him to bury O'Toole in it."

"With something concealed in it? It's surprising that McDivitt noticed nothing strange about it."

"Well, he didn't. And he was not happy to have Cy suggest that he should have."

"What now?"

Phil frowned. "The shed where this atrocity took place is not that far from where the two grave diggers were shot."

"Lolly and Maxwell." Father Dowling had offered Mass for these two all-but-anonymous casualties of whatever was going on.

"Bringing a suit to McDivitt is not a crime. We can't arrest Giorgio for that. The way we question him about it is important. It is amazing how rascals like the Pianones are sticklers for legal niceties. What the lab is working on is possible matchups between the evidence gathered at the scene of that execution and the Pianones."

"You don't sound too sanguine."

"Optimistic? Of course I'm not optimistic. Now we know the reason behind various recent screwball events, but it looks like that is about all we have."

"Are there indications in the shed as to who might have done it?"

"They're still working out there. The lab people. Heidegger can't identify the man he surprised and who then knocked him out."

"Do you believe him?"

"Cy does."

"Ah. Surely you'll be talking with Giorgio."

"He has been out of town since the day before yesterday."

"You're sure?"

"Salvatore Pianone says so."

And that was good enough for Robertson, the chief of police. In his view, the Pianones had cooperated like good citizens to this point, answering questions that were being put to them on a very questionable foundation. He did not want them harassed any further.

"But the suit?"

"Salvatore said that of course they sent a suit over to McDivitt. Would we like the bill of sale? It was a new suit, bought for the occasion. They paid for the whole funeral. O'Toole was an employee. Clothing the deceased for burial was merely part of that."

All the elation with which Phil had arrived was gone. After weeks of confusion, an explanation was found and he had reached a familiar obstacle. The untouchability of the Pianones.

Marie looked in to say that Lieutenant Horvath was on the phone. She had answered it in the kitchen. Phil lumbered down the hall to take the call in the kitchen. Several minutes later, he was back, a wary look of returned elation on his face.

"Someone turned in a gun that supposedly killed those two men."

"Lolly and Maxwell?"

"Yeah. Said it could be found wrapped in

a handkerchief in a bush by the entrance to Pirandello Savings and Loan."

"The Pianone bank?"

"That's right."

"Was it there?"

"Agnes Lamb just picked it up. It's on its way to the lab."

"Well."

"The caller said the gun belongs to Giorgio Pianone."

# Father Dowling

## 36

The call telling the police where they could find the gun with which Giorgio had killed Lolly and Maxwell turned out to be accurate. But it was by no means clear what could be done with the accusation, given the absence of prints on the gun.

"And of course it was a stolen gun."

Father Dowling smoked his pipe and listened to Phil Keegan reflecting on the present state of the investigation into the strange matters of recent weeks.

"Giorgio's being there when we exhumed the body points to the Pianones as the ones who were out there Hallowe'en. When they find out the vault is empty, what do they think? Someone there had to remove the body before burial. Naturally they are going to think someone bought Lolly and Maxwell because that's what they would have done."

"And then gotten rid of them?"

"Most likely."

"Then maybe they themselves had enlisted the two men. If so, they couldn't leave them alive, knowing what they know."

Phil thought about it. "Maybe you're right. That is simpler."

"Have you talked to Giorgio?"

"He has an ironclad, watertight alibi for three days either side of the estimated time of death of Lolly and Maxwell. Mickey, McDivitt's chauffeur, identified Giorgio on the films taken at the funeral, but she can't pick out the man who commandeered her vehicle."

"Are you sure that happened?"

"You're being very skeptical tonight."

"Is she still alive?"

"Agnes Lamb has been assigned to keep an eye on her."

"Then you already had the same thought."

"Oh, she's vulnerable either way. Either she agreed to drive the body out of there or she saw the man who commandeered the hearse."

Father Dowling had not spoken with the hard-luck chauffeur, but Phil and Cy Horvath had told him of her and he had the image of someone between disasters.

"What a bizarre series of events."

An underworld figure, Vincent O'Toole, is gunned down. Father Dowling is summoned by the wife and gives absolution to the apparently repentant man before he dies. The underworld from city and suburb shows up for his funeral and it seems over. The police, perhaps pardonably, fail to use all of their resources to find out who was responsible for the death of Vincent O'Toole. He had worked for the Pianones and they had paid for his funeral, but he may have been a victim of his employers or perhaps of a group envious of the Pianones and making a first effort to move in on them. On Hallowe'en there is a half-hearted effort to dig up the buried O'Toole. The upset widow, persuaded by Cy Horvath, decides to disinter her husband and have him buried in the cemetery at Barfield, having been told by Marie of the alleged appearance there of the Blessed Virgin. The body is exhumed, the vault lifted out of the ground, unbolted and opened, only to be found empty. The casket of Vincent O'Toole is not there. The only explanation is that it was never put there. On the day of the funeral, mourners had left the grave site after Father Dowling said the final prayers, and at that time the casket still stood above the grave, resting on the apparatus by which it would be lowered into the ground by the cemetery workmen before they filled in the grave. The vault had been closed and put in the grave and covered, but the casket was not in it. Someone must have taken it away in the interval. But who? When the vault was opened, Giorgio Pianone had appeared and seemed as surprised as anyone else that the vault was empty. He had come to the sexton's office where Lolly and Maxwell told again and again what they remembered of the day of the funeral. Their story was that, when they arrived at the grave, the closed vault had already been lowered into the hole, simplifying their task. They had only to fill in the grave, which they did. A month and a half later they were brutally murdered at the back of the cemetery. Where was the missing casket and the corpse of Vincent O'Toole? And for what diabolical reasons might someone want a dead man?

That question had now been answered. The grim findings in the corrugated metal shed at the back of the Riverside Cemetery made it clear that it was the clothing that had been put on the body that was wanted. Apparently the casket and body had been hidden in that shed, in a vault, among dozens of yet-to-be-used vaults, as good as disguise as any. Today it and the casket it contained had been opened and poor Vince O'Toole pulled out and stripped of his suit jacket — the jacket that had been provided by the Pianones.

Phil sat listening to this summary by the pastor of St. Hilary's. "That leaves the Pianones off the hook."

"Does it?"

"Why would they bury a suit and then retrieve it in a few weeks?"

"They can explain why the suit was so valuable, even if they weren't the ones who ripped it off that body."

"All they did was provide clothing for the deceased. That is what they will say. It is not a criminal offense. Whoever tried to get the coat thought it was valuable, but all the Pianones have to do is say they have no idea why the coat was thought to be valuable."

"You've become their lawyer."

"I know these guys, Father."

"You're just going to let it go?"

"Certainly not. We will go on questioning them. We will keep getting the runaround. Eventually it will all be forgotten."

"Even Lolly and Maxwell? Don't you have the gun that killed them?"

"Yes."

"A gun you were told belonged to Giorgio Pianone."

"It wasn't the Pianones who told us that. Obviously Giorgio has an enemy. So what's new?"

"Then there is someone other than the Pianones responsible for the deaths of those men and the desecration of the body of Vincent O'Toole."

"Look, Cy is on the case. If anyone can solve it, he can."

Marie was beside herself at the philosophical attitude of Phil Keegan. She of course had become the sturdy oak on whom Mimi O'Toole leaned for emotional support. Mimi had a great appetite for private revelations and Marie had supplied her wants until she became wary. Mimi was also convinced that her late husband was with her, a ghostly presence with whom she could commune.

"He's here with us now," she had said to Marie, smiling metaphysically.

"I suppose all the angels and saints are."

This had alarmed Mimi, whose concern for her husband's soul had not abated. The ghoulish events that had transpired since his death provided her with an unwelcome occasion to think that her husband did not lie easily because of the great weight upon his soul. She began to ask Marie for information about surefire novenas, ways to rescue a soul from eternal punishment and boost him up the ladder into bliss. Marie had mistakenly told Mimi of the vision of hell that had been shown to the children at Fatima. Father Dowling heard the frightened cry from his study and went into the kitchen to investigate.

"What are you talking about?"

"Hell."

"It is a chilly day." Now in early January the temperature was in the teens with the wind chill factor well below zero. But neither of the women was to be so easily diverted.

"Do we have to believe in it, Father?" Mimi pleaded.

There is a time for sound doctrine and a time to shelter the shorn lamb. "We must believe in God's mercy."

"And his justice," said Marie.

"But if he's merciful, how can he be just? I want mercy, not justice."

"As do we all, Mimi. God will never treat us unfairly."

But Mimi was worried about fair treatment. It was one of those times when Father Dowling wished that Marie would not undertake to instruct the faithful.

The further outrage when Vince O'Toole's body was found, rather than increasing Mimi's anguish, seemed to assuage it. "It's such a relief to know where he is."

"He will be put to rest in peace at last," Marie said, and Mimi took it as the confident judgment that her husband was saved.

McDivitt would conduct this second burial, which would take place in Barfield, at Buddy Walsh's cemetery.

"That won't solve all these mysteries," Marie said to Father Dowling when Mimi was gone, dropped off at her door by Phil Keegan.

"Cy Horvath is in charge of the investigation."

What had happened had promise as a Russian novel, perhaps, but it was all but incredible in the unimagined real world. A widow whose husband's body had been stolen on the day of his burial only becomes aware of it when she decides to have his body exhumed so he can be reburied in St. Teresa's cemetery in Barfield. Now the body had finally been found and the reburial could take place. The dreadful business in the corrugated iron shed at Riverside enabled *finis* to be written to the saga of Vince O'Toole. And none too soon.

Mimi's confusion had been compounded by the fact that two other deaths were linked to what had happened to the remains of her husband. Lolly and Maxwell had of course been there when the grave of Vincent O'Toole was opened.

"The men who did the digging?" Her eyes were round with horror. "If I had only left matters alone."

"It's not your fault!" Marie cried. She was usually more shocked by people taking too little rather than too much responsibility. "How could you have known?"

"I should have known."

"That's crazy."

It was a sign of how close Marie and Mimi had become that the housekeeper could say that without causing a flutter from the widow of Vince O'Toole. Marie suspected, and Father Dowling thought she was right, that Mimi was deriving too much satisfaction from her troubles. Morbidity was just around the corner.

But Marie told him that Mimi could still be distracted by gossip, as when Lulu Maiers came by to tell them about all the excitement at St. Vincent DePaul. Apparently someone had come and bought up every item of men's clothing in the store.

"We refused at first. The clothing is for people who can't afford much better. Anyone who could buy up all our stock isn't such a person."

"So what happened?"

"Oh, we sold it. It turned out that there was an emergency at some mission in Africa and this man wanted to Air Express all the clothing he could lay his hands on over there."

"Just men's clothing?"

"He said other people were taking care of the women."

"Isn't that amazing."

"Now we're hunting frantically for new stock."

"Just think," Mimi murmured. "I gave all Vince's things to St. Vincent DePaul. I wonder if his clothes . . ."

"It could be," Lulu said. "Of course we don't keep inventory."

"Vince was such a racist too."

"Why do you say that?"

"Maybe he really wasn't. He just said he hadn't met any good ones yet."

Lulu wanted to know who had been on duty when she donated her husband's clothes.

"Edith Hospers took care of it for me."

"Then I received it. Just a few weeks ago?"

So the three of them rang the changes on the likelihood that Vincent O'Toole's clothes would end up on the backs of African men who had been the victims of a disaster.

"What kind of disaster?" Mimi asked, as if it were important to have all the details straight.

"A flood, I think."

"What country?"

"I could ask, if you would like."

"I'd appreciate it very much if you would."

Marie imagined Mimi bent over an atlas, seeking the country where her husband's clothes had ended up.

"I think she thought I would distribute them to those who come to the center," Edna said, lifting her eyes.

It was a preposterous thought, and one that would not occur to Mimi now that she had more experience of the center. The center had proved to be Mimi's salvation. Under the direction of Edna Hospers, the center had flourished as a place where senior members of the parish could get together during the day, for cards, for games of various kinds, for excursions to the malls that Edna arranged. These were not impoverished people, even if some of them lived solely on their Social Security checks. More than once, Marie had heard people say that they could live comfortably on Social Security alone, but those who said it had other income as well, so maybe not.

Marie told Edna Lulu's story about the flood in Africa.

"I had a flood in Africa," Edna said in a strange voice and then, somewhat embarrassed, explained that she was parodying a line in a movie. "My kids are always doing that. It's catching. Did you ever see it?"

"What?"

"*Out of Africa.*"

"I almost never go to movies." The last movie Marie had watched all the way through was a replay of *The Song of Bernadette* on television.

"What country did they go to?"

"Lulu was going to find out."

Vince O'Toole's second burial at St. Teresa's in Barfield would be a simple thing. There would be no crowd of mourners — just Mimi and her son. At first he refused to come, and when he did he was dressed for more clement climes than the Chicago area in January. His saffron robes whipped in the wind like a foreign flag. Cy, who brought him, tried unsuccessfully to get Sonny to take his overcoat for the occasion. Apparently, he wanted to suffer visibly to punish his mother for making him come.

The earth had been jackhammered open to receive at last the mortal remains of Vince

O'Toole. McDivitt's hearse led them through the cemetery gates. McDivitt was in the limousine with Mimi and Marie Murkin. Father Dowling could see Cy Horvath in the car behind him. The four men acted as pallbearers, carrying the casket over the snow to the grave. It was the same casket.

"This is only the phenomenal order," Sonny said to Father Dowling.

"As opposed to what?"

The large eyes rolled upward. How to explain to the uninitiated?

Father Dowling remembered when Sonny had served as an altar boy. Perhaps he had acquired his taste for flowing garments then.

"It makes no difference whether I am here or there."

"It does to your mother."

A sigh that was visible in the frigid air. Cy managed to slip his suit jacket over Sonny's shoulder. He kept his overcoat for himself. A gesture worthy of Martin of Tours. In any case, it worked.

"Of course I'm charging nothing," Cecil McDivitt had said.

"That's generous of you."

"I just want to see him buried."

Well, he got his wish, and so did Mimi.

She clutched Marie's arm as the casket was lowered into the hole. There was some clattering as it settled into the vault. A bearded man went in after it and bolted the top on the vault. After he had been helped out and a few symbolic handfuls of frozen dirt were dropped on the body, a small excavator began to push the mounds of dirt into the hole. Satisfied at last, Mimi allowed herself to be taken back to McDivitt's limousine. Sonny followed, clutching Cy's suit coat around his massive body, the skirt of his gown whipping about. It was this dramatic figure who attracted the film crew that had been lurking out of sight, recording the event. So much for privacy.

When the others were gone, Father Dowling hurried over to the parish house for a visit with Buddy Walsh.

"Was that a camera crew?"

"A Fox River station."

"I don't want any publicity!"

"How are things going?"

"She has gone public, in a way."

He meant the amateur golfer who had told him the Blessed Virgin had given her a message that she could not divulge. She had opened a web site on which could be found enigmatic paragraphs purporting to be the words of Our Blessed Mother.

"You'd be surprised how concerned Our Lady is about Illinois," Buddy said. "That's all she talks about."

"The woman?"

Buddy made a face. "She claims it's Mary."

"Apart from that, how are things?"

"Prospering. I have an assistant and am promised another. Sometimes I think everyone in Illinois is moving to Barfield. And I dreamt of a sleepy little country parish."

Buddy wanted to hear about St. Hilary's, and Roger Dowling told him a bit, but he did not want his old classmate to covet his assignment. It was Father Dowling's prayer that he would remain in Fox River until, like Vince O'Toole, he was carried off.

"Are the police just going to drop the investigation now that the man is finally buried?"

What continued to puzzle Cy Horvath was the involvement of the Pianones. That they were in it, up to their chins, he did not doubt, but the counterindications did not permit a coherent explanation. Had they been involved in the theft of Vince O'Toole's body? Then why had Giorgio been surprised to find the vault empty? If they had not been involved, they seemed unlikely suspects for the murders of Lolly and

Maxwell. Giorgio had been accused of the executions and a gun purporting to be his had been made available to the police. It was the gun that had killed the two men, but there was no way to tie it to Giorgio. Whoever had used it had done so wearing latex gloves. In any case, the phone call made it sound as if someone were trying to frame him.

McDivitt's chauffeur, the little woman who had been driving the hearse, had belatedly identified the man who had commandeered her vehicle on the occasion of Vince O'Toole's first funeral.

"He is a Pianone man," Phil explained to Roger Dowling, but he himself still looked perplexed.

"She also identified the man who took over the hearse."

"Who?"

"Giorgio Pianone."

"But that makes no sense," Phil cried.

Cy listened as Phil explained why that wasn't possible. If Giorgio was in on the removal of the casket he would not have been so eager at the exhumation to find out what was in the vault.

"He had to know the vault was empty."

Father Dowling tapped his pipe stem against his teeth. "Anyway, that's possible.

What are you suggesting, Cy, a falling out among the Pianones?"

"They've gone to a lot of trouble to find out something they already know. Giorgio snatched the casket and opened it. Why should he be fooling around on Hallowe'en or jumping up on the truck bed when the vault was open, as if he doesn't know it's empty?"

"Perhaps because he doesn't want others to know that he already knows," Father Dowling said.

"But who? Healey must know as much as Giorgio."

A moment passed.

"Salvatore," Phil said, as if he were just remembering the name. "But why would he conceal that from his father?"

Father Dowling tipped his head. "Of course you don't know what anyone would be looking for in Vincent O'Toole's casket. Or in the clothes in which he was buried."

"All we have to know is that it's important. Valuable."

Father Dowling said no more. A visit that morning to Dombrowski's Rare Books on North Michigan had turned up more than he had gone there to find.

"Manzoni?" the dealer had said. "Here is a beautiful leatherbound Mondadori edition."

"I don't want the whole set. I already have several of them. All I want is *La morale cattolica*."

"Then you are in luck, Father Dowling."

Dombrowski had a three-volume edition of the work edited by Romano Amerio.

"The author of *Iota Unum*?"

Dombrowski's face lit up with delight. He urged Father Dowling to take the volumes into his office and look them over, make up his mind. It was like asking an early riser to smell the coffee but not take a cup. He was looking over the introductory volume as much as its uncut pages would permit when Dombrowski came into the office, shut the door carefully, and sat down.

"I am afraid for my life, Father Dowling."

"Are you serious?"

"I am." He sat back. "Of course this is all confidential."

"Of course."

Dombrowski feared that his dealings with Salvatore Pianone made him a marked man. He told Father Dowling about the dealer Cordelia Fabro, who had located some books for Pianone, charged too much for them, and then disappeared.

"Disappeared?"

"Pffft."

"What did she find for him?"

"It doesn't matter."

Dombrowski had found D'Annunzio materials. Father Dowling had not been much taken by the little D'Annunzio he had read, but that scarcely prevented others from running up the price of the holograph. In books and authors, as in so many other things, *de gustibus non disputandum est.*

"Whoever took it is a dead man."

"Surely you don't know . . ."

Dombrowski's hands flew up as if to fend off physical danger. "Good Lord, no. I did find it for him, however. Our dealings are known only by the two of us. That is why I wanted to tell you. In case . . ."

"Does Mr. Pianone suspect anyone?"

"Oscar Hanley."

"Oscar! Why would he be interested in the holograph?"

"He too is a collector, Father Dowling. His first purchase from me was a very rare *Huckleberry Finn.* He has a very impressive collection of early printings of that novel."

"But Italian?"

"He has been studying it, and making rapid progress. He is a very gifted young man."

"But I thought Oscar was going to marry Angela Pianone."

"Salvatore now thinks that was just a ruse to get into the house and at his collection. Which is, by the way, superb."

"He thinks the boy wooed his daughter only to steal a manuscript?"

"He assumes the lad has the same tastes he does. And he is right. Oscar Hanley is also a customer of mine."

Now Dombrowski's fear could be elaborated. A man who thought that a young man had pursued his daughter and actually become engaged to her only as a means to steal from his library was capable of imagining a conspiracy between the thief and the dealer who had gotten the holograph for him in the first place.

"Do you think Oscar would do this?"

"No."

"Do you think he is still alive?"

Dombrowski shuddered. "They would not harm him until Salvatore had gotten his D'Annunzio holograph back."

"But what would the thief do with it? Bury it?"

On the way back to St. Hilary's with the three-volume edition of Manzoni's *La morale cattolica* on the seat beside him, Father Dowling found himself wondering if that is what had happened to the missing holograph. Dombrowski had said young Hanley had a collection of printings of *Huckleberry Finn*. But hiding money in the coffin of a man about to be buried is a central event in that novel. Had Oscar Hanley slipped the holograph into Vincent O'Toole's casket?

But what Cy had just said made that unlikely. If the holograph had indeed been put into O'Toole's casket and it had been stolen and opened the day of the funeral, the Pianones would have either found it or known that is not what had happened to it. Yet weeks later, Giorgio and another member of the Pianone gang are at the cemetery obviously eager to see what a vault they knew to be empty contained. It made no sense. Later someone has desecrated the coffin, pulled Vince O'Toole out of it, and taken the jacket in which he had been buried.

Even more perplexing was the coming together of Father Dowling's apparently different concerns: the widow of Vincent O'Toole and the fiancée of Oscar Hanley, Angela Pianone. No matter which way he turned, there was a Pianone connection.

# Father Dowling

## 37

Angela Pianone had never asked that Mass be said for his soul, only for his welfare, spiritual and corporal. His name was Oscar.

"He was a friend?"

"He is my fiancé."

More she had not said, and of course Father Dowling did not press her. The proper name of the one for whom the Mass was offered was all he needed; even a vague description would do if the name were unknown. It would have been highly inappropriate to suggest that he needed to know more in order to fulfill her request. For that matter, she had not told him that she herself was Angela Pianone. She handed him money he could not accept.

"That is far too much."

"But I want . . ."

"Could I make a suggestion?" he asked, the first time she came.

She waited. Her expression was that of Mary as the pietà. Great dark eyes, olive skin, her thick hair tucked away under the scarf she wore over her head. He might have been giving her a penance, but then she seemed to be already punishing herself.

"We need help in the parish center. It's a gathering place for older people now."

"I will be glad to help."

He had taken her over to the school and introduced her to Edna Hospers. From then on she attended his noon Mass, as if she was afraid to miss those offered for Oscar. If she had been less mournful, he would have asked her if she were related to the Pianone on the police force.

"What is Peanuts's real name?" he asked Phil Keegan.

Phil had to think. "Why do you want to know?"

"I'll tell you when you think of it."

"Stefano. Now why do you want to know? What's he done now?"

"His sister is helping Edna."

"You've got a Pianone working here?"

"You have one on the force."

They had talked of the family then and Father Dowling had surmised that Oscar was Oscar Hanley.

"Requiem Masses?" Phil asked.

"Just Masses."

"I guess the whole family still thinks he's alive."

"The whole family?"

Phil reminded him of the break-in at the Loyola law school. Roger Dowling had read of this at the time, in the inattentive way one reads a story even as he is turning the page of the newspaper, and had not noticed any mention of the detail Phil stressed. One of the items missing had been a letter from Oscar Hanley.

"The Pianones must think he is still alive," Phil said again.

"Then they can't have killed him."

"Or they thought we'd think that when we consider the break-in."

"I wouldn't have thought of them as all that complicated. If you assume they stole the letter, why not just assume that Oscar Hanley is still alive?"

"Roger, it is very difficult to disappear from the face of the earth without dying."

"Is it?"

Marie seemed increasingly curious about Angela and her visits to Father Dowling, but of course the housekeeper could not or would not simply ask. He would have told her that it was a pastoral matter, which was true enough, but he would only be teasing. He realized that he was waiting for the chance to tease her. Ashamed, he went into the kitchen.

"I thought I heard Angela Pianone out here."

"What would she be doing in my kitchen?"

"I was wondering the same thing."

"But she's not in my kitchen."

"I must be hearing things."

"Not that she doesn't stop by often enough."

"She does. You must wonder why."

"She comes to see you and that is your business and we'll speak no more of it."

"She wants Masses said for her fiancé."

Marie actually got to her feet. "She's engaged?"

"That's what she tells me."

"Well, isn't she the busy little bee. When I was young, being engaged meant that you stopped flirting with other men."

Father Dowling rubbed his forehead. "I am trying to imagine Angela flirting with anyone. She is one of the most lugubrious people I have ever met."

"What does that mean?"

"That of the lugubrious people I have met, she deserves the appellation most."

"What does *lugubrious* mean?"

"Melancholy. Depressed. Low spirited. Lachrymose. Sad."

"She is a sad thing. Usually."

"But not when she flirts?"

"You're not going to forget I said that, are you?"

"It will be our secret."

Later, stopping by Edna Hosper's office in the former parish school, he asked whom Angela Pianone could be flirting with. Edna laughed.

"Who says she's flirting, Marie?"

"You find it implausible."

"She has become absolutely devoted to old Mr. Fenster. It has always seemed to me terrible for the family to just drop him off here in the mornings. He needs constant watching and the other old people find him too grim a reminder of what might lie ahead for them. Angela has been a godsend in that regard. She is at his disposal all day long."

"Is her manner toward him flirting?"

"Father, do you know who Mr. Fenster is?"

"Oh, yes."

"It taxes his powers to be told where he is, let alone to be flirted with."

He had prolonged the conversation only to neutralize her question about Marie. Why two good women should be so antagonistic toward one another was more than he could understand, but neither could miss an opportunity to take a dig at the other. For all that, things went well, very well in each of their domains, and well enough with regard to their coexistence in the same small parish.

He came upon Angela as he was returning to the rectory. She was at the shrine and there nodding in his chair was old Fenster. But it was Anton Jarry who came up to say hello, looking over his shoulder at Angela as he did so. Anton said something but Father Dowling had to lean forward to hear him. It seemed he was thanking him for turning the school into a center for seniors.

"How long have you been retired?"

"This is my first year not working. I was a watchman."

"A jeweler?"

There was a moment of silence before Anton laughed. "No, I looked after things nights."

"That sounds like a lonely job."

"It was. That's what I liked about it. I have trouble getting along with people. Even here where everybody's in the same boat."

He spoke in matter-of-fact tones, but it was a sad admission.

"What did you watch over?"

"I worked for Feibleman Construction. First thing they did on a new site was put up my guard shack. We moved it from place to place. That made me think I was always in the same place, sort of."

"I can see that it would."

"I read a lot."

"Did you?"

"I read everything Louis L'Amour ever wrote."

"Romances?"

"No, no. Westerns." He looked around. "They've gone."

He meant Angela and Mr. Fenster. "She found out I was watchman when the Crocus Building went up. That's the headquarters of her family. We had a nice talk about it. The old man, Fenster, is really out of it, isn't he?"

# Angela Pianone

She wrote to her sister, now Sister Maria Madeline, but Laura seemed to think that Angela wanted to enter the convent herself. Maybe she would have if she believed that Oscar was really dead, but she did not believe that, she would not. She had read Kafka, she had read Dostoyevsky, and she had enjoyed their dark tales of irrationality, but what she was living through was worse, if only because it was she who was living through it. If she pressed her eyelids closed, tightly, she could imagine that Oscar was there beside her, she could hear his breathing as if he were about to speak. She listened and listened and could not hear him, but felt the defect was on her side. She had to make an effort to find him in order to hear what he had to say.

And now there was proof that he was alive. He had been living in an apartment at the cemetery. But her elation was mingled with anger that he should treat her this way. Why didn't he come to her? Why didn't he at least call?

But deep deep within she thanked God.

Her fear had been that her family had done some harm to Oscar.

The last time she had seen him, they had been working late in the law school library. She was finding it hard to concentrate because of the conversation they had had earlier. It was about her family. Neither of them had mentioned before what her family was involved in. No one in her family ever discussed it with her, because they were certain she did not know, but Laura had told her everything before she went off to the convent. Going off to a convent was crazy enough, but saying such things about their father!

"I don't believe it, Laura."

"Of course you don't. Neither did I. Even now when doubt is impossible I find it difficult to believe. But it is true. I cannot accept a life in any way dependent on money earned in that way. I am giving my life for the family, Angela. May God forgive us all."

Laura herself would not have believed anything evil of the family unless it was all true. Laura must be mistaken! She had not gone into particulars, and Angela did not want to hear them anyway. After Laura was gone, Angela had become convinced that her sister was right. There were a hundred clues if one knew how to read them. Angela began to attend more closely to conversations among the Pianone men. Their Italian was a slang from Palermo, which they spoke in a kind of shorthand. She realized that, while referred to in only the most innocuous phrases, awful things were being talked about.

Going out with boys was pleasant but she did not know if they knew how the Pianone family had become wealthy. This made her reluctant to date. If she ever became serious about a boy she would have to tell him the truth about her family. She did not think she could ever do that. Until Oscar. She felt that she could tell Oscar anything and he would still love her. But when she did, he already knew. He had reached out and put his fingers to her lips, stopping her.

"It doesn't matter."

"Are you sure?" She had clung to him then, certain now that he was the means by which she could escape the shameful secrets of her family.

"My dad's a private eye."

As if that was the same thing, but she loved him for saying it. His parents were wonderful, particularly his mother, who had died so suddenly, shortly after Angela met her. Mrs. Hanley's funeral had given Angela the opportunity to meet some of his sisters, the Emmies, as he called them, but that did not make the occasion less sad. They liked her, though, as if any doubts they might have had had been swept away by Oscar. His father tried, but she could see that he was anything but delighted to have his only son marry into the Pianone family.

Her own family accepted Oscar. He was of course surprised that her father was such a cultivated man. And he really was.

"What do you know about Gabriele D'Annunzio?" he had asked Oscar.

"Nothing."

"You went to college and now you're in law school and I know more than you do."

"About — what was his name?"

"D'Annunzio, Gabriele. Not his real name. Nothing about him was real. He and Mussolini were big friends for a while, but that was a mistake. He was a poet. I have everything he ever wrote."

In Italian, of course, the edition published by Mondadori. "His name is Oscar, too," her father said, as if this had special significance. "Oscar Mondadori."

"I'm studying Italian."

"What for?" Her father was instantly wary. Of course all the family business was conducted in the mother tongue.

"So I can read Dante."

"Read Leopardi. Save Dante for when you're old."

Angela formed the belief that her father was able to live in the way he did, split into two distinct lives, because he intended at the end to repudiate the one and make his peace with God. In the meantime, he didn't want to think about it, it was too upsetting. She wished that she could talk to her mother about it but her mother seemed to be really unaware of what her husband and brothers-in-law and all their sons did for a living.

"Stefano," she asked her brother whom she never called Peanuts. "What do the police say about us?"

"What police?"

"The ones you work with."

"What do you think they would say?"

"You tell me."

"Don't think about it. I mean that." His eyes narrowed. "Has Oscar been asking you about us?"

Stefano was almost fluent in Italian, but his English was chancy and this gave people the impression that he was stupid.

"What could I tell him if he did?"

"Nothing. That's the way it ought to be."

The unknown and forbidden exercises an

irresistible attraction. Angela began to explore her father's study during the day when she was not likely to be observed. There was nothing incriminating to be found, there was nothing at all that suggested the family's line of work. How antiseptic it all was.

While she was in the study, she took down a volume of D'Annunzio's *Il Libro Segreto*. It was just a paperback, she would lend it to Oscar and he could surprise and delight her father with his knowledge of D'Annunzio.

On this thoughtful but quite unplanned deed was to hang her certainty that her family had not killed Oscar.

It was a quiet Sunday afternoon several weeks after Oscar's disappearance. Her brothers and uncles were napping. The women were still busy in the kitchen. Angela was in the dining room putting away silver when there was an explosion in her father's study. He began to bellow with rage. He rushed out of the study and stood looking wildly about.

"Where is my D'Annunzio?" he demanded. She had never seen him like this. He looked as if he could kill with his bare hands. And then he noticed her. She had not spoken to him since Oscar's disappearance, as if her silence could punish him for what she was sure he had done. All the warmth and politeness had been a sham. He had no intention of letting an outsider into the family. Now he rushed to her and grabbed her wrist in a painful hold.

"Where is that D'Annunzio?"

"You're hurting me."

"That's what he was after, eh? He got it and then he left, is that it?"

Her head was spinning, her wrist hurt awfully, but she could have cried out with joy. He was telling her that Oscar was alive.

She explained that she had given Oscar D'Annunzio's *Il Libro Segreto*, describing the impulsive act in her father's study. "It was just a paperback," she said. "I thought you wouldn't mind."

He stared at her for a moment, then turned away.

Since her father's outburst, with its indication that Oscar was still alive, her sorrow had altered. Now it was her agony to think that Oscar had gone in order to be free of her. She sometimes thought it would be better if the worst had happened and he was dead, and she could mourn him and hate her father. As things now were, she was caught in a fundamental ambiguity. Of late it had been some relief to talk to Mr. Fenster about it. But she could have told him his nose was on fire and he wouldn't have understood.

Then Anton Jarry had told her he had been a watchman on the construction site of the Crocus Building. The crocus was her father's favorite flower, so the name of the building signified that it was his. Legally it was owned by a corporation linked to one of her uncle's in the most tangential way. It was from this firm that Salvatore Pianone rented most of the building.

Anton Jarry was trying to impress Angela with the importance of the work he had done, and she listened patiently. Edna said that a good part of old age seemed to consist in preparing a carefully edited version of one's earlier life. How could a watchman's life be interesting?

And then Anton began to tell her of the night the van had come to the site. He had let it through the gate and it had left hours later.

"The next day we began to pour concrete."

# Phil Keegan

"He's so dumb he'll probably tell us things about his family he shouldn't," Captain Phil Keegan had said years ago when Cy Horvath expressed surprise that Peanuts was being taken onto the force.

"I heard that no one had ever done worse in the tests."

"I said he was dumb."

"But is his family?"

"How do you mean?"

"Do you think they'd let him become a cop if they thought he was going to become a stoolie?"

"Maybe he doesn't know anything."

"So what's he doing on the force?"

"He makes the rest of us look good."

The Pianone family in its relation to Fox River officialdom presented a perplexing problem. With apparent sincerity, politicians said they were going to wipe out vice. Citizens against pornography were assured that their pleas were finally being heard in city hall. And something was done. Out on the west side, a square block was designated for the smut industry and the Pianones shut down everything and moved their various sleazy operations to this new location. Hustlers hung around the porn parlors, so that prostitution too was more or less confined to the area. It received the name No Man's Land from a journalist, not a happy choice, but it did not stick, however apt. No Man's Land was the space between your front line and the enemy's. Smut City was what the police, and eventually everyone else, called it. It was the enemy's territory. And it was territory the police did not disturb.

"We are permitting evil, Cy," Phil said.

"That's for sure."

"I mean, there's always going to be evil, right?"

Cy had learned that there were questions best left unanswered.

"It goes back to St. Augustine. Father Dowling can explain it to you."

Keegan knew that Cy and lots of cops would like to close down Smut City and run the mob right out of town. But the local paper crowed about the victory over vice represented by sequestering it in a limited area and keeping it away from decent neighborhoods.

"What you might do, Cy, is have a talk

311

with Ray Hanley. His son's a missing person."

"The one who was engaged to Angela Pianone?"

"They're still engaged, according to her. She helps out at St. Hilary's with the old folks. She has dedicated her life to the proposition that he is still alive. I suppose the alternative is to face up to the fact that her family got rid of him."

There it was again. Phil Keegan, who was as upright a cop as there was, assumed that the Pianone family was responsible for the disappearance, probably death, of an innocent citizen, and did nothing about it. Few emotions ever made their way to the surface of Cy's Hungarian face or were betrayed by his expression. The fact is, he had but one expression. Behind it now was a single question. Why didn't they pull all the stops and find out what had happened to young Hanley and let the chips fall where they may? Who was in charge of the city anyway?

Ray Hanley had been after them to find his son ever since he disappeared. On the other hand, Ray was a private investigator who had the skills and even more motivation to discover what had indeed happened to his son. When word came that Oscar Hanley had been hanging out in an apartment at Riverside cemetery, Cy got Ray talking about his son.

"So where is he now?"

The look of anguish on Ray's face made Cy wish he had put the question less impatiently.

"I keep running into blank walls."

"Walls protecting the Pianones?"

Hanley had a suite of offices in a building on Dirksen, just across the street from the Crocus Building from which Salvatore Pianone ran his far-flung network. The suite was not all that better than the offices at police headquarters, but then Ray had Earl O'Leary answering his phone and looking as if he knew more than he did when someone came calling.

"He's a male secretary, but don't tell him. He thinks he's my assistant."

"He type and everything?"

"There's a computer out there. Everything's computer now."

"Phil Keegan and I were talking about your neighbor across the street and he says you wonder why we haven't done more to find Oscar. The reason we were talking is that I wondered the same thing."

"So what's the answer?"

"What have you been able to do?"

"He assign you this?"

"That depends."

"On what?"

"Our conversation."

"What's the magic word?"

"Pretend I am as dumb as I look. I know nothing about the case. Tell me about it."

It sounded different, looked at from the inside, and that's where Ray Hanley was, whether he liked it or not. His son Oscar had fallen for the Pianone daughter, a good-looking girl by anyone's standards, and the kid wouldn't listen when Ray tried to tell him about the Pianones.

"You meet the family?"

"Yes. Eileen and I got to know Angela, but it was after Eileen died that I was asked to come by one Sunday afternoon."

"The famous Sunday afternoons."

"Are they?"

"Classical music, talk about books, food to a fare-thee-well. Everyone takes a nap and goes home, all rested up and ready for another week of extortion, prostitution, pornography, on and on. It sort of tugs at the heart strings."

"When you're there, you'd never believe he did anything but sell insurance and handle a little real estate. The women obviously think that's all it is. They couldn't act the way they do if they knew. Angela didn't know. Oscar assured me of that when I finally convinced him that they were what they were said to be, the mob in Fox River. But even then he thought they showed real civic spirit when they moved all the garbage out to Smut City."

"So does St. Augustine."

"What?"

"Keegan told me so. Lay it out chronologically, Ray. The last day or so you saw your son, how you figured he was missing, what you've done after he became just a file downtown."

Cy did not have any kids; it was the great sorrow of his life. He and his wife couldn't even talk to one another about how bad it was seeing their friends with their kids, all that excitement, something new all the time, helping them get ready to take on the world. But Cy could see there was a dark side to it too. People with kids had an extra vulnerability. Whatever happened to the kid happened to them and they suffered but they couldn't take away the suffering from the kid himself. For the first time, Cy realized what Ray had been going through. For the first time, he sensed what the immunity of the Pianone family looked like to one of their victims.

"Why would they get rid of him?"

A gray cloud passed over Ray's face at the way Cy put it, but they weren't going to get anywhere if they didn't tell it like it was. "That's the mystery, Cy. They liked him, really liked him. And it looked to me that they were determined to keep him out of their dirt the way they kept their women out."

"How'd your son feel?"

"What do you mean?"

"Any chance he wanted in?"

The gray cloud was darker when it passed over his face this time. "You wouldn't say that if you knew him."

"I didn't know him. For me he's just X. So I imagine a young man falls in love with a girl. He may or may not have known beforehand about her family. Say he did, though, and that was part of her attraction. His old man makes a modest buck, he's smart and in law school and we all know about lawyers." Cy held up his hand. "Indulge me. Let me go on. Maybe he didn't know about them at first, but he finds out after the engagement. You attended one Sunday afternoon. He's there every Sunday? More or less? His father thinks that Sal Pianone is a bastard but he wouldn't try to corrupt the young man who will marry Miss Pianone. When did Sal become such a nice guy? Maybe he tried to recruit Oscar, maybe your son took the bait, or even sought the bait, but then he saw what he was getting into. By then he was past the point where he can just break off the job interview. By then it's go ahead or disappear."

Ray listened, trying to appraise this version of what had happened. It got his nod. "I never thought of that. Here's another: Oscar gets to know more than he should, not because he's being told, but because he is a smart kid. He can put two and two together. Somehow it dawns on Sal that Oscar knows too much. It's a problem because Oscar is engaged to his daughter, but we know who would get favored in solving that problem."

"They got along?"

"Oscar was learning Italian," Ray squeaked. "So he could read the authors Sal talked about."

"He was learning Italian," Cy mused.

"Angela knows Italian too, of course. That was another motive."

A lover's code, a language others would not know? Outside of the family, of course.

"Cy, remember that break-in at the Loyola law school?"

"I don't know anything, remember?"

"I think I led the Pianones to the stuff they took. I went down and talked to the dean's secretary. Faye. Oscar had sent in a letter requesting leave of absence and I wanted to see it."

"Leave of absence? Why?"

"Catch his breath. He had been going to school nonstop for all those years. His record was top notch so they told him okay, but send in a letter. That's the letter I wanted to see. She had it in her desk. Her miscellaneous file. She finds the letter. It's in an envelope which also contains a smaller envelope addressed to Angela. Cy, I don't know why I didn't just grab the damned thing and tear it open. I decided to come back after business hours."

"You let yourself in."

"No problem. When I get to the dean's office, the outer office, I see a light in the secretary's office. At the same time I get clobbered from behind. I came to out back, draped over a Dumpster."

"They should have killed you."

"Thanks a lot."

"You know what I mean. Take no prisoners, leave no witnesses."

"I didn't see a thing."

"You know that. How could they be sure?"

"Cy, this is what it means. Forget about what they didn't do to me. They have a tail on me. Still. Probably since Oscar disappears. There was a guy in the waiting room while I'm talking to the secretary had a plug in his ear and was supposedly listening to his portable CD player. I figure that's my tail, listening in on me and Faye. They made the same decision I did and got there sooner. But, Cy, they must still be trying to figure out what happened to Oscar!"

That was possible. On the other hand, they would want to keep anything interesting out of Ray's hands. If his son left a letter for Angela at the dean's office, he could be saying things they don't want said, whether or not Oscar is alive. But he let Ray keep his theory.

"Okay, what do you want done?"

Ray stared at him. "What do I want done?"

"That's right. You must have thought about this. What could the police do that they have not done, given the situation we both know and deplore?"

"It's not going to be all-out war against the Pianones?"

"Not likely. Guerrilla war. So what do we do?"

"I been out to the place he was staying at, the cemetery."

"Me too."

"I found this." Ray had it in his wallet, a

little wad of paper. He handed it to Cy after he had unfolded it.

"Whose number is this?"

"Earl's."

"Your assistant?"

Ray nodded. They observed a moment of silence, thinking about it. Had Earl O'Leary known all along where Oscar was? Chances are he knew where he was now.

"Is he in?"

"He's on a case."

"Where does he live?"

Ray didn't even have to look it up. "One twenty-three Fourth."

# Marie Murkin

Marie Murkin's domain was the rectory and any other part of the parish operation she could lay claim to, but the senior center, located in the former parish school, was Edna Hosper's, and she was determined that Marie should make no encroachment on it. This led to a testiness in the relations between the two women: Marie might concede the loss of a battle but never the loss of the war. The rectory housekeeper did not think of herself as an employee or as entrusted with a limited range of responsibility. Her writ ran as wide as the pastor's since she considered herself to be his stand-in.

Not that Marie could be numbered among that small band of discontented women who imagined that they should be ordained priests. A female priest made as much sense as a male nun so far as Marie was concerned. There was not a revolutionary bone in her body. Once pastors of St. Hilary had had younger priests to help them in their work, men to whom they could delegate clerical tasks — baptisms, wed-

321

dings, funerals. Marie of course did not aspire to preside at any of those functions. The truth was that she considered her mandate to be far less restrictive than that of an assistant pastor.

Once there had been other housekeepers with whom she could share this conception of her function. The woman out at St. Teresa's in Barfield might be such a one, but Barfield was distant and Marie was past the age when the making of new far-flung friends attracted her. Besides, she did not need support in her conviction. Perhaps she had never expressed it even to herself, but, in a nutshell, she considered the pastor's business her business. How then could she concede hegemony over the parish center to Edna?

For all that, Marie was a diplomat. She knew all about the spoonful of sugar, at least theoretically, though putting this sound doctrine into practice was not something that came easily to her. But it was important that relations between herself and Edna did not become open warfare. Nonetheless, she had come to think of Mimi O'Toole as a spy behind enemy lines.

"Is she married?" Mimi asked.

"It's a sad story."

"I thought there might be some tragedy

there. No wonder I feel drawn to her."

"Not at all like your own case, Mimi."

"How do you mean?"

It was a delicate moment. Marie was not sure what she had meant. She had spoken to retain Mimi's loyalty and had not really thought of what she was saying.

"Her difficulties occurred years ago. Your loss is fresh."

"Her husband's dead?"

Marie told the story, how could she not? It wasn't as if it were slander or calumny. Marie's husband was in Joliet and unlikely to emerge for many years to come. Mimi brightened. No prosecution of Vincent O'Toole had ever been successful.

"That makes it all the stranger," Mimi said.

"What?"

"It probably doesn't mean anything."

Mimi obviously wanted to be coaxed. But Marie knew the human heart. She ignored the tantalizing remark.

"Then again, it might."

"What?"

They were in the rectory kitchen, Marie with her cup of tea, Mimi with a cup of very strong coffee that Marie had fetched from the study. Mimi sat forward, resting her forearms on the table.

"Do you remember when I brought all of Vince's clothes to Edna, thinking others over there might want them? It was a very touchy thing. I didn't realize then that it was all wrong. Anyway, she was very good about it."

"Took them all to St. Vincent DePaul's, as I remember."

"Not all."

"Oh?"

"Yesterday I was in her office and she opened the closet and there was a man's suit hanging there."

"No."

Mimi lifted her hand. "I swear."

"One of your husband's suits?"

"Of course, I'm not sure of that."

Marie did not for a moment think that there was anything in Edna's personal conduct that deserved reproach. In another world, the discovery of a man's suit in the closet of a woman whose husband was languishing in prison might have suggested hanky-panky. But rivalry had not clouded Marie's mind concerning the goodness of Edna Hospers. She was self-reliant, she supported her family and was raising her children in an exemplary way. If there had been the glimmer of an accusation in Mimi's voice, Marie would have scolded her properly. And then something occurred to Marie.

"It must be her husband's."

"Her husband's!"

Marie's eyes went to the window where great soft flakes of snow drifted down, covering the world with the innocence of winter. She was touched by the thought that Edna had a suit of her husband's in her office closet. It was a kind of sentimentality of which she thoroughly approved. In her room over the back of the rectory, Marie had an ugly brass ashtray that her husband had fashioned. It still bore the aroma of tobacco and there were moments when she lifted it and inhaled the aroma with tears running down her cheeks, breathing in all the joy and happiness of which she had been deprived when her husband deserted her. Her mood communicated itself to Mimi, whose eyes teared as she looked across the table.

No need to tell Mimi that it made little sense to think that Edna would have kept a garment of Vince O'Toole's in her closet. It became a little project to find out about the suit. Marie wanted to see it with her own eyes, the better to come up with an explanation for its being there. But she favored the view that it belonged to Edna's husband.

Did she dream of the day when she could take the suit to Joliet and bring him home clothed in it?

When she mentioned it to Father Dowling he seemed about to give her one of his scoldings, but he didn't. After a moment, he shrugged. Marie beat it back to the kitchen.

# Sonny O'Toole

The Daybreak Temple of Contemplation was located on Dempster Avenue in Skokie, in a storefront that had been converted into a residence and house of worship by Pacific Hugon, a dissident who had left a more traditional establishment in Evanston and marched down Dempster with the half dozen disciples — including Sonny O'Toole — who found in his protest a vision closer to their own aspirations. They had come upon the whitewashed windows of their eventual home. A Realtor's notice was pasted there.

A month after they had moved in and had established a routine, begging in the morning or afternoon, two monk crews alternating at the airport and on city streets, the newspapers were full of the death of Sonny's father. Under the tutelage of Pacific Hugon, Sonny had begun the laborious spiritual journey from bondage to his body to enlightened mind. He thought that he was making progress. The indifference he felt when he read of the bullet-ridden body of his father seemed proof of that. He mentioned it to Pacific.

"He was your father?"

"Of my earthly body."

But Pacific waved away the correction. His eyes traveled over the newspaper account with obvious interest.

"We will all attend the funeral," Pacific announced.

Sonny thought about that. He had an intimation of the impression he alone would make if he appeared at his mother's door. Her shaved and sandaled son in a wraparound garment that looked as if it would glow in the dark would be much for a mother to absorb. It had been months since he had contacted her, even by phone.

"I think I should go alone."

"You are still in need of reenforcement from the brethren."

Did Pacific wonder if he would be back? Sonny had never known such peace as was his since they had moved to Skokie. When begging, he was aware of the looks of distaste — even of hatred — he received when he extended his bowl to people. But his costume and shaved head were a disguise and he found that he was immune to the general disapproval. He came to relish it, as if the sneers and frightened looks proved that he had overcome his attachment to the world these people still inhabited. Eventually they would have to make the journey he had already begun, undergo the purgation he was engaged in even now. After all, he and they and everything else were really one. The trick was to erase the differences, which were merely appearances in any case, and become lost in ultimate identity. In his imagination Sonny likened it to falling asleep.

"Whoever killed my father might not like all of us there."

"You mean you'll be in danger."

"Not alone. My father had friends as well as enemies."

When he saw it in this light, Pacific urged Sonny to go mourn his father, in the earthbound way, but to meditate at six and noon and at six again in order to remain in communion with his brothers on Dempster Avenue.

"Jesus!" the man who answered the door had said, leaping back. Sonny shook his head.

"Not quite."

"Sonny!" his mother cried, pushing her bodyguard aside and embracing her son.

Can nothing shock a mother? Any adjustments she had to make to his new appearance took place in a matter of moments. She led him off to the back of the house, the sun porch, where on Sundays his father had cut off the beautiful view by pulling the blinds so he could watch sports on television. Sonny sat next to his mother on a wicker couch and held her while she cried. A lump formed in his own throat, moved by her grief rather than the loss of his father. His father wasn't lost. He was where everyone and everything would be eventually. Sonny tried to explain this to his mother, but she shushed him.

"He received the last sacraments. In the hospital. He is at peace with God."

"God is at war with no one."

"Father Dowling just happened to be there."

"Nothing happens by chance."

"Shut up and listen."

She wanted to re-create the scene for him and of course he let her. Her telling him to shut up and listen was a welcome. Any grievance she had felt against him was gone. Sonny felt at home again. What would it be like without his father there? But any inclination he might have felt to return to his former life disappeared when he accompanied his mother to McDivitt's. All that depressing emphasis on death and grief told him how radically changed he was. There was less difference between life and death than between sleeping and waking. A closed eye shuts in the light, as Pacific said. Talking with Father Dowling had been the greatest test, but he passed it.

"What attracted you?" the priest had asked about Sonny's new life.

"Contemplation."

"What had you known of contemplation in the Christian tradition?"

"Only that it is egocentric."

The priest did not contest this, though his smile suggested he did not accept it. The truth was that Sonny knew next to nothing about Christianity. It didn't interest him. He felt if he looked into it he would find others like himself, like his family, caught up in the things he had heard of all his life. Father Dowling did suggest he read someone called Saint John of the Cross. But it was the cross that would have prevented his interest. Pacific, who had been a Franciscan once, had come to see that the crucifix tugged the mind down toward the body and pain and time and life — all the things one must transcend. Sonny smiled the smile he had been working on. But he felt no more tendency to quarrel than the priest did.

At McDivitt's he had been similarly amused when his mother rejected the burial clothes offered by the Pianones and insisted that his father be buried in the suit he had worn for their thirty-fifth wedding anniversary. As if it mattered. He took the gift suit from her, noticing how heavy it was compared to the simple costume he wore. Carrying it out to the car he felt that he was holding up a shield against the world.

He was reminded of that when his father was buried a second time, on a bleak cold day in January. It was difficult to concentrate and see that the cold he felt was only an illusion. He refused the offer of an overcoat, but later, when a suit jacket was draped over his shoulders, he suffered it to remain. He was still wearing it when the cameras turned on as they walked back to the cars.

# Earl O'Leary

## 42

Ray Hanley had been elated when he learned that Oscar was alive and had been living in the gatehouse apartment at the cemetery, but as time passed and his son did not get in touch with him, gloom descended once more on Ray. The news that his son was alive might have been false.

"He'll be back," Earl said.

Ray looked up with a haunted eye. The victim on the rack, wondering why this was happening to him. He had known emotional pain, and now he was being led deeper into agony. He sought out Angela, leaving the office in Earl's hands. Not that there was much to look after. Potential clients came and talked with Ray and left as neither potential nor actual clients. In his present condition, Ray did not exude confidence.

The morning after he spent some hours with Angela, he came to the office in a better mood.

"It's harder on her than it is on us, Earl."

"It has to be, although that's hard to

imagine. Not that I am comparing my grief to yours."

"Oscar really liked you, Earl."

This was true enough. But then Earl had worked on his friendship with Oscar. Oscar was Giorgio's main interest, and he had supplied the defeated rival for Angela's hand with more than enough information to make him unhappier than he already was. He sensed that there was something emotionally masochistic in Giorgio's curiosity and he felt a bit like a brothel keeper in catering to it.

"Why would those monsters do a thing like this?"

"It had to be them," Earl agreed.

Ray brought his fists down on the surface of his desk and shook with frustrated anger.

"An idea," Earl said, after a minute.

Ray turned his haunted look on Earl, the dull glitter of hope deep in his reddened eyes. The appetite for hope is not quelled by disappointment. "What?"

"You know about the Trojan horse?"

"At Southern Cal football games?"

Earl made a notch in his mind; he would laugh about this later. He sketched for Ray the plight of the Greeks outside Troy. They had the city under siege but they were the ones being punished. What to do?

"Infiltrate. Get inside the enemy's camp."

"What are you talking about?"

"Why don't I try to get inside the Pianone operation?"

Eyes, it has been said, are the windows of the soul. For a brief instant, Earl caught a glimpse of a dark corner of Ray Hanley's, a node completely dedicated to avenging the disappearance of his son, by whatever means. Earl himself, having tasted danger, was drawn to the role of double agent. There was something deeply satisfying in knowing what others do not know. At present, it was only Ray Hanley who did not know his true role. This gave Giorgio an advantage over Hanley, but also in a way over Earl. He would be justified in thinking that Earl was his tool, part of a plan that Giorgio had concocted in order to discredit Oscar Hanley.

"Mr. Pianone really loves his books," Earl had observed a few months back when Giorgio was unable to spill his guts about how hurt he had been to hear Oscar playing the role that was his, being instructed by the great man.

"They are like part of the family," Giorgio had said fervently. "You have to see them on the shelves, the leather, the gold embossing, the lettering. That's just their outsides."

Earl had seen the books. Shadowing Giorgio on several Sundays and on the few weekday occasions when he went to Salvatore's house, he had been impressed by the security, but only to a point. Several times he entered the house, wearing a workman's coverall in case he ran into anyone. But he ran into no one. Already imprinted on his mind was a floor plan of the house based on Giorgio's answers to some casual questions Earl had asked.

"We could arrange for Oscar to steal a book."

Giorgio's reaction might have been a prayer, but it was profanity, whispered in admiration.

"If he thinks Oscar lifted a book, Oscar is dead."

"What title would you suggest?"

"Earl, if you think I am going to take a book out of that library . . ."

"I'll do it."

Giorgio laughed. The Wright brothers had been mocked when they said they could fly like birds, Lindbergh had been scoffed at, and so too the space program had been the subject of knee-slapping jokes. Earl waited patiently for Giorgio to stop laughing.

"Breaking out of prison is a piece of cake compared to getting into *Il Gabiano.*"

"What book would make Salvatore angriest?"

"You're serious, aren't you?"

"You hired me to discredit Oscar Hanley. This looks like a good way of doing it. Yes, I am serious."

"What is your story when you get caught?"

"Giorgio hired me."

Giorgio's face twisted in anger and his arms lifted, his hands splaying their fingers. He stared at Earl's throat as if it were a keyboard.

"I won't get caught. But if I do, I take this." Earl held out his closed hand and turned it over. Slowly he opened it. In the palm of his hand lay a small capsule. His eyes met Giorgio's.

"Geez."

Giorgio agreed to discuss it as a what-if plan. He was giving no orders. If Earl did this, it was on his own responsibility.

"I would suggest something by D'Annunzio," Giorgio said. He thought. "He has something in the author's own handwriting. If that were gone and he thought Oscar took it . . ." Giorgio drew a finger across his throat, making a gurgling sound.

Two days later, Earl called Giorgio. "It's done."

"Wait. I'll call you in ten minutes." Never assume a caller is who you think he is. This was something Giorgio must have learned from Salvatore.

Giorgio called back in five minutes, using an outside phone from the sound of the background noise. "You did it?"

Earl chuckled. "I'll turn it over to you whenever you want."

"No! You keep it. And keep it out of sight. You got the handwritten thing?"

"Do you doubt me?"

"It was in a box, tied with a ribbon?"

"A green ribbon. Giorgio, I didn't take this risk in order to make a mistake. I did this to earn my second payment."

Giorgio hesitated. "You'll get it. But I still want you working for me."

As if to bind him more closely to the operation, Giorgio asked Earl to come along the following night. A manager of one of the skin palaces in Smut City was skimming from the take.

"What will you do?"

"Break his arms."

Having earned his spurs, Earl was asked along on other occasions. He had been there on the night they took care of Cordelia Fabro, red Volkswagen and all.

"What's she done?"

"Crossed the Pianones."

"Uh huh."

Earl drove the van with the Volkswagen in back, which is why that watchman got a good look at him going in and coming out. Inside, he took one end of the body bag when they swung it once, twice, and then let go and watched it drop into the open trunk of the Volkswagen like a penalty shot. Giorgio drove the vehicle down into the hole prepared for it. He didn't want Earl shoveling the dirt back in. He wanted a division of labor to insure that everyone along was a party to the deed. Let Healey operating the little earth mover do it. Giorgio actually said a prayer over the covered hole.

"You sure they're done digging and moving earth around down there?"

"Tomorrow they pour cement."

On the way out, Earl had the feeling his picture was being taken when the watchman looked at him, then hunched a shoulder. Big shot.

"Who's the watchman?" he asked Giorgio.

"He's just a watchman."

Earl went back the next day to watch. The

cement truck came and laid several yards of freshly mixed concrete within the frames provided. Then the workmen began the task of smoothing the surface.

"So long, lady, whoever you are," was all Earl could manage in the way of a prayer. He would have removed his cap if he wore one.

# Marie Murkin

## 43

When the body of the Eastern monk was discovered it was described as a hate crime and
members of the Skokie Nazi Party were
called in for questioning. There was no iden-
tification on the body and two days passed
without anyone reporting the man missing. A
phone call suggesting that a similar community in Evanston be consulted met with a
ringing denial by Eminent, the leader.

"I never knew him," he pronounced.

It was the description of the slain man's
costume that caught Marie Murkin's eye.
She gasped and ran into the study with the
paper. Phil Keegan was there with the
pastor but she did not feel she was inter-
rupting. It was an occasion when Phil
Keegan was not at the St. Hilary rectory.
She spread the paper out on the desk before
the pastor and pointed to the story.

"Did you win the lottery, Marie?"

"This on top of everything else will drive
her mad."

Phil puffed on his cigar, a picture of indifference, and Marie was suddenly angry.

"I suppose you won't investigate this one either. What do you care about a simple monk?"

"Who do you think it is?" Father Dowling asked.

"You know who I think it is."

"That's quite a jump, isn't it?"

"It's him. You'll see."

Of course she was right. The body was the body of Sonny O'Toole. His mother had to identify him and Marie and Father Dowling accompanied her to the morgue. She regarded the mortal remains of her only child with ominous quiet. She nodded in agreement at the suggestion that he be moved to McDivitt's. Marie waited for the outburst, the wail of despair, the cursing of her fate, but Mimi O'Toole remained in control of herself, almost as if she were being influenced by her dead son. Marie was determined to keep at her side, to be there when the inevitable outburst came.

"No," Mimi said, when McDivitt suggested that Sonny be buried in ordinary clothes. "Bury him in his habit."

"I'll check at the morgue to see if they have any of his clothing there."

Marie was certain that this hint that the body was unclothed would do it, but Mimi gripped the arms of her chair and closed her eyes. "I will buy a new one."

They found bolts of cloth that approached the hue of Sonny's garment, but nothing, Mimi thought, was exact. But then she had an idea.

"White silk," she told the clerk. "Eight yards of white silk." She said to Marie, "I will bury him in white."

For all her insistence on Sonny's being buried in his monk robe, Mimi wanted Father Dowling to send her son off with a requiem Mass. The pastor wondered if she thought this would be the right thing to do.

"We never discussed the matter at length," he said. "But he made it clear he had put Christianity far behind him."

"But he was a monk. Aren't monks Christian?"

Now it will come, Marie told herself. If Father Dowling refuses to conduct a funeral for Sonny, Mimi will lose control. He did not refuse. Mimi grabbed Father Dowling's hand and pressed it to her lips.

"God bless you, Father Dowling. God bless you."

Marie was not a hand kisser, but even so she was almost as glad as Mimi. Not that she had ever doubted the pastor. If he had managed to get Vince O'Toole through the pearly gates, Sonny's flirtation with Eastern mysticism would not prove to be an insuperable hurdle. Father Dowling's understanding caused Mimi to waffle.

"I wish I'd kept that suit they brought for Vince," she confided in Marie. "Maybe have McDivitt bury Sonny in that."

"What happened to it?"

"St. Vincent DePaul."

Marie wondered if it had been among the stock bought and sent to Africa.

The initial verdict that Sonny had been beaten to death with his heavy wooden begging bowl was changed. At most, the beating was auxiliary, begun before the young man had died and continuing mercilessly after he had gone from this world. The principal cause of death was strangulation with the robe, which had been unwrapped from the body. It was conjectured that he would not have struggled, almost as if he had welcomed the assault. The robe was retained as evidence and probably would not have been available as a shroud even if Mimi had not decided on a white robe for her dead son.

"Do you think it's connected with his father's death, Phil?"

"That's pretty far-fetched."

"How many Eastern monks have been killed lately?"

"About as many as Western monks."

"It's quite a coincidence."

"That's what I said."

Gerry Quinn called when he heard Roger was going to bury Sonny from St. Hilary's.

"Did he come back to the faith, Roger?"

"How do you mean, Bishop?"

"Had you talked to him about his becoming — what exactly was he, an Eastern monk?"

"Of a sort. Apparently there had been a split in an Evanston community and he fled into Skokie with a splinter group. They had different views about unity."

"Was he serious about it?"

"I think he liked the community life. Remember the sixties?"

The auxiliary bishop accepted the analogy and withdrew any objection he had called to make. His only advice was discretion. Roger assured him that discretion was his middle name. But the truth was he had misgivings about the matter himself. Of course it was wrong to ignore the stated wishes of another, and while Sonny had not said anything about his eventual burial, something they both would have believed to be a far distant future event, he had pretty clearly stated that he had dropped the faith in which he had been raised. The result was a liturgical compromise.

Father Dowling said the Mass of the day, with a commemoration of the soul of Sonny O'Toole — prayers for the dead are not confined to Catholics — and the casket was placed where it would have been if there were an ordinary funeral Mass. None of Sonny's brethren came.

# Father Dowling

Father Dowling often received odd requests, but it was his experience that they were usually motivated by intelligible reasons, if only one could elicit them.

"You want me to bless the basement of the building where your father works. Angela, wouldn't it make more sense to bless the whole building?"

"Not for my purposes. Perhaps my father would like that. I am interested only in the basement."

"You must have a reason."

"Not one that I can tell."

As a rule, a priest should put himself at the disposal of the faithful. He was, in an important sense, their servant. The pope himself was designated servant of the servants of God. It ill behooved a simple priest to balk at a request to bring God's blessing down on someone or something.

"A month ago I blessed a cat. I did so only after some hesitation. But then I noticed in the book we use that contains various sorts of blessing that it was once customary to bless farm animals. And I bless cars. So why not a cat?"

"You think I'm crazy."

"I think it must be a very important reason if you cannot tell me what it is."

Angela burst into tears. For all Marie Murkin's faults, and he did not mean to suggest that she had many of them, she never resorted to tears. It was the most disarming tool in the female arsenal, particularly when used as a weapon on a priest. A husband might console and soothe, but a celibate had nothing but words, and words are notoriously ineffective in altering emotions. All he could do was wait for her to stop. When Marie Murkin appeared in the doorway of the parlor, drawn by the sound of Angela's weeping, Father Dowling could have cheered her curiosity. He got to his feet.

"I'll leave you women alone for a moment, to compose yourselves."

"There, there," Marie was saying as he left the room, her arm around the shoulders of the girl that shook with grief. In the study he relit the pipe that he had put down to receive Angela in the front parlor. There are times when the male sees the female as of another species — strange, unfathomable — and this was one of them. Imagine asking him to come bless the basement of a downtown building.

Minutes later, Marie came for him. "She's all right now."

And indeed she was. Her eyes were dry but her smile was a bit sheepish. "I'm sorry, Father. I was overwhelmed."

By the thought of blessing a basement?

"Your suggestion that my father have the whole building blessed is a good one. Do you mind if I pass it on to him?"

"Of course not."

He would have agreed to bless the whole downtown, he was so relieved to have her back to her usual melancholy self.

Marie joined him as he stood in the doorway watching her hurry back to the school. "The poor thing," Marie murmured. "It's a wonder she hasn't gone mad."

The fiancé who had run away? Of course.

"The basement of the Crocus Building!" Phil cried when he told him of the strange request. "She wants you to bless a grave."

"A grave?"

"What else could it be? Let me use your phone."

Phil did not wait for permission. In a moment, he had Cy Horvath on the line. Listening in, as he could hardly avoid doing, Roger Dowling realized he had come up with something the police had been looking for.

"That's got to be it, Cy. Who did the construction on that building? It doesn't matter. They could have made a deposit without the contractor knowing and he unwittingly lays a concrete cover over the burial site."

While the thing to be done seemed clear — to tear up the concrete floor of the basement of the Crocus Building and unearth whatever body or bodies might be there and then charge Salvatore Pianone with whatever could be made to stick on the basis of that evidence — the way to do it required thought. First, a court order would be needed before men with jackhammers could be let loose on that concrete floor. But the judiciary being in somewhat the same ambiguous relation to the Pianones as the police and city hall, it was imperative to get a judge who would not alert the Pianones to what was in the air. The threat would call for drastic action, and it was not conceivable that they would blow up the Crocus Building rather than let the police have free access to the property.

All this was on the assumption that there was a body buried beneath the concrete floor of the basement of the Crocus Building, and Roger Dowling felt obliged to tell Phil that he was making a logical leap of epic proportions.

"Angela made no mention of a grave."

"She didn't have to. She gave you the message and she assumed you would do what you have done — pass it on to the police."

Roger Dowling did not like that, either as an abstract idea or as an appropriate description of what Angela was likely to do.

"What she did say was that she would ask her father to have the whole building blessed."

"What a mockery that would be. He might just as well ask you to bless Smut City."

"I suggested that whole buildings rather than basements are usually blessed. And she said she would pass the suggestion on to her father."

Phil was on his feet. "As soon as she tells him that . . ." He stopped. An unusual smile spread across his face. He picked up the phone as if in a trance, and dialed.

"Cy? Do nothing for the moment. I've got a better idea. Let's have Pianone tear up the basement for us."

He replaced the phone and sat once more, his smile having become beatific.

"Do what she asks, Roger. Suggest to Sal Pianone that he have the Crocus Building blessed. The whole thing. All four floors and of course the basement as well."

Roger shook his head. "No, Phil, I won't do that. As liturgical matters go, blessing of buildings is not anywhere near the front rank. But I will not put it to a utilitarian purpose. You're going to have to achieve your ends more straightforwardly."

Phil was undisturbed. "It will be enough if the daughter passes on the suggestion to him."

After Phil left, Father Dowling continued to have mixed feelings about recent events. Phil had thought Angela was trying to use him in a way similar to the way in which he now proposed to do. But Phil had not seen and heard her cry. Those were not the tears of a conniving young woman.

He stopped himself. It would be better not to claim any competence in the appraisal of feminine behavior. Or masculine, for that matter. If Angela's reason for wanting the basement of the Crocus Building blessed was correct, it was not just any burial site that she had in mind. Was that not the meaning of her tears?

Obviously, having listened to Anton Jarry, she thought Oscar Hanley was buried beneath the concrete floor of the Crocus Building, interred there by her own family.

# Cy Horvath

## 45

When Cy asked Ray Hanley where his assistant Earl was, Ray said he was on assignment. Ray had made an effort to remember before he said that. He had to remember some more to wonder if it was true. "I suppose he's run off too."

Since then Cy had gone by Earl's place at 123 Fourth but without any luck. After a couple of days, he began to think that Ray was right. It looked as if Earl was out of town.

"Was the assignment out of town, Ray?"

"Out of Fox River?"

"Where was the assignment?"

"We got a call from Indiana, someplace. I told him to take care of it."

"What was it about?"

"What's it usually about? Some husband fooling around."

"I'd like to talk to him."

"Yeah? I'd like to talk to Oscar. The last time we talked we quarreled. I hit him. I have to see him again. My God, I've got to do something, Cy. Have you any idea what it's like?"

For a moment Cy thought Ray was going to cry. He could imagine what it was like for a father to have his son just disappear.

"The odds are even that he's safe, Ray. Remember, you thought the break-in at the law school showed the Pianones think Oscar is still alive. That means they don't know where he is. That means his disappearance cannot be explained by anything the Pianones did. So let's ask what reason Oscar might have had for taking off."

"None. Cy, I've tried this. But he had everything going for him. He's got real talent, lots of different talents, but he decides to get a law degree so that his life will have a stable financial base. He is among the top three students in the law school. He will be able to write his own ticket. Cy, in a couple years he will be making more in a year than you and I ever dreamed of. He's got a girl, a beautiful girl, an innocent girl."

"A Pianone girl."

"Who is abject at his disappearance. Cy, we get together and cry about it. She doesn't say it but I know she thinks her family is responsible."

They went over it several times and later Cy went to Tremble's Tavern and took a beer into a back booth that was like a confessional. It fostered thinking.

What they had was one missing young man and neither of the obvious explanations seemed to fit. The first and obvious explanation was that he had somehow antagonized the Pianone family after having been on remarkably good terms with them, and they got rid of him. Keegan thought the story about the nighttime visit to the construction site of the Crocus Building might tell them where the body was buried. If they dug up Oscar, that was it. But it could not be overlooked that Salvatore acted as if Oscar was still alive. He clearly thought that the young man had gone off, taking with him something that had destroyed the peaceful spirit of a Pianone Sunday afternoon. But Ray insisted that his son had not gone off on his own accord. To what? What could be more attractive elsewhere than what he had right here?

A stopper. The thing to do was to back away and take a wider view. Oscar has been done away with and if it isn't the Pianones it is X. Who is X? Was there someone who had taken advantage of the situation, gotten rid of Oscar and counted on the present impasse? The police would assume the Pianones did it and X was safe. As in algebra, you had to use known quantities in order to find what X stood for.

Angela Pianone was as beautiful as he had heard, but her manner was cold. "Isn't it late to be taking an interest in Oscar's disappearance?"

"I was hopeful that you would be of help."

Her coldness evaporated like dew before the morning sun. Cy astonished himself by thinking in simile. Angela could bring out the poet in any man.

"His father tells me that Oscar is a poet."

The present tense won her. "That's how we met."

"Between the lines."

She tipped her head and looked at him through her lashes. "I criticized some poems of his that had appeared in a student magazine when we were both at Northwestern. He looked me up to defend himself. The poems weren't that bad. They were really very good. But I objected to their world-weary air. As if he had lived a full life, tasted every experience, and was writing from the edge of the grave."

Immediately she regretted putting it that way, and Cy did not say that on the edge of the grave was where he might have been.

"We fell in love. I think he thought of us as

a kind of Romeo and Juliet, because of my family."

"Who were your common friends?"

She was surprised by this sudden shift in his interest. He explained to her what he was after, and why.

"If it isn't your family and he didn't just run away, there has to be a third explanation."

"Explanation of what?"

"At least of his running away."

"If he could communicate with me, he would."

"He hasn't?"

"No."

"Not even a letter?"

"None that I received."

"Then we have to assume the worst."

"No! My father thinks Oscar is alive."

"That's why we are taking your father to be innocent and exploring another avenue."

She could hardly be disappointed by the prospect of her family being thought innocent, however distasteful it was to return to the assumption that Oscar Hanley was dead.

"I want to hear about your friends. Was there any rival among them?"

"Rival!" She laughed, but the musical cadenza might have been counting off smitten males who had longed to substitute for Oscar. But she was not being coy. She refused to accept the premise of his question. Oscar loved her and she loved Oscar and that was it, they were meant to be.

"I'll never marry now."

"Like your sister?"

"I will remain in the world." She thought. "I could take care of his father."

"Ray Hanley?"

"Yes. He has lost his wife and now his son."

"Doesn't he have daughters?"

"Lear had daughters!"

Cy waited but she didn't explain the remark.

"The way you help out at St. Hilary's?"

She began to tell him about Mr. Fenster, an elderly man for whom she took special responsibility when she was at St. Hilary's center.

"That could be my vocation."

"I thought you were a law student."

"I was. Neither Oscar nor I was fitted for that." Angela looked at Cy. "How well do you know Mr. Hanley?"

Cy shrugged. "I know him."

"What do you think of Earl O'Leary?"

"I have been looking for him."

"What do you mean?"

"He's out of town on assignment."

After a moment, Angela smiled. "I keep forgetting that he works."

"Were he and Oscar close?"

"Oh, yes."

Cy decided not to tell her that there was reason to think that Oscar telephoned Earl during the time he was hiding out at the cemetery. He tried again.

"It's hard to believe Oscar has not gotten in touch with you."

This was obviously a sore spot. If he loved her as she said, it would be cruel not to let her know he was alive. But that seemed to be what Oscar had done while he was in the gatehouse apartment — nothing. Except maybe telephone Earl.

When Cy called the St. Hilary rectory, Marie Murkin told him Father Dowling was away.

"On assignment?"

"What do you mean?"

"Tell him I called."

The sight of Tuttle with Peanuts in the cafeteria set Cy's mind going. He sent Agnes for Peanuts.

"What do you want him for?"

"Nothing. I want to have a talk with Tuttle."

"Without Peanuts around."

"You got it."

Five minutes later, he sat across from Tuttle. "What do you know of Earl O'Leary?"

Tuttle looked over both shoulders so rapidly his tweed hat did not change directions. "In what respect?"

"He and Oscar Hanley were pretty close. Oscar had Earl's telephone number with him when he was at Riverside, that apartment over the gatehouse. Presumably he called him. That means Earl knew where Oscar was when everyone else, including his father, thought he was dead."

"He's close to Giorgio too."

"Giorgio . . ." But before he could say the family name, Tuttle grasped his arm frantically and shook his head. This time his hat moved too. Then he nodded.

"Tell me about it."

"Peanuts may come back."

Cy took Tuttle to his office and closed the door. The little lawyer told him the story of tailing Earl's car after drinking with Ray Hanley and then taking up a vigil behind the parked Earl.

"A car came and he ducked down. It went into his driveway and ten minutes later came out again. Only afterward did he go inside."

"And Giorgio was in the car."

"Driving. It was a Lincoln Town Car."

Cy stood. "Thanks, Tuttle."

"What are you going to do?"

Cy just looked at him, saying nothing. It was like the frozen frame of a film.

"Okay, okay. Just asking."

On his way out, Cy told him again, "Thanks, Tuttle."

Judge Griswold was thirty-two, had been elected municipal judge in a mix-up last fall, and still thought of herself as an independent, autonomous servant of the people. Unlike Dr. Pippen, the assistant medical examiner, Judge Griswold was not beautiful, but Cy liked the scrubbed openness of her face and the gray eyes that did not blink.

"A search warrant should not be issued except for the most serious reasons."

"A member of the most powerful underworld organization in northern Illinois paid a visit on a man who has been contacted by a missing person. That missing person is persona non grata with that same mob."

"Is this address correct?"

"One twenty-three Fourth. That's right, Your Honor."

"Good hunting."

He did not reply tallyho. Griswold was a

stalwart woman and he hoped that she would resist the tug toward compromise and eventual corruption that her position exposed her to.

# Earl O'Leary

## 46

Whenever Earl made what should have been a masterstroke, he found himself deeper in doo-doo than before.

He had made a preemptive strike, implementing the plan he had worked out with Giorgio ahead of schedule, intending to lay claim to the holograph. After the ghoulish effort in the cemetery shed, after the unnerving experience of being surprised at such work by Heidegger, after getting the coat off that putrid mess and fleeing — after all that to find that the coat did not contain the holograph.

He had thrown it into his trunk, not wanting the accompanying stench inside the car, and come immediately home, driven into the garage and lowered the door. At the workbench, holding his breath as much as possible, he laid out the coat. From the very beginning he had the sense that something was wrong. Feeling the coat did not reveal the hidden holograph. The seam that he had opened and then closed again did not look as if it had ever been altered. But he tore the coat open anyway. It was empty, as empty as that vault they had pulled up out of O'Toole's grave. Then he inspected the label. This was not the coat they had brought to McDivitt.

The undertaker had been vague about what had happened with the clothing provided, but finally he came clean. He had not put that suit on Vincent O'Toole. Earl had not needed McDivitt to tell him that. Mrs. O'Toole had taken it with her. She had gotten rid of her husband's clothes, within a week, or ere those shoes were old with which she followed her husband's body, like Niobe, all tears. Earl frowned. Where had that come from? He smiled. Oscar. Oscar spouted memorized lines like a geyser on the least provocation. The clothes had gone to St. Vincent DePaul.

Having discovered the boxes from St. Hilary's still in the back of the store, and being surprised by the night watchman when he had, Earl had returned the next morning and bought up everything in back for the missions.

"We get more than we can use," the manager said, sucking on his teeth. "You may want to come back again."

"I wouldn't be surprised."

The man worked at his teeth with the nail

of his little finger. He held a Fig Newtons cookie in the other hand. He stood by while Earl got the boxes into the truck he had rented.

"Don't forget those over there."

The boxes from St. Hilary. Earl had hoped the manager would notice that he had nearly overlooked them. He put those in the cab, on the driver's seat, then drove to the rental company where his car was parked. He transferred the St. Hilary's boxes to the trunk of his car and left the others. It didn't matter. He had rented the truck in the name of Oscar Hanley. An antic thing. The name just sprang to his lips when the clerk was filling out the application. That could have been embarrassing when he asked for Earl's driving license, but it was the date of expiration he looked for and then Earl had whipped it away.

Back to the garage then, hoping against hope that (1) these were the clothes that Mimi O'Toole had left at St. Hilary, and (2) that the suit containing the holograph was among them. It wasn't. He tore open the boxes one by one, scattering their contents as he searched for the suit. Suits he found, awful gabardines and glen plaids, sports jackets that must have glowed in the dark, and a dozen neatly folded pairs of slacks, all with multiple pleats, probably to conceal Vince O'Toole's pot. But there was no black suit.

Earl went inside, opened a beer, sat on the couch from which Giorgio had removed Oscar, and tried to figure out what had happened. Somewhere along the line, Giorgio had stolen a march on him. He must have heard of the shuffle at McDivitt's. He could have plucked the suit out of an O'Toole closet weeks ago and kept mum about it ever since.

Militating against this was Earl's estimate of Giorgio's intelligence. He simply did not believe that his supposed ally had the cunning to pull off such a double-cross. A brutal unequivocal piece of treachery. Earl had taught himself that the moment when he and Giorgio together slit open the suit and removed the holograph would be the moment of maximum danger. He would have served his purpose so far as Giorgio was concerned. Giorgio could execute the rest of the plan himself; it would not give him a moment's pause to put Earl among the faithful departed.

While he sat there he had picked up the remote control and turned on the television, letting it run mute for a while, then turning on the sound. Vincent O'Toole, whose body had figured in the news in recent days, was being reburied. There was a tall pouting pudgy figure in a kind of dress, but it was the coat thrown over his shoulders that brought Earl to the edge of the couch. That was the son McDivitt had mentioned. My God, that must be the suit jacket.

It is not an easy matter to track down a monk. Inquiries at the O'Toole home, using several disguised voices and bogus claims, failed to get him the information.

"Somewhere in Skokie," Mrs. O'Toole said impatiently to a supposed inquiry from the United Fund.

"And where in Skokie would that be? They may be eligible for the fund."

"How did you hear of them if you don't know where they are?"

"A member of our board spotted one. In a robe."

"They beg with bowls on the street."

So Earl was reduced to cruising the streets of Skokie on the lookout for mendicant monks with wooden bowls. It seemed a definition of futility. But then, near Northwestern University, he saw two of them. Not Sonny O'Toole — these people were short and skinny. But they were hurrying along Dempster as if their lives depended on it. They could not be going far on foot, Earl reasoned, so he parked and followed them walking. They walked for three miles before ducking into a storefront. The place had been turned into a meditation center. Did they live there? Earl went inside. There were a few chairs and he staggered to one, put his face in his hands, and swayed from side to side. Minutes went by before he felt a tap on the shoulder. He shook his head and remained hidden in his hands.

"Nothing is real," a voice said soothingly. Earl took away his hands and looked into the full moon face of the man he recognized as Sonny O'Toole.

"I wish that was true."

"It is." The pale fat hand emerging from the saffron robe made an arc. "None of this is real. There is manyness, but being is one. The many are an illusion."

"I see."

"Why were you groaning?"

"Did I groan aloud?"

"My heart went out to you. You reminded me of myself, not long ago, when I first came upon such a place as this. It was the most important thing I ever did."

"Tell me about it."

Sonny was more than happy to tell Earl how he had become a member of the community. He was careful to leave everything before that day obscure, but that was all right with Earl.

"Do you ever leave the community?"

"We are together wherever we are."

"Do you live here?"

"Come, I'll show you."

In the back was a little warren of cells. It was the metal armoire in each that caught Earl's eye. When they got to Sonny's the monk stepped inside and Earl, using the bowl he had picked up along the way, brought it down on the ovoid expanse of Sonny's skull. The bowl bounced off with a bonk and Sonny turned, surprised.

"You struck me."

Earl struck him again, using a plaster of paris statue this time. Sonny's eyes literally crossed before he sank to the floor. Earl took a loose length of Sonny's robe and wound it tightly around his neck, lifting his chins to get it in place. Then he rolled him on his side, so as not to see his face, and twisted the fabric until he could twist it no more. A small struggle, a twitch, and then relaxation. Earl rose and opened the metal armoire. It was empty. Empty! There were two metal hangers and that was all. They set off a musical complaint when he swept his hand angrily across them. He left the cell, closed the door, and started away, but halfway toward the open area, he stopped and went back. Inside the cell again, he looked under the cot. Nothing. There was no other place where anything could be hidden. Earl closed the door on the late Sonny O'Toole.

"Are you the head monk?"

"You want Pacific."

Pacific. The man looked more like Erie.

"I have a silly question."

"No question is silly. Or rather, all questions are silly."

"My father visited here and left his suit jacket and I wondered if . . ."

"His suit jacket?"

"Yes, he took it off and must have hung it somewhere and when he left he just put on his topcoat . . ."

The monk was shaking his head. "No one ever left a suit coat here."

Would he lie? But the staring eyes seemed incapable of dissembling.

"I said it was a silly question."

That had been stupid, but what could he do? He had killed Sonny so he could not identify him and then he made a spectacle of himself with the head monk. His only hope was that they would think that none of this was real.

It was now time to think of what Giorgio

was thinking. Either Giorgio had pulled a fast one on him or he had not. Earl did not really believe Giorgio was capable of it. That meant that both of them had failed. Only Giorgio wouldn't think so. He would know that Earl had taken the coat from Vince O'Toole's body and would assume that Earl had possession of the holograph.

But he could learn that McDivitt now claimed he had used Vince's own suit to bury him in.

So what? He would go through the same thought process Earl had, wondering when Earl had made the big switch. Only Giorgio had been spared the additional defeats of St. Vincent DePaul and Sonny O'Toole.

And then it occurred to him that Oscar was probably dead. When he had told Giorgio he could pick up Oscar at his house, he had not explicitly formulated in his mind that he was delivering Oscar Hanley over to his assassin. What if Oscar's body were found now. . . . Thinking of Ray Hanley, of his job, turning over a jumble of thoughts, Earl made a quick decision.

Remembering renting the truck in Oscar's name played a part in it. If the dealer made a fuss, it would appear that Oscar was alive and well and renting trucks. Earl had sought to establish the same thing before

Oscar himself had gotten into contact with him. Ray Hanley was a lot easier to work for when he had the hope that his son was still alive.

He left a message for Ray Hanley. A new client in Indiana, Earl would be on the road for a few days. He drove to Michigan City, checked into a motel, and got into bed and slept for twenty-four hours.

# Father Dowling

## 47

Roger Dowling tended to be skeptical of religious vocations that were triggered by some great tragic event, completely reversing the path of the person involved. This was a prejudice, of course, and he did not wish to be unfair to Sister Maria Madeline, but even her choice of a name in religion had a touch of the dramatic about it. Father Dowling drove off one day to the convent in which Laura Pianone, now Sister Maria Madeline, was enclosed. He was concerned about Angela, and thought her sister might be able to offer insight into her state of mind.

Sister Porter listened to him like a character in the poetry of Dante Gabriel Rossetti, the blessed Damozel looking out from heaven at this worldling come to the convent door.

"Tell her I have come about her sister Angela."

A prolonged sigh. "We have all heard of Angela."

"What I have to say is for Sister Maria Madeline alone."

She left him in a spick-and-span room

that had a table without cloth on which stood a simple vase filled with flowers. There were two chairs. On the wall was a crucifix that did nothing to prettify the agony and torture that Jesus endured for our sake. There was no carpet on the floor. At least ten minutes went by before a discreet clearing of the throat and a young nun who might have been Angela's twin glided into the room, immediately taking the chair across from Roger Dowling.

"How is Angela?"

"Sad, very sad. But she has not despaired."

"Thank God."

"She wants to believe Oscar is still alive."

"Oh, but he is!"

"I mean on earth."

"So do I, Father. He came to see me."

"Here?"

She smiled. "I never leave. Yes, here."

"When was that, Sister?"

Her expression became preoccupied. "Normal time means less to us here. It is the church year that governs our lives."

"What feast was it near?"

"I would say it was a week ago, almost exactly a week ago. Today is Thursday?"

"Yes, it is."

"It was the Feast of Saint Blaise."

Roger Dowling was trying to adjust to this

extraordinary revelation. He had spoken to Angela only yesterday, and she knew nothing of this. Was it possible that the two lovers were reunited and he had made this trip in vain? He told Sister Madeline how confused he was by what she had said.

"He came to ask me what he should do."

"I wouldn't have thought he needed directions on that score."

A small smile. "His concern was my family, not Angela."

"You had a similar experience, I believe."

"Now I thank God for it. It brought me here."

"Sister, have you let Angela know that Oscar is alive?"

"Does she doubt it?"

"He has been missing for weeks. She has been going frantic. Did Oscar ask you to get word to Angela?"

"That would be very difficult for me to do."

"Did Oscar know that?"

"You tell her, Father. Reassure her. I hope I haven't caused her more pain."

When she asked for his blessing and he had given it, she slipped back into the obscurity of her life. Father Dowling hoped his questions would not occasion troubling distractions when Sister Maria Madeline was engaged in prayer.

# Anton Jarry

## 48

Gratified by the reception of his story about the incident at the construction site of the Crocus Building that had taken place while he was watchman, Anton Jarry was tempted to expand his repertoire of interesting episodes from his past life. And he succumbed to these temptations, conjuring up manufactured memories of his days with the mob.

"I'm surprised Father Dowling lets him come here," Anton overheard a chirping woman say one day, perhaps intending that he overhear.

"There is more joy in heaven over one repentant sinner," began another female voice, leaving the completion of the quotation to her companion. Anton turned to see who had spoken second. It was a sweet-faced woman with silver hair whom he had seen at Mass where she wore a black mantilla that made her hair even more beautiful. She was called Mimi. He caught up with her when she came out of the noon Mass.

"Who was that priest?" he asked her.

"Some Franciscan."

"How can you tell?"

"Their feet."

"Is something wrong with their feet?"

She stopped and took his hand as she laughed, the physical contact seemingly meant to assure him that her laughter was not mocking.

"They wear sandals."

"Not very practical in this climate, are they?"

"They wear socks with them."

"You're quite an expert."

"I grew up in a Franciscan parish."

They wandered on to the school where the cafeteria was now open. Mimi said she wasn't hungry, she would just put a few things on his tray. Some yogurt, a mixed salad, iced tea. She didn't have a spare pound on her and maybe this diet was why. Anton lived by the principle that if some of him was good, more was better, and he ate with an eye to expansion. She grew fluttery and chiding as he kept loading up the tray.

"You can't eat all that!"

"Oh yes I can."

They were like kids at school here, he had noticed that before. Now he noticed it in himself. He led her to a far table, where they could be by themselves.

"I appreciated your coming to my defense this morning."

"Oh, you heard us."

"You're right about me. I've got a lot to make up for."

"We all do, Anton."

His eyes raised to the ceiling. "I wish my account was as light as yours."

She was as susceptible to stories of his mob connections as others had been.

"Isn't it dangerous to talk about such things?"

"If they were going to kill me, they'd have done it long ago."

Her hand went to her mouth when he said kill.

"Not that they haven't tried."

"Oh, don't tell me. You don't know what you're saying. I've heard nothing."

This was a variation on the preretirement self he had been constructing. In earlier accounts he had been a witness or at worst a forced collaborator in dreadful deeds. "I should have said no," he would say, and others would object. "And be killed?" "There are some things worse than death?" "Name one." Now with Mimi, he became the target of mob vengeance. He was a walking time bomb, knowing what he knew. He could be writing a book, he could be

378

making a recording for the police to be delivered to them at the appropriate time.

"I could bring down the whole thing," he said, and for the moment he believed it. It gave him a tremendous sense of power as well as vulnerability. "That's why I keep to myself most of the time."

"I don't understand."

"I don't want to take anyone with me if they strike."

Mimi sat straighter in her chair. "Well, they don't scare me. They can't do anything more to me than they already have."

He put his hand over hers. "What do you mean?"

"Do you know who I am?"

"Mimi . . . What is your last name?"

"O'Toole."

"You look Italian."

"O'Toole is my married name."

Mimi O'Toole. O'Toole! He looked at her. My God. She was the widow of Vince O'Toole who had been gunned down. He was a man whose picture in the paper Anton had recognized.

Mimi's response was what he had expected when he spoke to Angela Pianone, but obviously it had been a mistake to suggest that they were both in the same boat.

"How can outsiders understand?" he

had asked Angela.

"Understand what?"

She asked the question in a way that discouraged an answer. Spinning Mr. Fenster around, she wiped the corners of his mouth, and then pushed him toward the school.

"What can outsiders understand?" he said to Mimi now. She squeezed his hand.

After lunch, he and Mimi strolled the walkways of the parish, going as far as the rectory, stopping for a moment at the grotto, then around the church and up the street walk in front of the rectory. Two men were getting out of a car parked at the curb. Anton stopped, his hand tightening on Mimi's.

"What is it, Anton?"

But he couldn't speak. For days he had been enjoying talking about his adventures with the mob, but the young man with blond hair and beardless face brought back the one true memory Anton had exploited. The older man nodded toward the old couple who seemed rooted to the walk. The young man glanced at them and then looked back at Anton, who could not get the terrified expression off his face. Then they went on to the rectory.

"He recognized me," Anton said hoarsely.

"I thought he did."

"He drove the van," Anton croaked. "I'll never forget any of those faces."

"He looks like an altar boy."

"At a requiem Mass."

# Angela Pianone

## 49

Angela was in ecstasy and in her joy her imagination ran riot.

*The condemned is sentenced to be executed. He is led out into the courtyard. The sun bounces off the white wall, hurting eyes that have not seen daylight for weeks. The firing squad stands out in stark silhouette against the chalk-white wall. The blindfold is tied tightly around his head and he is led to the post where his arms are drawn behind him, around the post, and then manacled once more. He hears commands being given, there is the sound of rifle bolts sliding cartridges into position. A first command is barked. Eternity is a breath away. Suddenly there is a great commotion. A horseman has ridden into the courtyard. There is pandemonium. The blindfold is stripped away. He sees that the horseman has come to a halt between him and the firing squad. He is sinking to his knees, to thank God for this reprieve, when he hears the horseman's announcement.*

*"He is to be hung, you idiots. Not shot."*

Angela had actually written this, as an exercise, as a spoof, when they were at Northwestern, and for a time it seemed that they would both devote themselves seriously to creative writing. Her parody of Dostoyevsky might have been the script for her own tortured life since the disappearance of Oscar. She vacillated between the certainty that he was dead and the wild hope that he was alive so many times that she had begun to distrust her emotions. In a secret corner of her heart was the desire to have the whole awful thing behind her, the period of mourning ended, and life continue on some new basis. Had Laura ever known this temptation? There were days of such depression that even Giorgio seemed a welcome ticket out of the slough of despond.

And then, without warning, against all expectation, Father Dowling called her in and told her. Oscar was alive.

She wanted to feel pure joy, feel nothing but gratitude. She felt like running to the grotto and kneeling there for hours in the winter air, telling Mary how grateful she was that her prayers had been answered.

She felt almost guilty to be so happy. And to think that Laura had been the instrument of her joy. What would her sister have done if the obstacles to her own love had fallen away? Not that Jimmy Cantori could be compared with Oscar, but then Laura had no ambitions beyond the most traditional: a husband, a home, children. The very naturalness of that ideal made Angela painfully aware of all that had been closed to her. When Laura had turned from Jimmy it had been to a lifetime that conferred immortality on Jimmy and her thwarted love. She might strive never to think of him in her convent cell. When she sent up prayers from her place in chapel, there might be room in her mind for God alone, but her whole vocation was an offering of her thwarted love for Jimmy.

When Angela had received the request to come see Father Dowling in the rectory, she went to Edna Hospers.

"What'll I do with Mr. Fenster?"

"Park him out in the sun. He's not likely to run away."

"I'm worrying about him rolling away, Edna. That lock on his chair wheel doesn't work."

"Put a rock under the wheel. Before you came, we just let him sit, Angela. He doesn't know, one way or the other."

She asked Mimi if she would look after

him for some minutes. "I read that they know a lot more than we think."

"I'll do it, dear. Have you seen Anton?"

"Not today."

Anton. Apparently it was true that he was entertaining everybody with stories about his days in the mob. He had said something to her, as if they could exchange a secret handshake. How Mimi could care about such a man was beyond Angela. But she herself had believed what he said about the basement of the Crocus Building. How could she not wonder whether it was Oscar who lay buried there? Angela went along the walk to the rectory door.

Marie Murkin wore an unusual expression when she came to the door, as if she was bursting to say something but didn't dare. She took Angela's hand and hurried down the hall with her.

"Here she is!" she cried.

Father Dowling looked the same. He was standing up. "We can go into the parlor where you won't have to breathe all this pipe smoke."

"But I love the smell of tobacco."

Tobacco smoke retained the power to evoke Sunday afternoons before everything fell apart. Her father smoked huge cigars, and between dinner and his nap he smoked one until it nearly burned his fingers, the burning of the cigar measuring the reading of one of his favorite authors. If she sat in the study, he would read aloud. To hear him read a poem once was to have it imprinted on her memory. "She lived beside untrodden ways, beside the springs of Dove, a maid whom there were few to know, and very few to love." How he could pronounce each word as an individual musical phrase and still keep the continuity of line and stanza and poem was one of the mysteries of his reading. "She lived unknown and few could know, when Lucy ceased to be, but now she's in her grave and oh, the difference to me."

She was hardly seated when Father Dowling began to speak.

"I visited your sister yesterday and she said something you should know. I thought of calling you last night when I got home, but I thought it would be best to tell you face-to-face."

"What is it?"

"She told me that Oscar Hanley had come to see her."

The horseman had arrived, the commands stopped, the blindfold was removed and the news was wonderful. She was aware of crying out and then she fainted.

Marie Murkin was patting her face with a cold cloth when she came to. Father Dowling looked down at her with concern. Marie helped her back into the chair. For a horrible moment she thought she had dreamed what he said.

"No. That is what she said."

"But when? Why to her? Why hasn't she let me know?"

"When was a week ago. Why, apparently he felt it was safe to let your sister know he was still alive. He apparently didn't realize that she couldn't just pick up a phone and call you."

"But she should have. It's cruel that she didn't." Then why was she laughing? She was giddy with joy. A long nightmare was at an end and Dostoyevsky was welcome to her tragic vision. Angela wanted a happy ending, to be once more in Oscar's arms. She just babbled and she didn't care that Marie Murkin was still there, hearing everything she told Father Dowling. Maybe he had asked her to stay. What an unstable character he must think her. Breaking into uncontrollable tears, fainting and then babbling like an idiot. She said again that she had wanted to be there the first time Laura met Oscar. And then an awful thought came.

"What if you hadn't gone to see her? Did she know you were coming?"

"No."

"Father, she has known for a week. A whole week when I have been left to think. . . . Oh what if you hadn't gone?"

From babbling to weeping, and he was obviously glad that Marie Murkin was there. She was led away to the front parlor then, where Marie continued to soothe her.

"It's that awful tobacco smoke," Marie crooned. "It's enough to knock anyone out."

Angela laughed even as she continued to cry. She even gave Marie Murkin a big hug. If Mr. Fenster were there she would have kissed him.

# Father Dowling

## 50

There might have been less taxing alternatives but Father Dowling decided to make the trip again himself, armed with a photograph of Oscar Hanley. He had told Phil of his interview with sister Maria Madeline, and both had the same thought: How could she possibly know if the man who visited her was, in fact, Oscar Hanley? Until they knew for certain, rejoicing in his return was ill-founded. Sister Maria Madeline had never met Oscar, and of course she would have no reason to doubt what he said.

Sister Porter was a tad less receptive this time. He waited again in the little sitting room but the nun who came after a twenty-minute wait was the superior, Mother Ismelda Marie. There was a smile on her lips, but Roger Dowling was put on the defensive by her manner nonetheless.

"Mother, I visited last week on an errand of mercy. The fiancé of Sister Maria Madeline's sister has disappeared . . ."

"He has been here. He sat in the very chair you do. When he told me why he was here, I relented."

"A question has arisen as to whether your visitor was who he said he was."

Her glasses were gold rimmed. In this setting they seemed a wild extravagance. "I find that difficult to believe."

"If you saw him there is no need to disturb Sister Maria Madeline." He put the photograph on the table. She did not look at it. He turned it toward her. She continued to look directly at him. Custody of the eyes. "I have brought a photograph."

She dipped her head, glanced at it, then looked once more at him. "Who is he?"

"You have answered my question."

"What do you mean?"

"This is a photograph of Oscar Hanley."

"That is not the same man who visited here."

"That is what I came to find out." He put the photograph back into its envelope.

"But why?"

"We would have to know the man who came here in order to know that."

"Let me see the photograph again."

He took it out and laid it before her. She studied it. "He was younger than this. A young man. Almost still a boy, but he wasn't. His hair was not dark but light." She put the small finger of one hand on the photograph. "The ears of children are on the same line as the eyes. With age, as the face lengthens, they are slightly above the eyes. The line of his ears and eyes was the same."

"I didn't know those things."

"I am an artist."

"Ah."

"What reason could he have to want to deceive Sister Maria Madeline?"

Father Dowling pondered that question all the way back to Fox River. If he had listed his thoughts, suggesting more coherence than they had as they tumbled through his mind, the list would look like this.

- Oscar Hanley meets Angela Pianone and they fall in love.
- The Pianones' source of income is an impediment to their love: Men who marry into the Pianone family are already or become part of the family enterprise.
- Laura Pianone, in a similar situation, discovered what activities her family was engaged in, and fled to the convent to live a penitential life.
- Oscar surprisingly is accepted by Salvatore. The Hanleys are delighted with Angela. Oscar and Angela will marry and Oscar will become a legitimate lawyer.

- Suddenly, without prelude, two months ago Oscar disappears.
- There are two theories: one, that he is dead, the victim of the Pianones who for whatever reason saw him as a threat; two, he just ran away.
- The first seems more plausible, the body being disposed of in the typical mob way, with the basement of the Crocus Building a favorite possibility.
- Salvatore's rage when he finds a holograph missing from his library and his claim that Oscar took it suggests Sal thinks Oscar is still among the living.
- Oscar visits Sister Maria Madeline, as Roger Dowling discovers when he visits her to see what light she can cast on the mystery of Oscar's disappearance.
- How would his visit ever have been known if Father Dowling had not chanced to visit the convent?
- The man was not Oscar Hanley.
- Angela is about to experience a new agony: Her sister's visitor was an impostor.

Why?

It was by any standards an odd way to send a message to Fox River. Perhaps he assumed that Sister Maria Madeline would contact Angela. But cloistered nuns do not engage in regular correspondence, even with members of their family. If the impostor knew this, would he have visited the convent? Did Sister Maria Madeline tell him she would get word to his fiancée, her sister? Nothing in Father Dowling's conversation with the young nun suggested this.

If the impostor did visit on the assumption that his visit would become immediately known in Fox River, he would have been disappointed, at least for a week, when nothing happened.

But why would anyone want to impersonate Oscar Hanley? What possible purpose other than causing yet more suffering to Angela and Ray Hanley could it have?

A sign told him that he was twenty-seven miles from Fox River. He had gone away confused and was returning more confused. There was still a lost sheep. Father Dowling, influenced by the sense that he personally had been toyed with, however accidental that was to the impostor's visit, was determined like a good pastor to find that sheep. But in the jumble of his thoughts that biblical allusion was joined by a phrase from a police bulletin. Dead or alive.

# Earl O'Leary 51

Earl parked on Third and came through the intervening yards to home, awakening dogs near and far as he went. The growl of a nearby dog lifted the hairs on the back of his head, an animal reaction to his fear of that particular animal, shades of childhood experiences when the only routes between his home and school gave him a choice of which barking dogs to confront. When he reached the fence, on the other side of which was the backyard of his house, he stood on tiptoes and studied the dark silhouette of 123.

Why this precaution? Earl the mastermind, the man in charge, found his careful plans unraveling. Had anything at all gone right? His great regret at the moment was in having turned Oscar over to Giorgio. Without the holograph, Oscar was of little use to Giorgio. Standing in the still of night, looking at his darkened house, Earl realized how alone he was in the world. Yet he and Oscar had been friends of a sort. They could have been real friends, true friends, if Earl had not been conspiring to betray Oscar.

The plan with Giorgio apart, they had gotten along. Earl even liked Oscar's poetry when he thought about it.

Angela? Yes, she was beautiful. Maybe too beautiful. How could a man stand being married to a woman who looked like that? Perhaps after a few months you didn't really see the other, the surface where beauty lies. Once when Earl asked Ray Hanley what Eileen had been like, his employer had fallen silent. After a moment, he shook his head.

"I wouldn't even try to describe her."

"Don't you have photographs?"

"She never took a good picture. Not even home videos. She just didn't come through, not the real Eileen."

What lay beneath the beautiful exterior of Angela? Would a man speak of her as Ray Hanley spoke of his wife? Earl eventually did see pictures of Eileen, a plain woman with a nice smile and beholding eyes. That was all.

But photographs give surfaces, skin-deep imitations of the real. A slow smile formed on Earl's face. Here he was, standing outside in the night thinking of reasons not to love Angela when he had no reason at all to think that she even liked him. But she loved Oscar. His smile faded.

Satisfied that his house was indeed deserted, Earl vaulted over the fence, crossed the yard, and let himself into the house by the back door. In those minutes by the back fence, he had resolved to do what he could to undo what he had been doing for Giorgio. When he turned on the kitchen light, he heard a groan from the other room. He froze and immediately turned off the light and moved several feet from where he had been standing.

Again he heard the groan. His hair responded as it had to the growling of the dog. He waited, but no further sound came from the other room. Thoughts flickered in his mind, making no sense. He imagined that he had not telephoned Giorgio to tell him Oscar was here, lying on the couch in the living room. He tried to dismiss as hallucinatory his memories of waiting in his car outside, watching Giorgio come and go, presumably taking Oscar away. What if none of that had happened and Oscar was still in there on the couch?

He swiftly crossed to the doorway, put his hand around to the opposite wall, and felt for the switch. There it was. He flicked it. The light in the living room went on. Earl had stepped out of sight when it did. He waited. A groan!

He dropped to his knees and looked stealthily around the doorway at the couch. Something lay upon it, a carpet, rolled up, with feet emerging from it. My God! Earl sprang to his feet and ran to the couch and touched the carpet roll, pressing it, bringing a muffled cry from it.

"Oscar?"

And then he recognized the shoes emerging from the carpet. They were Oscar's. The carpet was tied with rope, thick rope. It was a wonder that Oscar could breathe, let alone make any noise.

"Wait, Oscar. It's Earl. I'll get you out of there."

He ran back into the kitchen, pulled open a drawer, and took out a carving knife. He had started back to the living room when the doorbell sounded. He wheeled and looked at the door, undecided. Then someone began pounding on the door. Before Earl could move, the door smashed open and Lieutenant Horvath burst in. He was carrying a gun.

"Drop the knife!"

A black woman came in after him, also carrying a weapon. She struck a stance and leveled her gun at him, holding it with both hands.

"I'm just going to cut him free . . ."

But Horvath had not come to talk. He swept the knife from Earl's hand and grabbed his wrist in the same movement, spinning him around and bringing the wrist up painfully behind his back.

"Agnes."

A movement and then Earl felt cold metal click in place around his wrist. In a moment, the other wrist too was manacled behind him. Earl looked at Horvath with what was meant to be a condescending expression.

"Meanwhile there is a very uncomfortable Oscar Hanley in the other room."

Horvath left him in the care of the black officer called Agnes. From the other room he called out, "Agnes, bring that knife."

She pushed Earl ahead of her into the living room. Horvath was kneeling by the couch, his ear cocked toward the rolled carpet on the couch. For the first time Earl was aware of the odor in the room. It suggested that Oscar had been incontinent. How long had he been rolled up like that?

Horvath cut through the ropes and they fell away. Then he began very delicately to unroll the carpet. At one point it threatened to roll off the couch and Agnes sprang forward and got a knee under it, holding it in place. Horvath completed his work until, like a scruffy moth emerging from its co-

coon, a smelly, bearded, blinking Oscar came into view. The gag had worked its way half free and when Horvath removed it, there was a whimper of pain. Oscar's mouth was swollen and dry.

"I'll get water," Agnes said, heading back toward the kitchen.

"Better start with wet cloths," Horvath advised. "And call the paramedics."

He was standing now. Oscar's eyes were mere slits to ward off the light. But gradually he was able to look around. When his eyes came to Earl they widened and he tried to rise. There was a wild look on his face now and his swollen mouth twisted in anger. Agnes came then and began to apply a damp cloth to his lips. He fell back and closed his eyes.

"I found him there when I came in," Earl said, happy that his voice sounded so matter-of-fact.

"Have you been keeping him here all along?"

"Keeping him here! I went for that knife to do what you did with it. I just got home."

Horvath stared at him for half a minute, then shook his head. "We've had the house under surveillance. You've been in here all along."

"Without any lights on?"

"When the lights came on, we approached the door. The knife was reason enough to come in."

"You sound like you're rehearsing."

"I'm arresting you for kidnapping Oscar Hanley."

"Kidnapping?"

From the couch, muffled by the damp cloth, came the first words from the victim. "Arrest the sonofabitch."

"Oscar," Earl said in disappointed tones.

Apparently Horvath had alerted others before coming through the door. They arrived now, uniformed officers and a pair of paramedics. Oscar was the center of attention, but Earl was not forgotten.

"Take him downtown and book him for kidnapping. I'll be down to write a report."

"I want a lawyer," Earl cried, for the first time really believing that he was in trouble.

Horvath looked at him. "Sure. How about Tuttle?"

"Good. I know him."

But Horvath had lost interest in him. Earl was led from his house by uniformed cops. All the way downtown he thought of things he should have said to Horvath. He should have said he had parked on Third and come in the back way. He should have said that he was just back from Indiana and he could prove it. He should have said so many things. The trouble was he felt guilty as charged. He had colluded in the kidnapping of Oscar. Finally a thought he had been avoiding came home.

This was Giorgio's doing. Giorgio had taken Oscar away but he had brought him back again. Had he told the police they could find the missing Oscar at 123 Fourth? That was the bitterest pill to swallow. Earl was booked and led away to a cell after telling the desk sergeant that his lawyer was Tuttle and he demanded to see him.

The closing of the cell door was the most definitive sound Earl had ever heard. He wanted to cry out in protest. He did not belong here. He was not a common criminal. He was Earl O'Leary.

He became aware of being looked at from neighboring cells by indifferent, hostile, or merely vacant eyes. His fellow criminals.

"This is all a mistake," he heard himself say.

From up and down the cell block came the sounds of derisive laughter.

# Giorgio Pianone 52

Dumping the Hanley kid back on Earl's couch accomplished that but not much else. They had gone through the house, not as thoroughly as they might, but pretty thoroughly. Nothing. Not that Giorgio had expected Earl to be dumb enough to leave the holograph in the house.

"Come have a look out here, Giorgio."

Healey had taken the garage, Giorgio the house. On a workbench in the garage was the coat they had prepared for Vince O'Toole. The lining was ripped open. It was empty. That bastard Earl had already removed the holograph. So he did have it. Giorgio realized that to this point he had entertained doubt as to whether Earl had double-crossed him. Someone had popped open O'Toole's casket and stripped that jacket from him, but who? It had to be Earl, but until he knew, it was possible it was someone else. The torn-up suit jacket in Earl's garage settled it.

"What's with all these clothes?" Healey asked.

There were boxes of old clothes, the stuff hanging out of them as if they had been packed in a frenzy. Or unpacked.

"It doesn't matter. Come on."

He checked on the kid rolled up in the carpet. What a smell. The coat in the garage smelled too. Giorgio wanted fresh air. He wanted to call the cops right then, and tell them to check out 123 Fourth if they wanted Oscar Hanley, but he stopped himself. From now on he was doing nothing until he got the okay from Salvatore.

He dropped Healey off at Smut City, he couldn't take him to his uncle's house. Salvatore wanted only family there. Others who worked for them were just mercenaries, family was blood. Giorgio was trying to think of how he could tell Salvatore of Earl O'Leary's treachery without involving himself.

"I think I know who stole the D'Annunzio holograph."

Uncle Salvatore sat at the desk in his study. Light fell from the lamp onto the page he was reading. He closed his book. His eyes rose to Giorgio.

"Oscar Hanley had the help of a man who works for his father, Earl O'Leary."

He got no help at all from Salvatore. There was no indication how this was affecting him. Giorgio knew how his uncle had reacted when he discovered that the holograph was missing. He had expected the same kind of outburst now, but with the difference that now something could be done about the thief.

He was still standing. He could not sit unless he was asked to. Salvatore's eyes bore into him. Giorgio wished that he had gone over this thoroughly in his mind before coming to his uncle. He wished that he had kept control of Oscar Hanley. If he was found by the police he would deny everything Giorgio said. It was when he said that Earl and Oscar had hidden the holograph in Vince O'Toole's casket that the first reaction came. Salvatore rose from his chair.

"Where?"

"In O'Toole's casket. In his clothing. That's why they opened the casket. . . ."

Salvatore came around the desk and took Giorgio's arm in a viselike grip.

"How do you know this?"

"It's true."

"How do you know it?"

Salvatore must have pressed something while he was still seated at the desk. Two men were standing in the doorway of the study, Salvatore's bodyguards. They were almost never in evidence in this house.

"Healey and I went to his house. In the garage we found the suitcoat that had been stripped from Vince's corpse. I saw right away what that meant."

"What did it mean?"

"That Earl and Oscar had stolen Vince's casket. They opened it the other day and were surprised by the cemetery sexton. But they got the coat off the corpse. The coat we found on the workbench in Earl's garage."

"Where is it?" Salvatore's manner was less menacing. Giorgio stared at him. He felt about three years old.

"In his garage, on the workbench."

"You left it there."

"The smell, uncle, you wouldn't believe it."

"The smell I'm getting here I don't believe. Go get it."

"Now?"

But Salvatore had gone back behind his desk and sat. His hand went out and rested on the book he had closed.

"Now. I'll go now."

And without Healey. On the way he tried to remember how simple the plan he had worked out with Earl had seemed. Why had he agreed to sewing the holograph into the lining of Vince O'Toole's burial suit? He should have recognized a shell game when he saw it. All that business of snatching the casket and hiding it in that metal shed. None of that would have become known if the widow hadn't decided to dig up her husband and bury him somewhere else. All because Earl had thought it would be funny to mess up the grave on Hallowe'en. That started it, that's when things began to go wrong.

Earl had known the casket was not in that hole. But he also knew that he was going to double-cross Giorgio and get the holograph while Giorgio was conveniently out of town in Racine disposing of Oscar. What was his game? He wanted to get me into trouble, Giorgio thought. He wanted to frame me. Well, by God, that suit coat would hang Earl O'Leary. He may have taken the holograph from the lining, but the suit proved that it had been Earl who desecrated Vince O'Toole's body.

123 Fourth was all lit up when Giorgio arrived and a paramedic van was backing out of the driveway. Patrol cars, at least half a dozen, were everywhere. Up and down the street, people stood in huddles, wondering what was going on.

"What's going on?" Giorgio asked an officer.

"Just routine."

"Someone hurt in there?"

"What's your interest?" the black woman next to him asked. She turned out to be a detective.

"I know the guy who lives there."

"What's his name?"

"Earl. Earl O'Leary."

"Come on inside."

That easily, Giorgio got inside the house, but when he was led into the living room and saw Horvath he wondered how smart this was.

"Giorgio Pianone," Horvath said.

"That's right."

"He says he knows Earl O'Leary."

"I wondered if something happened to him."

"Why would you think that?"

"Look, I saw the ambulance leave."

"How do you know Earl O'Leary?"

Giorgio took a deep breath. "He works for Ray Hanley. Hanley's son goes with my cousin Angela." It cost him much to say that.

"You mean Oscar Hanley?"

"Yeah."

"The man who has been missing for months?"

Giorgio shook his head at being reminded of this terrible thing.

"We just carried him out of here," Horvath said.

"No."

"We found him rolled up in a carpet lying on that sofa. Did Earl ever tell you he had anything to do with the disappearance of Oscar Hanley?"

"Why would he tell me a thing like that?"

"Why would you be dropping by his house at this hour of night wondering how he is?"

"Hey, I was just driving by. I'm sorry I stopped. I'm out of here."

He turned and all the way to the back door he half expected Horvath to stop him. He shut the door behind him and stood panting, watching his breath form and dissipate in the cold night air. The door of the garage was open. Giorgio looked toward the street. The officers were returning to their cars. They were wrapping up. He could leave and come back when they were all gone. But the open garage door exercised a fatal attraction. He moved toward it, devoid of will power.

Inside, he hurried to the workbench. The coat was still there! He snatched it up and, hugging it to him, ran out of the garage. He ran right into Horvath.

"What have you got there, Giorgio?"

# Tuttle

## 53

"I'd do it as a favor to Ray Hanley, if nothing else," Tuttle assured Earl O'Leary. He tipped back his tweed hat and thrust his face at Earl's. "You didn't have anything to do with Oscar's disappearance, did you?"

"Come on. We were friends."

"But they found him all trussed up on a couch in your house."

"He was there when I got home. Someone left him there."

"Who?"

It was Earl's turn to lean forward. "The Pianones."

Tuttle sat back abruptly. He had a private room in which to interview his client, but the place was probably bugged. He frowned at Earl and shook his head.

"Don't you believe me?"

Tuttle brought a finger to his lips. He took out a piece of paper. "We can't talk here."

When Earl read the note, he took Tuttle's pencil and printed in large letters, WHERE?

"Wait a minute."

Tuttle stepped outside and caught the attention of a guard.

"I want to take my client into the main visiting room."

"Lawyers get private rooms."

"My client has claustrophobia."

The guard led Earl into the buzz and distraction of the main visiting room where they found a table.

"Can we talk here?"

"Would you want a tape of this noise?"

Earl was actually shocked at the suggestion that an interview room might be bugged.

"Wouldn't you, if you had the chance?"

Earl thought about that, then shrugged.

"So tell me how they came to find Oscar Hanley all tied up and lying on the couch in your living room."

Listening to Earl, Tuttle thought of the clipped account he had gotten from Horvath when Cy called to tell him Earl O'Leary wanted him to represent him. "What's he done?" "He's under arrest for kidnapping." "Who?" "Oscar Hanley." As a friend of Ray's, Tuttle hesitated. But then he remembered that Earl worked for Hanley. If Hanley's assistant was in the slammer, Tuttle wanted to hear from him what he had to say to the charges.

"Did I lock him up out there at Riverside?

I didn't know he was there."

"But he left there."

"I know. He called me from there."

Tuttle nodded. Earl's phone number had been found in the gatehouse apartment. Earl seemed to be leveling with him.

"Why would anyone drop off a tied-up Oscar at your house?"

"Because we're friends! How's he doing, by the way? Would you check on that?"

Tuttle thought of being parked up Fourth a block from where Earl had been sitting in his car. He had sat there while Giorgio Pianone came and went in his Lincoln Town car. Was it possible that Oscar had been brought to Earl's house then? But that would mean that he had let his supposed friend lie tied up for days.

"You know Giorgio Pianone?"

"Why do you ask?"

"He was seen coming and going at your house."

Earl lit up as bright as Smut City on a moonless night. "He was seen at my house?"

"Drove right in the driveway, stayed awhile, then drove away."

"So why are they holding me? That's the explanation, don't you see? Giorgio is framing me. He must have had Earl and he

411

dropped him on my couch."

"I still don't see why he would do that."

Earl was getting impatient. "Because I'm Oscar's friend."

"There's a big problem with that, Earl."

"What's that?"

"It was four nights ago that Giorgio made that visit."

Earl sat back. The guy could be eighteen years old with that baby face. He looked like an altar boy. Ray had laughed and said Earl's youthfulness was like a disguise. Earl sat forward again.

"I've been out of town."

"Were you out of town four days ago?"

He frowned in thought. "Yes."

Tuttle expected clients to lie to him, but it was not often that he knew *when* they were lying. Earl was going on, his memory was clearing up, sure, he had been in Indiana that day.

"Okay. That's enough for now."

"What do you mean, for now? Tell them Giorgio is responsible, tell them to let me go."

The far door opened and a parade of people came in, heading for the desk. There was Horvath and Agnes Lamb, a couple of cops, and Giorgio Pianone. Earl saw Giorgio and rose to his feet. Giorgio

412

stopped and stared at Earl. The two men looked as if they would rush at one another, but there was no chance of that. They shouted enraged accusations at one another and then a silence grew that was as thick as the hatred shining in both their eyes. The whole room had quieted.

Earl said to Tuttle, "You're right. That's enough for now."

# Father Dowling


**54**

It was a prosecutor's dream, with Earl O'Leary providing rope to hang Giorgio Pianone and Giorgio returning the favor with a vengeance. Phil Keegan wore a look of vindicated satisfaction and was not disturbed when Marie Murkin asked him what in the world the police had done to solve the horrible crime.

"Which one, Marie?"

"Which one!" Marie looked pleadingly at Father Dowling. "Ask Mimi O'Toole which one, she'll tell you."

Father Dowling agreed to the extent that many if not most of the mystifying happenings of recent months seemed connected to the posthumous fate of Vincent O'Toole. While the question of who had shot O'Toole down had never been answered, it seemed that he had provided an occasion if not a cause for the series of wicked deeds that Giorgio attributed to Earl and Earl attributed to Giorgio. Marie sought to shield Mimi from the slings and arrows of outrageous fortune but had been

414

supplanted by Anton Jarry.

"Isn't that the man that was smitten with you, Marie?"

"He is the man who was reported missing when he had simply taken a bus to Nashville to visit the Grand Ol' Opry."

Phil Keegan was less disposed to think of Jarry as a harmless figure. "He's the guy that claimed there is a body buried in the basement of the Crocus Building."

"I think Angela Pianone was convinced it was the grave of Oscar Hanley, Phil. She wanted me to bless it."

"I thought you did."

"The whole building, not just the basement."

He had been met at the door by Salvatore Pianone and all the employees of the Pirandello Savings and Loan and the Empedocles Real Estate Company, men on one side, women on the other. They encircled Father Dowling and there was a tearful embrace of father and daughter. Sounds of sympathetic sobs came from both sides of the entry hall. Father Dowling sprinkled them all and the place in which they stood with holy water and called down the blessings of Almighty God upon them, asking that all deeds done on the premises might redound to the greater honor and glory of

God and to the eternal salvation of the agents.

"That was beautiful," Salvatore said afterward. "Did you write it?"

"No. I never compose liturgies. That would be their negation." He showed Salvatore the book from which he had read.

"It was the way you read it."

It was doubtless fanciful to see in Salvatore Pianone a tragic figure. Giorgio was a nephew, not a son, but the plight of the nephew had opened the door at last to frank and full discussion of the Pianone enterprises. A demand that Smut City be closed would be debated before the City Council and the session would be televised. The *Fox River Tribune*, which in the past had saved its moral indignation for far-off turpitude, suddenly became aware of what had been going on under its nose for decades and professed to be shocked.

"Round up all the usual suspects?" Father Dowling asked Phil.

"I think this time we may do something." But he extended a hand to show his crossed fingers. "If nothing else, we've got Giorgio. There is no way in the world they can get him off."

More tests in the lab had found a partial print from Giorgio on the gun that had been turned in by an anonymous caller. This was the gun that had been used to assassinate Lolly and Maxwell. When this became known, Oscar Hanley was placed in a difficult position by Earl O'Leary.

"My client says there is an eyewitness to the killings," Tuttle announced.

The trial was weeks away but the battle had been waged in the media from the time of the arrests of the two suspects.

Gretchen Phillips, Giorgio's lawyer, wore pinafores and bows in her hair and looked so young she made Earl O'Leary seem old. She looked wide-eyed into the camera and said that she hoped that Mr. Tuttle's client would not claim to be that eyewitness.

"But then I suppose the one who shot those men can be called an eyewitness."

Tuttle scoffed at this with the air of a man who held three aces and had one showing. "The eyewitness to whom I refer and who will be produced at the appropriate time is not Earl O'Leary."

"I know that boy," Mimi O'Toole said, having seen a clip of Earl on television. "He came to visit me."

Cecil McDivitt stopped by the rectory to tell Father Dowling that both Giorgio and Earl had come to see him. "Both wanted to talk about the clothes in which Vin

O'Toole was buried."

"Giorgio had brought a suit to Cecil," Phil Keegan noted.

However convenient it was for the prosecutors to permit the two men to pummel one another via their lawyers, it seemed clear to Father Dowling that they had acted in concert, at least in the matter of the desecration of Vince O'Toole's remains.

"I had nothing to do with killing those two men," Earl said to Father Dowling when he visited him in jail. Word had been sent to the pastor of St. Hilary's that Earl wished to see him. "I'll swear that on a stack of bibles."

"Let your speech be yea yea or nay nay."

"Nay nay, then. I had nothing to do with it."

"But the other things?"

"Is this confession?"

"Are you Catholic?"

"I was. I still am."

"Have you confessed your sins regularly?"

"They never told us about that."

Whatever Earl knew of confession he had picked up from movies and television. Well, it was a time-honored plot ploy. But Earl's danger did not come from his confessor, not that he wanted to confess.

"It might be easier than you think."

"Do you go to confession?"

"Of course."

"To yourself?"

"Even a priest needs a priest, Earl."

"I have to talk to somebody but I'm not ready to go to confession."

"Anything you say to me will be just between the two of us."

"Promise?" But immediately Earl put a hand on his arm. "I'm sorry. I know you mean it."

The story Earl told was more subtle than the one Tuttle told on his behalf, and of course it contained details that Earl had not shared with his lawyer. The events Earl admitted to as well as others of which he claimed to be as innocent as a priest took on intelligibility once the holograph was mentioned. Of course. The precious relic of the Italian writer that Salvatore had so venerated.

"Did you intend to sell it?" Father Dowling remembered the half-terrified Dombrowski and wondered where a purchaser for the holograph could be found.

"Sell it? Oh, no. Giorgio meant to make it look like Oscar had stolen it. That would enrage Salvatore, Oscar would get the heave-ho, and Giorgio could move in."

"But I understood he was already close to Salvatore."

"Move in on Angela. He wants to marry Angela. She was promised to him when they were kids but she fell in love with Oscar."

"And you helped him?"

"I pretended to," Earl said quickly, but the very facility with which he spoke indicated it was a lie.

"After all, you worked for Ray Hanley."

"And Oscar was my friend. So was Angela. Giorgio thought he had convinced me to betray Oscar, and I went along with him, figuring that was my best chance of knowing what he was up to and stopping him."

"Ah."

"And he double-crossed me. I don't know how he did it, but it was like sliding walnut shells around on a table. The suit he gave to McDivitt was not the one the holograph was sewn into."

"When did you learn that?"

Earl stared at him. His face had not lost its look of innocence. Would any jury vote to convict such a chorister? "Everybody knows that."

Had Earl been the silhouetted man Heidegger had surprised in the metal shed at the back of Riverside Cemetery, the man who had attacked him and then fled with the suit jacket that had been torn from the dead body of Vince O'Toole?

# Cy Horvath

## 55

The prosecutor sought to counter the Pianone ploy of hiring Gretchen Phillips to defend Giorgio by appointing two very junior prosecutors who had the undeniable merit of being female, young and castable as ingenues. Carol Coaster was assigned to prosecute Giorgio and Felicia Solomon would make the case against Earl O'Leary.

"You think they can handle it?"

Preswick looked brave. "I'll be at the table with them. They'll be backed up by the whole office. We're going to win these two."

Until Tuttle and Phillips stopped making the prosecutors' case, it looked as if a summer intern could have won those cases. But suddenly silence fell and ruminative pieces began to appear in the *Tribune*. The nature of circumstantial evidence was rehearsed in long plagiarized pieces. Accusations of the planting of evidence by overly zealous or vindictive police were written about. A woman who had served twenty years for murder was released when the real murderer, dying of cancer, had confessed.

The released woman went from station to station, from talk show to talk show, and what ordinarily would have been treated as a one-in-a-million possibility was made to appear only normal. The unstated suggestion was that the prisons are full of innocent men and women, suffering for the crimes of others. Phil Keegan did not take kindly to this treatment. He refused to be interviewed and was written up on that account.

"Cy, these cases have to be absolutely airtight."

"Nothing guarantees conviction, you know that."

"Juries," Phil said with disgust. But he might as well have said prosecutors or defense lawyers or journalists. Even detectives. Until Giorgio Pianone and Earl O'Leary were proved guilty, they were innocent, even if only Earl looked innocent.

Ray Hanley was whiplashed between joy that his son was still alive and shock at Earl's perfidy. But for the first week or so, joy triumphed. Oscar lay like a potentate on snowy linen at St. Jude's. Sustenance trickled into him through tubes that ran from bottles dangling from stands beside the bed. On the wall every aspect of his system was monitored and translated into digits and dials and pulsing lines. He was well on the way to recovery. Doctors doted on him, nurses spoiled him, residents honed their inchoate skills on him, Angela was with him night and day.

"I won't go home until they have removed all that." Her pretty hand gestured at the tubes and bottles and dials and digital displays.

"I'll stay too," Ray promised, but this meant he slept in a chair with his mouth open and snored so loudly even terminally ill patients complained. He was persuaded to go home. It was there, in his kitchen, that Phil Keegan and Cy and Ray sat down with a new quart of Jameson's before them. Ray splashed generous amounts into glasses and handed them round.

"That is my last bottle."

"Save it," Cy suggested, arresting his glass on the way to his mouth.

"I mean I'm quitting. In thanksgiving. As soon as Oscar is released from that hospital with a clean bill of health, I am on the wagon in perpetuity."

Phil nodded. Cy said nothing. Neither of them believed a word of it. In any case, it did not interfere with their enjoyment of the bottle before them.

"When's he come home?"

"Maybe in two days." Ray brought his glass swiftly to his lips at this threat of abstinence on the horizon.

"Have you talked to him about what happened?"

"No."

Ray had clamped a total embargo on questioning Oscar until the boy was out of the hospital.

"It might do him good to talk about it."

"I doubt it."

"We don't want him forgetting anything."

"Oscar? Not on your life. Know what he was doing, wrapped up in that carpet, being starved to death and bounced around like a cord of wood? Composing poetry."

He spun it out of his memory now and Angela wrote it down. None of it seemed to have anything to do with the trouble Oscar had been in.

"He called it therapy. He tried to think about anything but himself. He never believed he would die."

"Well, he was right."

"He has a destiny," Ray said, and washed it down with Irish whiskey.

Thanksgiving gave way to resentment.

"I was nursing an adder at my bosom," Ray said. "I thought Earl O'Leary was Os-

424

car's friend, and mine too, and all the while . . ."

"All the while what?" Cy asked.

"All the while he was setting me up."

"He says he was cooperating with Giorgio to protect Oscar."

"Giorgio says he called and told him Oscar was at his place and pick him up."

Which Giorgio had done. Tests on the Lincoln were devastating to Giorgio. There was evidence that the carpet in which Oscar had been tied up had been in Giorgio's trunk. Fibers that had been missed when Giorgio put his car through a wash. The tire marks that had been cast from the scene where Lolly and Maxwell were killed matched the Lincoln too.

"You got your man," Tuttle had said to Phil earlier downtown. "Let Earl go. He will be your best witness against Giorgio."

"Is Earl innocent?"

"Of course he's innocent. You know the law."

"On that basis Giorgio is innocent too."

"I know the evidence you got on him, Keegan. You've got nothing on Earl."

Would Tuttle be able to convince a jury that the fact Oscar had been found tied and bound on Earl's couch was happenstance, proof that Giorgio was trying to frame him?

Would he be able to explain away the suit jacket that Giorgio had been taking from his garage?

" 'Taking'? Who says so? You probably caught him in the act of planting evidence."

"He was running out of the garage."

"He probably heard you coming."

"People at St. Vincent DePaul can identify him, Tuttle."

"He isn't denying going there to buy clothes for the missions."

"He didn't get around to mailing them off."

"The poor you have always with you," Tuttle said unctuously.

"Why did he visit the Pianone woman who is a nun?"

"Who says he did?"

Cy studied the twill in Tuttle's tweed hat. A million threads, wound, twisted, shaped, but capable of reshaping at will. The likelihood of getting Sister Maria Madeline to testify in a criminal trial involving her nephew and Earl O'Leary was unlikely. Father Dowling had said that the mother superior identified a picture of Earl O'Leary as that of the man who visited the convent claiming to be Oscar Hanley. It would take days in court to establish that sequence even if the nuns agreed to take the stand, which was probably against their religion to do. Would Father Dowling testify to what he had learned during those two visits to the convent?

"I hope that won't be necessary, Cy."

"You could be subpoenaed."

"What could I say except what others told me?"

# Marie Murkin

## 56

Marie remained convinced that Earl O'Leary was innocent and that he would not even be brought to trial.

"The man is a private detective," she explained to Father Dowling. "He works with Ray Hanley."

"Have you spoken to Ray about him?"

"The poor man has been influenced by all this ridiculous speculation in the papers. I know what they're up to."

"What's that?"

"It's a conspiracy to draw attention away from Giorgio Pianone."

"I don't think anyone has forgotten him, Marie."

"Link him with a nice boy like Earl O'Leary and the jury will think Giorgio is innocent too."

"There will be separate trials."

"We'll see if there are two."

Mimi had told her what a nice visit she had had from Earl O'Leary and at a time when it had done her a lot of good. The young man had a kind heart, there was no doubt about that.

"What did you talk about?"

"That was the thing, he just let me chatter, and it was just what I needed. We talked of the funeral and McDivitt and how I donated Vince's clothes to St. Vincent DePaul."

Phil Keegan regarded all this cynically, talking about the clothing Marie was certain Giorgio Pianone had been planting in Earl O'Leary's garage.

"Marie, they remember Earl at St. Vincent DePaul."

"Doing what? Asking about clothes to be sent to the African missions?"

Mimi was inclined to skip those particular merits of Earl O'Leary. She said again that Vince would have had words to say about his clothes ending up in an African mission. Marie was winding up for a little homily on that topic when Anton Jarry came along the walk from the school. Mimi spied him coming and laughed nervously.

"I don't know how he always finds me."

Marie suspected that Mimi had told Anton where she was going before leaving the parish center. Well, she wasn't going to have any middle-aged lovebirds cooing in her kitchen. She rose with Mimi and took her own coat from the rack. Mimi's was draped over the back of her chair.

"I'll walk back with you."

So the two women, buttoning their coats on the back steps, confronted the grinning Anton Jarry. He bowed to Marie but his hand went out for Mimi's, and she let him take it. There had been a moment when Marie wondered if Anton had ever told Mimi of his interest in her. It crossed her mind to mention it to Mimi. And she might have if Anton did not seem even less attractive to her than before. A simpering male is intolerable when it is for another that he simpers. Mimi was welcome to him. Her critical faculties, perhaps never acute, had disappeared. Mimi had apparently forgotten entirely all of those fanciful anecdotes of Anton's years working on the edge of the mob and of witnessing a burial in the basement of the Crocus Building while it was under construction when he was the night watchman. He had half fooled Father Dowling with that story and he had been persuaded by Angela to bless her father's building.

"Ten thousand dollars," Marie had exclaimed when she took the check Salvatore Pianone had placed in the envelope he handed to Father Dowling after the blessing of the Crocus Building.

Father Dowling had just sat still behind the desk in his study.

"Stop joking, Marie."

But she could see the concern in his eye. She handed him the check. He held it for a moment, his head back, looking at the ceiling.

"I'll send this back."

"You can't do that."

But he had taken a parish envelope from the desk and slipped the check into it. He scribbled something on parish stationery, folded it, took out the check and slipped it into the folded note, and sealed it all in the envelope. While he was addressing the envelope, Marie said, "Why do you think it is tainted money? All money is tainted."

He licked a stamp and put it on the envelope. Then he rose to his feet. "I'll mail this now."

"The mailman will pick it up at the door."

"And notice the address."

Marie gasped. Of course. She was seeking desperately for some argument that would cause him to change his mind. It was insane to refuse a check like that. Still, she admired him for it, in a way.

"They'll never convict him," Anton Jarry said as the three of them shuffled along the walk to the parish center.

"Earl O'Leary?" Marie asked brightly.

"Ha! I mean Giorgio Pianone."

"But he's guilty as sin."

"When was a Pianone ever convicted in this town?"

Mimi did not enter into the conversation, its topic being somewhat too delicate. She and Anton might trade stories about the Pianones, but Mimi was trying to let her husband's associations fade from memory.

"There is an eyewitness to his shooting those grave diggers."

"According to Tuttle."

Marie was placed in a novel position, defending Tuttle. She was glad when they got to the center.

"I'll run up and say hello to Edna."

Edna Hospers had her office in what had once been the office of the principal of the school. Her tasks were not wholly unlike those of a school principal. Marie went into the outer office and stopped.

"Yoo-hoo, Edna."

No answer. The inner office was empty. Marie's eyes went to the closed door of the closet. She hesitated only a moment before crossing to it and pulling it open just a crack. She had to open it wider before she could see that it was still there, the suit Marie imagined Edna thought her husband would wear when he was released from prison.

It was so touching that her eyes were misty when she went back down the corridor. She did not want to run into Edna now. She was still sniffling when she got back to the rectory.

"Are you getting a cold?"

His question was opening enough. She told Father Dowling all about the closet and the suit and Edna Hospers's dreams.

# Cy Horvath

The monk was told that he couldn't beg in the courthouse and was hustled into the street. He came back in again and his gown got caught in the revolving door so that when he walked into the area under the rotunda he almost undressed himself before the screaming began. This time they brought him upstairs where Cy Horvath saw him sitting cross-legged in a corner of the waiting room.

"What's he doing here?"

"Waiting to be processed."

"For what?"

Brenda picked up a slip and brought the appropriate portion of her trifocals to bear on it. She glanced at the monk. "Indecent exposure."

"For wearing a gown?"

"It says he tried to take it off in the rotunda."

Cy took the charge sheet and went over to the monk. "Excuse me."

The monk's eyes were closed and his lips moved in what might be prayer. His head was totally hairless, his legs were crossed, and he held a wooden bowl in his lap. There were pieces of what looked like chalk in it. The eyes opened.

"I am Lieutenant Horvath."

"Ah." He rose in one unbroken motion which, given his weight, was impressive. Cy doubted that he could get up from that position without help. "I wish to report a murder."

"A murder."

"It's an old one. But you may be interested in it."

Cy took him to his office. The monk's name was Pacific Hugon and he lived with his community on Dempster Avenue in Skokie. The bowl was filled with pieces of plaster. He wanted to tell Cy about his community and what they did.

"I'm a Catholic," Cy said in defense.

"I used to be a Franciscan."

"Tell me about the murder."

"You may know about it already. I am told it was in all the papers. I was interviewed many times." He seemed inordinately proud of this. "We do not read newspapers, of course, nor watch television, so I cannot say what exactly was reported." He took a breath and looked around. "I don't know how long it has been since I was last in an office like this."

"Were you ever arrested?"

"Oh, many times."

"What for?"

"Protesting this, protesting that. I was very militant while I was a Franciscan."

"Are we talking about Sonny O'Toole?"

"That was his name in the world."

Well, he was out of the world now, but it was still his name as far as Cy was concerned. Ever since he had seen the monk, an image had been trying to form in his memory, and when it did he asked the question about Sonny O'Toole. The crime had occurred in Skokie so that, while they had been informed of it, it was not in their jurisdiction. Pacific did not know whether the Skokie police were still investigating Sonny's death. He had been found dead in the street.

"We took him out of the center and left him lying in the street. Of course, the body is just an envelope."

"He was dead."

"He had been beaten and strangled to death."

The monk was ashamed of the way the community had stayed out of the investigation of Sonny's death. Now, with all the publicity of the trials in Fox River, he had decided to come forward.

"I know who killed Gladness."

"Gladness?"

"Sonny O'Toole."

"You saw the murder committed?"

Cy wished he had spoken with the Skokie police before having this conversation with Pacific Hugon. If this involved a quarrel in the monks' community, the Skokie police were welcome to it. It would be difficult to pick a culprit out of the lineup if all the suspects were dressed in gowns and had shaved heads. From somewhere in the folds of his gown Pacific produced a newspaper page.

"I saw this on a newsstand." He bit his lip. "I should have been recollected but perhaps there was a purpose in my being distracted. I recognized him."

Cy took the newspaper page and unfolded it. There were photographs of both principals in the celebrated Fox River case. Giorgio Pianone and Earl O'Leary.

"Which one?"

"The boy."

He meant Earl. "Tell me about it."

Earl must have been crazy making himself known at the meditation center in the way Pacific described. That was not the behavior of a murderer anxious to cover his tracks. On the other hand, Pacific had no doubt at all about the fact that Earl O'Leary had been in their center on Dempster. He had talked with Sonny and before leaving had sought out Pacific.

"Are you the superior?"

"That is not the term we use."

He sang something, apparently his title. Then he shifted his bowl.

"What do you have there?"

Pacific upended the bowl and poured its contents onto Cy's desk.

"One of the brothers swept these up so the cell would be clean if the police came."

"What is it?"

"They are pieces of a statue of Buddha. What that boy struck Gladness down with."

"Did the brother handle these pieces?"

"No one has handled them."

They sat in silence for a while. It occurred to Cy that unless he spoke no one would. He thanked Pacific for bringing the pieces of plaster of paris. The monk rose then and gathered his gown about him and then stood holding his bowl. Cy put five dollars in it.

"You're welcome," Pacific said and left.

Cy thought about the monk's last words. It did not seem likely that he was being sarcastic because Cy had not thanked him for bringing the pieces of plaster. Perhaps he assumed Cy was grateful for the opportunity to contribute.

"Hello," Cy said when he passed Brenda, the dispatcher.

She squinted at him. "You've been here all day."

"I'm going to the lab."

"Hello?"

"Same to you."

Lab tests found several unmistakable prints of Earl O'Leary on a large chunk of the broken statue. Preswick was delighted and professed to be completely confident that what the monk had brought in his wooden bowl would prove the undoing of Earl O'Leary.

# ✧ Epilogue ✧

Giorgio Pianone was convicted of the murders of Lolly and Maxwell in late March and two weeks later the jury in the Earl O'Leary trial found the defendant guilty of the murder of Sonny O'Toole.

"What about Vincent O'Toole?" Marie cried.

"They'll both be in prison for life, Marie."

She looked knowingly at Father Dowling. "Ha. You know what a life sentence means nowadays. They'll be out before you can say Jack Robinson."

"I never say Jack Robinson."

"You just did."

It was a lovely day and Father Dowling had taken his breviary outside to read it in a lawn chair by the tulip tree. Marie had come across the lawn to tell him of the O'Leary verdict, which she had just heard on the radio.

"Just think if that so-called monk hadn't come to Cy Horvath."

"So-called? His name is Pacific Hugon."

"He used to be a Franciscan."

440

Marie did not care for Franciscans. Friars had been in charge of St. Hilary's for some years before Father Dowling was assigned to the parish, and Marie had stories.

"Marie, you don't think . . ."

"It's hard to tell with a shaved head."

"I would never have guessed. What color was your real hair?"

She ignored him. He was not to be encouraged in such a facetious mood. Father Dowling was more relieved than he let on at the successful resolution of the events that had wracked Fox River and the parish of St. Hilary since last autumn. Marie and Phil Keegan had been witnesses when Mimi O'Toole married Anton Jarry. Marie had not been amused when the pastor suggested that they might just as well make it a double-header while they were at it. But the housekeeper was clearly jealous of Mimi. Not that she thought that highly of Anton Jarry. It was Marie's skepticism about his stories that had led to a somewhat grisly discovery.

"I don't know how you sleep nights," she had said to Jarry a few weeks before the wedding.

"Oh, I'm nervous," he replied, patting Mimi's hand. "Don't let looks deceive."

"I was referring to your story about the basement of the Crocus Building."

441

"Let sleeping dogs lie."

"They buried a dog!"

Jarry sat back and brought his hands together over his bulging stomach. "No, a car. A Volkswagen, the original kind, the bug."

"A car!"

"An import."

"And all along I thought you meant a human being."

"Oh, she was buried with the car."

She? Marie's skepticism mounted and she took great pleasure in passing the story on to Phil Keegan the next time he visited the rectory. Cy Horvath had come with him, not to stay, but to be there when the pastor was told the Giorgio verdict.

"A Volkswagen bug? I'll check it out."

"He will, too," Phil said when his lieutenant was gone, and there was pride in his voice.

What Cy discovered was that Cordelia Fabro, a bookseller, had disappeared along with her automobile, a red Volkswagen bug, without a trace. It seemed irrelevant to Anton Jarry's story until Father Dowling suggested that Cy talk with Dombrowski. The following day, Cy had a court order to do a sweep of the basement of the Crocus Building. Sophisticated equipment would tell whether there was anything suspicious under the concrete floor. The dials on the machine spun definitively at one spot in the basement and registered nothing anywhere else. The court order was extended to include excavation, despite the protests of the officers of Pirandello Savings and Loan and Empedocles Insurance. Six feet down, the Volkswagen was found and under its hood — the motor was in back — the remains of Cordelia Fabro. Anton Jarry was questioned concerning his memories of that night.

"You recognize anyone?"

Only after persistent questioning, which he seemed to enjoy, did Anton talk. He named Vincent O'Toole and Giorgio Pianone. And Earl O'Leary.

"Vince is dead and Giorgio and Earl are already taken care of," Keegan said to Father Dowling, reporting Chief Robertson's decision not to pursue the matter further.

"Maybe that's wise."

"I still don't get the reason for all these crazy goings on," Phil said, but was soon distracted by a spring practice game coming in from Sarasota. Even the White Sox were preferable to no baseball at all.

The human mind is a mysterious thing. Logicians have mapped the connectives between thought and thought, identified fallacies and legitimate inferences. But why do we put one thought with another in the first place? One afternoon in his study, trying to drive from his mind all the details of the trials still going on downtown, Father Dowling thought of the prison time awaiting Giorgio and Earl. His thoughts went to Edna and her husband and on to Marie's odd remark about the suit hanging in the closet of Edna's office.

He found that he had risen to his feet. When he passed through the kitchen, Marie asked where he was going. "I'll be back." The door closed on some remark of Marie's and he walked slowly up the path toward the school. It was a nice day and senior men and women who frequented the center were enjoying the sun. In what had been the auditorium, shuffleboard was being played and in a corner were two tables of bridge fanatics. Up the wide staircase that had once thundered with the feet of boys and girls and down the corridor to Edna's office. Edna looked up with a smile.

"Did someone leave a suit coat here, Edna?"

She laughed, then grew serious. "You're referring to those trials, aren't you?"

"Perhaps. Marie said she thought she had seen a suit jacket in that closet."

"I never use it."

"Could I see?" They went together to the

closet and Edna opened the door. A dark suit jacket hung there.

"For heaven's sake, is it yours?"

Father Dowling had taken it from the closet. His hand ran along the back of the garment. Edna was thinking. "Do you know where I think that came from?"

"Mimi O'Toole."

"How did you know that?" Edna's eyes widened. "It will never fit him."

"Who?"

"Anton Jarry."

"Do you mind if I take it."

"Of course not."

He sat then and they talked of other things. He might have been postponing the great test. On the way back to the rectory, he stopped at the grotto to say a prayer, but he made no special request. Marie looked up when he came in the kitchen door.

"What's that?"

He held it up. "A suit coat."

"I am taking things to the cleaner if you want me to send that."

"Maybe."

He closed the door of the study. He laid the coat open on his desk and examined the inner seam. He could not resist patting the fabric on each side of the seam. What he felt made him hurry. Which Pius had been named Sarto?

The tailor. Father Dowling was not papal material. It took him some time to open the seam. When he had he drew forth from the area between the lining and the back of the jacket the D'Annunzio holograph.

Pages written in a study in Italy. Great sums had been spent for them. Men had died for them, a grave had been desecrated, poor Sonny O'Toole strangled. And all along the suit jacket had been hanging in the closet of Edna Hospers's office in the St. Hilary senior center. If thoughts are put together randomly, a sequence of events can have the maddest logic of all.

No one had had any doubt where the trail would lead if the death of Cordelia Fabro were pursued. That was why Marie reacted so strongly to Salvatore Pianone's second visit to the St. Hilary rectory. There was a look of near terror on her face when she announced who had come.

"Bring him here."

"I put him in the parlor."

"He'll feel more comfortable here."

"I know what chair I'd like to put him in," Marie whispered.

"I'll tell him."

Salvatore's step seemed slow as he came down the hallway, and when he took a seat in the study he looked years older than he had on his last visit. Smut City had been closed and Phil had reported rumors, which he doubted, that the Pianones were going out of business. Salvatore looked around at the shelves of books.

"I am sorry that you sent back my check."

"For blessing a building?"

"My daughter thought that Oscar was buried there. That's why you blessed it, isn't it?"

"Yes."

Would he mention Cordelia Fabro and how she had ended up beneath the concrete floor in the basement of the building that housed Pirandello Savings and Loan?

"Angela will marry him, Father."

"He is a good boy."

"A poet."

"Will he go back to law school?"

"Perhaps. For now he is cataloging my collection. They will live with me."

"I met your daughter the nun."

"You are fortunate. She refuses to receive me there."

"She is praying for you."

"Perhaps it is working. This has been a terrible year."

Father Dowling opened the drawer of his desk and took out a sheaf of pages. "Here is your D'Annunzio holograph, Salvatore."

He looked at it for a long moment, his eyes lifted to Father Dowling. If his mind was trying to grasp how that missing document had ended up on the desk of the pastor of St. Hilary's, his expression gave no indication of it. He did not reach out for it.

"I had reconciled myself to losing it."

"There it is."

Salvatore took it then, not with the joy of possession, but as if he were mystified at his desire to own it. Recent events had caused him to find much in his life unintelligible. He wanted to go to confession.

Father Dowling closed the door and, in his function as stand-in for Christ, helped Salvatore examine his conscience. It had been decades since Salvatore had approached the sacraments. Father Dowling seemed to have been cast for the role of the priest who reconciles hardened criminals before it is too late.

"What did he want?" Marie asked, when Salvatore was gone.

Father Dowling brought a finger to his lips.

"I'll bet."

Lost sheep were not Marie's favorite animal.